I0779421

Guardians of the Ley Lines

by Greg Maxfield

Greg Maxfield

Silver Sage Books
– Est. 2024 –

© 2024 Silver Sage Books
The Library of Congress has catalogued this edition as follows:

Names: Maxfield, Gregory D, author.
Title: Legends of the ley lines / Greg Maxfield
Description: Silver Sage Books, 2024
Identifiers: | ISBN 9798218440343 |
| ISBN 9798218431952 (paperback) |
| ISBN 9798218440350 (ebook) |
Subjects: Fantasy Fiction, Science Fiction,
American Southwest, Mysticism, Indigenous Peoples, Cultural
Heritage
Classification:
LCC PS3605.A9854 GB1215-1239
Library of Congress Control Number: 2024909742

Printed in the United States of America
First Printing

Cover design by **raiba_svisuals**

This is a work of fiction. Names, characters, places, and incidents either are the product of the author's imagination or are used factiously, and any resemblance to actual persons, living or dead, businesses, companies, events, or locales is entirely coincidental.

For Dad, who taught me
without him knowing
to love the desert landscape
and the culture of the American west.

GREG MAXFIELD

Prologue

LUCAS GRANT SAT HUNCHED over his desk in his claustrophobic Eugene office, the twin monitors bathing his face in cold, flickering light. Papers were strewn across every available surface, their edges curling under the weight of too many revisions and too little sleep. Mournful notes from *The Hours* soundtrack kept time in the quiet. His fingers battered the keyboard, each keystroke tethering him to his crumbling ambitions. This lecture was his last chance—a final, desperate attempt to dismantle the myths of ley lines, to anchor his research in irrefutable science, and to claw his way to tenure before the academic tide swept him under.

The words "Redstone Study Begins" loomed on his calendar, stark against the monotony of his schedule. To anyone else, Redstone, Arizona would be just another dot on the map, but to Lucas, it was a battleground—where his data would collide with myths and where his career teetered on the edge of redemption or failure.

As he merged his latest data from the Blythe intaglios into his presentation, a chill crept down his spine. The new readings were erratic, defying the consistent patterns he had meticulously documented. Frustrated, he muttered a string of expletives and checked for technical errors, but everything seemed flawless.

The sudden chime of an incoming video call shattered his

concentration. Elana Rossi—his ex-wife and former research partner—filled the screen. Her curls framed a face he knew too well, her eyes carrying the legacy of a history neither of them could fully put down.

"You look like the Mojave ate you alive and spit you back out," she said, her voice soft but edged with something sharper—something familiar.

Lucas sighed and leaned back in his chair. "The final dataset just imploded. The readings are erratic, as if something—I don't know—something massive disrupted the entire field." He rubbed his temples, his voice tight with frustration.

Elana's expression grew serious. "You always did hate anomalies, didn't you? But what if it's not just noise, Lucas? What if it's something real?"

Lucas crossed his arms. "You're not seriously suggesting the ley lines are *responding*? Come on, Elana."

Her lips pressed into a thin smile—one he remembered from late-night arguments and half-finished bottles of wine. "Why not? You're so focused on disproving myths that you can't see the edge of something bigger. You used to love asking the hard questions. What happened to that Lucas?"

The words landed harder than she likely intended. Lucas turned away from the screen, his jaw tight. "I ask the right questions, Elana. But questions without answers are just noise."

She shook her head. "No, Lucas. They're possibilities. And sometimes, the noise is where the truth starts whispering."

Silence stretched between them, thick with old wounds and unspoken words. Lucas stared at the numbers on his screen, the erratic spikes and plummets in his data. He could almost hear the hum of something just out of reach.

When he closed his laptop, her voice lingered in the air.

The ley lines had always been about data, patterns, and cold, reliable conclusions. But now, they felt different—like a puzzle piece that didn't quite fit, yet hinted at a larger image just beyond his understanding. Something about them lingered, unsettling and insistent, like a faint vibration he could almost hear if he just listened closely. And somehow, despite everything, Elana still seemed to hear it.

———

Sierra Castillo hurried along the narrow path, her worn hiking boots crunching against the dry, cracked soil. The setting sun stretched amber shadows across the rugged landscape, turning the rocks golden and igniting the horizon with fire. Over her shoulder hung a weathered canvas bag filled with trusted supplies—a loyal companion on countless treks through Arizona's unforgiving terrain. The golden hour for painting was almost here.

Reaching the top of a ridge, she paused. The view unfolded before her—distant mesas rising like sleeping giants, red rock formations glowing in the sun's final light. It was perfect. Her pulse slowed, her breath evening out as the connection settled in. Here, where two ley lines converged, the air felt alive. Sacred. She set up her easel among the sagebrush and prickly pear cacti, her movements careful, deliberate.

But as she began to paint, something caught her eye. Her brush hovered mid-air. In the clearing below, the serenity shattered into discord. Crumpled paper bags, empty bottles, and scraps of half-eaten food lay scattered across the earth. Trampled plants—stems bent and torn—sprawled in every direction. Ancient stones had been shifted and displaced, their balance destroyed by careless hands.

Sierra dropped her brush and scrambled down the ridge. The closer she got, the worse it became. Kneeling beside a wilted desert marigold, she traced the crushed petals with trembling fingers. Dust clung to the fragile blooms, dulling their once-bright color. Her throat tightened as tears blurred her vision.

"I'm so sorry," she whispered.

Her voice broke, the apology escaping like a breath carried away by the wind. Around her, the desert seemed to hold its breath. The marigold, the scattered trash, the broken stones—they felt like accusations, each one pointing to neglect, to carelessness, to wounds that might never heal.

Sierra rose slowly, her gaze sweeping over the damage. Wildflowers lay flattened into smears of color against the earth. Stones—keepers of forgotten stories—bore fresh scratches, their surfaces marred. Somewhere in her chest, anger sparked, sharp and clear.

"Popularity," she said bitterly, her voice almost drowned by the wind. "Is this the price? They trample the heart of this land for a fleeting moment of wonder."

She turned away from the mess, her hands shaking at her sides. The silence around her felt hollow, stripped of its usual presence. Her breath steadied, and with it, her resolve sharpened.

"*We can't let this continue,*" she though. She felt a strength, something unyielding. "If they destroy the ley lines, they destroy more than stone and soil. They sever something ancient, something irreplaceable."

The sun dipped below the horizon, and Sierra stood still in the fading light. Her ancestors' stories felt closer now, their presence a faint but solid beneath her feet. Whatever came next, she would not let this place fade into silence.

———

Hiram Caldwell sat at the head of the polished mahogany table, the skyline of Salt Lake City stretching behind him in hues of gold and steel. His family's legacy, his father's empire, had been built on precision, control, and a relentless pursuit of profit—values Hiram had spent his career trying to soften, to redirect toward something more meaningful. The map of Redstone lay spread before him, its ley lines faintly etched across its surface like whispers from a history he couldn't quite touch.

"Why haven't we made progress?" His voice was calm, but a thread of frustration ran beneath it.

A man in a gray suit cleared his throat. "The resistance in the town is stronger than expected, sir. They've brought in a professor to prove that the phenomena people are seeing are just natural. The locals are rallying around them. It seems they are happy with Redstone just the way it is."

Hiram exhaled, his fingers tracing one of the faint lines on the map. "We're offering them real investment—better schools, jobs, infrastructure. Things that matter." He looked up, and his words were soft but firm. "Why can't they see that?"

A woman with sharp features and a neatly annotated notebook raised her voice. "They do see it, Hiram. But they're framing the ley lines as their personal cultural and ecological treasures. It's not just resistance; it's a narrative they believe in."

Hiram nodded thoughtfully, his brow furrowed. "They have every right to protect their home. But we're not here to exploit Redstone; we're here to honor it. My father would have bulldozed his way through—I refuse to do that."

The executives exchanged uncertain glances. Hiram stood, walking to the window, hands resting on the cool glass as he stared out over the city.

"This town isn't just another project to me," he said quietly. "My family's history is tied to Redstone in ways I'm only beginning to understand. If we're going to move forward, it has to be with trust—with transparency."

The sharp-featured woman spoke carefully. "Then perhaps it's time to speak with them directly. Show them your vision, your sincerity."

Hiram turned back to the table, his expression resolute. "I'll go to Redstone myself. I'll meet with them, listen to their concerns, and make sure they understand that this isn't about conquest—it's about building something together."

The room exhaled collectively, tension giving way to purpose. The executives began to gather their papers, but Hiram's assistant lingered by the doorway.

"Sir," she said, "is this about Redstone's future, or your family's past?"

Hiram's looked back at the map. "Both," he replied. "But this time, I intend to honor both."

Chapter 1

LUCAS TIGHTENED THE LAST TIE-DOWN STRAP on the bed of his Tacoma, the truck groaning under hastily packed boxes. Amid the clutter, a frayed photograph slipped into view, catching his eye. He picked it up: Tillamook Head, Oregon Coast. In the image, a younger Lucas grinned from the cliff's edge, eyes wide with boundless wonder. His thumb traced the glossy surface, worn smooth by time, and a pang of loss cut through him. That boy had once reveled in discovery, unburdened by the failures that now trailed him like shadows.

As he merged onto the highway, the truck's engine hummed steadily beneath him. Rolling hills and rocky outcrops gave way to stark desert vistas. On the passenger seat, a stack of papers and photographs threatened to spill, one showing Elana's forced smile from their last vacation together. His grip on the wheel tightened. How had the pursuit of truth cost him so much? His marriage had unraveled thread by thread, worn thin by the relentless pull of opposing beliefs.

The truck slowed as a pair of pronghorns crossed the road ahead. Their unhurried grace anchored him in the moment, pulling him from the spiral of his thoughts. He watched them vanish into the sagebrush, their fleeting presence leaving a faint echo of something he couldn't name. Perhaps this journey wasn't just about scientific validation.

At a scenic overlook, Lucas pulled over and stepped out. He leaned against the hood of the truck, the arid breeze brushing against his face, carrying the scent of juniper and sunbaked earth. The jagged peaks of the Cascades rose in the distance, sharp and unmoving, like sentinels guarding ancient secrets.

He reached for his notebook, hoping to capture a thought, an idea—something to ground him. But the page remained blank. Geophysical phenomena had always been an intellectual puzzle to him, a series of test results waiting to be charted. Yet now, they felt like something more. It felt as if significance danced at the edge of his awareness, just out of reach.

A hawk cried overhead, its silhouette cutting clean arcs into the pale sky. Lucas followed its flight, something shifting in his chest— an unspoken pull, as though the land itself urged him onward. He slid the notebook back into his pocket and returned to the truck. His skepticism softened, if only slightly, by the raw beauty surrounding him.

Glancing in the rearview mirror, he caught his reflection—worn, tired, but resolute. The photographs on the seat beside him seemed to watch, silent witnesses to the road ahead.

"Whatever truths await," he said softly, his voice steady, "I'll face them."

Chapter 2

SIERRA STEPPED INTO LADAWN'S BAKERY and the warm scent of fresh bread wrapped around her. For a brief moment, the tension in her shoulders eased. Sunlight filtered through the wide windows, glinting off polished frames on the far wall. She looked to the ley line maps that had always hung here—glossy paper dotted with colorful pins marking Redstone's sacred sites. Their paths wove across the paper like veins beneath skin—a mosaic of history and mystery.

But a new map caught her attention, a world map. In it, travelers to Redstone had begun to pin their hometowns to share how far they had traveled.

"Hank thought it would be good for business," Ladawn said from behind the counter. Her voice was light, but her shoulders were set, her movements brisk as she poured coffee into a to-go cup.

Sierra's lips pressed into a thin line as she regarded the maps. "They're not souvenirs, Ladawn. These lines aren't just stories to sell."

Ladawn sighed and set the steaming cup on the counter. "I know that. But the bakery has to survive. People are coming to Redstone for the ley lines—they want to see them, touch them, feel something *magical.*" She nodded subtly toward a nearby table where tourists huddled over their maps, fingers tracing inked pathways, voices rising with excitement.

Sierra turned back to the maps, her fingertips hovering over the delicate lines. "And what happens when seeing isn't enough? When they start taking—trampling places they don't understand, leaving behind damage we can't undo?"

Her voice was low, sharp with restrained anger.

Ladawn leaned forward, resting her elbows on the counter. Her coffee-stained apron bunched around her waist. "Sierra, I hear you. I really do. But I'm trying to keep this place alive. Do you know how hard it's since Robbie dies? I've been doing everything I can so that the kids and I can stay here. This bakery isn't just flour and sugar— it's all I have left."

Sierra's expression softened, her frustration ebbing into something quieter. "Then fight with me," she said, her voice earnest. "We can protect Redstone without turning it into a sideshow. Without letting tourists tear up everything sacred."

Ladawn hesitated. Her eyes flicked briefly to the tourists, then back to Sierra. Something flickered across her face—weariness, doubt, maybe both. "Maybe," she said. "But right now, I have to keep the doors open. If I don't, there won't be a bakery left to fight for."

Sierra nodded, her grip tightening around the coffee cup. Silence settled between them, sharp with unspoken fears and lingering hopes. "I understand, Ladawn," she said finally. "But we have to ask ourselves—what's the cost? Some things are worth more than money."

Ladawn watched Sierra settle at a corner table, her movements stiff, her expression drawn. The fragile balance between preserving the past and surviving the present felt impossibly thin, like a thread stretched taut over an open flame.

Out of the corner of her eye, Ladawn spotted her son Eli weaving through the morning crowd, a tray of pastries balanced in his steady hands. His flushed cheeks and bright energy stirred something in her chest—a reminder of why she fought so hard to keep this place alive.

But Sierra remained rigid, her fingers wrapped around the coffee cup, her knuckles pale against the ceramic.

"Mom, why is Sierra upset? Are the ley lines supposed to be a secret?" Jasmine's small voice cut through the murmur of the bakery. Ladawn glanced down at her daughter, whose wide eyes brimmed with earnest concern.

Ladawn opened her mouth, but Hank Jenkins spoke first. Leaning back in his chair, he filled the space with his low, confident voice. "It's nothing to worry about, Jasmine. We're just helping people understand the history of this town—the stories that make it special."

Sierra's head snapped up, her voice sharp. "It's not just history, Hank. It's sacred. We can't let it become a sideshow."

Marla, Hank's wife, joined in, her voice smooth, overly polished. "Sierra, maybe this tourism will be good for our local businesses, like Ladawn's. Think of the opportunities coming to Redstone because of it."

The air felt brittle around them. Sierra's reply came softer this time but firm. "I just hope it doesn't change what makes this place special."

Ladawn stepped in, her voice steady. "We'll keep an eye on things, Sierra. We all want what's best for Redstone."

Sierra hesitated. Her shoulders rose with a slow breath, and she turned away. The coffee cup trembled slightly in her hands as she walked toward the door.

But the morning crowd had other plans. A tourist couple stepped into her path, their smiles bright with excitement.

"Excuse me, miss," the man said, his voice brimming with polite energy. "Are these the ley line maps we've heard about? We saw some videos online and just had to come. Could you tell us more about them?"

Before Sierra could answer, Ladawn stepped in with a practiced smile. "Little lines and big legends," she said, her voice light. She turned to Eli. "Eli, why don't you share some of our town's fascinating history with these folks?"

Eli's face brightened as he stepped forward, his voice bubbling with enthusiasm. The tourists leaned in closer, captivated by his energy.

But Ladawn's gaze drifted back to Sierra, still lingering near the door. Together, they watched as three new pins were pressed into the glossy surface of the ley line map. The sight left a sour taste in Ladawn's mouth. Those tiny marks didn't feel like symbols of a thriving tourist trade—they felt invasive, like cracks spreading across glass.

Sierra turned and stepped outside, sunlight catching in her hair as she disappeared into the street. Ladawn stood still for a moment, unease settling somewhere deep and unspoken.

The bakery hummed back to life around her, but the tension in the air remained—thin, fragile, and impossible to ignore.

Chapter 3

As Sierra drove away, the door to Ladawn's Bakery swung open, the morning bustle stilled by a stranger's imposing presence. Ladawn glanced up from the counter, her smile faltering. Hiram Caldwell moved through the space with measured strides, his presence cutting through the bakery's warmth.

Ladawn glanced up from behind the counter, her practiced smile faltering.

Caldwell approached Hank and Marla Jenkins, who sat at their usual table. With careful precision, he lowered himself into the seat opposite them and set his briefcase down with a muted thud.

"Hank. Marla," Caldwell greeted, his voice calm but serious. "We need to resolve this now. I need that deed so we can start excavating."

Hank leaned back in his chair, his fingers drumming lightly on the edge of the contract resting between them. "We've been thinking, Hiram. Maybe this deal isn't the best thing for Redstone."

"Hank's been thinking, that is," Marla interjected.

Caldwell's brow furrowed slightly, but concern, not irritation, flickered across his face. "What's changed? The terms are solid. This project isn't just about money—it's about survival. About giving this town a future beyond faded memories and empty storefronts."

Hank's gaze drifted toward a group of tourists poring over ley line maps near the window. "It's not just about the money, Hiram. Redstone isn't Salt Lake City. The ley lines, the history… people here care about preserving that."

Caldwell exhaled slowly and leaned forward, his voice steady. "I understand that, Hank. I do. But sentiment alone won't keep the lights on or these tables filled with customers a decade from now. This town is fading, whether we admit it or not. And I can't stand by and watch that happen."

"Maybe," Hank said, his voice firmer than before. "But what kind of town will we be if we sell out our soul?"

The bakery door chimed as another group of tourists entered, their voices loud and bright. One of them gestured at a framed map, their camera's flash briefly lighting up the room. Marla's fingers tightened around the edge of the table as she followed their movements. For a moment, pride and unease crossed her face— pride in her town's stories, unease in how easily they were being reduced to glossy paper and fleeting fascination.

Caldwell noticed. His voice softened. "You see that? They're here because of the story. But stories alone won't keep this bakery open, won't keep your grandkids in school, won't stop families from leaving when the jobs dry up. We need infrastructure, investment— something real, something lasting."

Marla glanced at Hank, her hesitation etched clearly into the furrow of her brow. But before she could speak, Ladawn appeared at their table with a tray of coffee. Her movements were brisk, her presence sharp.

"You've stirred things up, haven't you, Mr. Caldwell?" she said lightly. "Everyone's talking about your project."

Caldwell met her gaze and offered a tired smile. The sharp confidence he usually carried was softer now, almost hopeful. "Change always comes with resistance, Ladawn. But it's the only way forward. If we want to protect what matters most, we have to build something that lasts."

Ladawn's expression didn't shift. "Maybe," she said, her voice edged with steel. "But some things are worth preserving, no matter the cost."

She turned and walked back to the counter, her footsteps crisp against the wooden floor. The space she left behind filled with silence, heavy with unspoken words.

Caldwell's smile faded. For a long moment, he sat still, his hands resting on the edge of the table. When he spoke again, his voice was low and steady. "Think it over carefully. This opportunity won't come again. And I genuinely believe it's what Redstone needs."

Chapter 4

As Lucas entered Redstone, the town unfolded before him like a patchwork quilt—adobe buildings stitched together with winding streets, verdant trees defying the desert's stark canvas. He adjusted his sunglasses against the relentless glare, his eyes catching on banners fluttering in the breeze, bright letters promoting the *Sunset Market*. There was a quiet pulse to this place, an unspoken rhythm of life he hadn't expected.

He stopped for fuel and breakfast at a local convenience store.

Memories surfaced unbidden, sharp-edged and relentless. His once-thrilling academic achievements felt hollow, eclipsed by the jagged remains of his marriage to Elana. What had started as spirited debates—firelit conversations alive with curiosity and mutual admiration—had decayed into a cycle of defensiveness and resentment. *Science versus spirituality.* The phrase had become a bitter refrain in their home, each repetition carving deeper cracks into the foundation of their love.

He could see it now—how he had wielded logic like a weapon, dismantling her beliefs under the guise of intellectual enlightenment. He had convinced himself he was saving her from illusion, yet all he'd done was drive her further away. In his relentless pursuit of empirical truths, he had invalidated the tender, intangible connection they had once shared. The irony wasn't lost on him: in trying to dismantle her spirituality, he had dismantled her love.

In the aftermath, he had fled—to California, to the ancient landscapes of the Blythe Intaglios—clutching at data and theories like lifelines. His article, *"Geomancy Debunked: A Rigorous Scientific Examination of Ley Lines and Their Purported 'Magical' Energies,"* had been a declaration, a manifesto masquerading as research. He'd cataloged geomagnetic fields, ionized air, telluric currents—all measured, stripped of wonder, presented in cold finality. But it wasn't the science that had cut Elana the deepest; it was his smug certainty, the way he had closed the door on her world.

Back in the truck, a splash of green against the desert's muted tones pulled Lucas from his thoughts. Trees stood resolute, their roots anchored deep in unseen waters, stubborn symbols of survival. Farmland patches, nourished by an invisible river, spoke of perseverance—of generations fighting to carve life from inhospitable earth.

The sight struck something deep within him. The contrast between Redstone's thriving heart and the surrounding desolation mirrored the tension within his chest—a push and pull between belief and doubt, reason and something older, harder to name. The town's defiant greenery stirred memories of his grandfather's garden in Oregon, where the air was thick with rain and the scent of damp earth. Those days felt impossibly distant now, like sunlit fragments slipping through his fingers.

Lucas's trained eye swept across the landscape, cataloging its features with clinical precision—rock formations, soil density, the faint shimmer of heat waves rising from cracked earth. And yet, the ley lines lingered at the edges of his thoughts. Folklore. Superstition. Words he had used to dismiss them in countless papers and presentations.

It was as if the town balanced itself precariously between past and present, honoring its roots while inching toward an uncertain future. A fragile equilibrium.

Could it hold?

Could he?

The sun blazed overhead. Lucas reached for his sunglasses again—an instinctive gesture for an Oregon native unaccustomed to such relentless brightness. Along the main street, posters for an upcoming art fair and the Sunset Market flapped in the warm breeze, vibrant splashes of color against adobe walls. The scene buzzed with life, with purpose.

There was strength here, Lucas realized—something resilient yet delicate, something worth understanding. The flicker of curiosity he'd felt earlier flared brighter now. For the first time in a long while, he leaned into the unknown, ready—perhaps even eager—to confront the mysteries waiting ahead.

Chapter 5

THE EARLY-AFTERNOON SUN HUNG UNBLINKING over the town square, its light pouring down in relentless waves. The air buzzed with the energy of sweating but eager merchants setting up their wares, movements brisk with anticipation for the evening market.

Sierra adjusted her canopy, grateful that the solstice arrived in June and not August. Under the thin shade, she arranged her artwork with practiced care, each placement deliberate. Her paintings and jewelry weren't just products; they were stories—tributes to her Hopi heritage and her deep, abiding connection to this sacred place.

Her fingers lingered on a necklace of turquoise and silver charms, their cool touch anchoring her. Sunlight caught the beads, setting them aglow with soft reflections. These weren't simple adornments—they were fragments of the desert's spirit, tangible echoes of survival and memory.

Unconsciously, her hand rose to the necklace around her neck— a polished turquoise stone set in delicate silver, etched with faint spiral patterns.

"Sierra!" A familiar voice called out across the bustle, warm and steady. "Those paintings—spectacular as always!"

She turned and found Joe grinning widely, his easy warmth disarming in its sincerity.

"Thanks, Joe," Sierra said, returning his smile. "I'm excited to share them. How's your pottery coming along?"

Joe held up a vase, its curves smooth and painted with earthy reds and deep blues. "Ready for the market crowd! Hoping for good sales tonight."

"Best of luck," she said. "I'll send some folks your way."

As Sierra finished arranging her jewelry, movement across the square caught her eye. Mayor Helen Jones strolled through the crowd, her salt-and-pepper hair glinting in the sunlight. Her steps were measured, her expression composed—an anchor of calm amidst the bustling marketplace.

"Afternoon, Sierra," the mayor said, pausing at the stall. Her gaze settled on a painting of the desert at dusk, shadows softening rugged peaks beneath a lavender and gold sky. She brushed her fingers lightly against the canvas. "You capture Redstone's spirit beautifully. Always have."

"Good afternoon, Mayor," Sierra replied. "I'm just finishing up here. What do you think?"

She hesitated, her smile fading as tourists scattered across the square, cameras flashing and maps unfolding. She leaned in closer, lowering her voice.

"Mayor Jones, we need to talk."

The mayor's brow creased, her focus sharpening. "What is it, Sierra?"

Sierra's eyes drifted toward the edge of the square. A family posed for photos near a patch of wildflowers—flowers that weren't meant to be trampled.

"I was out painting earlier this week," Sierra began, her voice tight. "I went to my favorite spot, where the ley lines converge. It was trashed, Mayor. Garbage everywhere, plants crushed, rocks moved. It was… it was heartbreaking."

The mayor's expression fell, concern clouding her features.

"I'm scared this is just the beginning," Sierra said. Her voice wavered despite her effort to steady it. "This rush of tourism and development—it's not sustainable. It's not good for the land. And it's not good for us."

Mayor Jones sighed, her shoulders dipping slightly. "I

understand, Sierra. Believe me, I do. But as mayor, I have to stay neutral. The town is divided, and I can't risk alienating either side right now."

Sierra's fingers gripped the edge of the counter. "Neutrality won't protect the ley lines, Mayor. It won't stop people from tearing up places they don't understand. Every careless step feels like a wound. This isn't just history—it's alive. It's sacred."

The mayor's expression softened, and her voice dropped into something quieter. "I'm working on something, Sierra. But we have to tread carefully. We need to bring people together, not drive them further apart."

Sierra closed her eyes briefly and exhaled. "I know. I just hope we're not too late."

Mayor Jones placed a hand on Sierra's shoulder. "Keep doing what you're doing. Your art, your voice—they remind people of what's at stake. They matter."

Sierra forced a smile. "Thank you, Mayor. I'll keep trying."

Mayor Jones gave her shoulder a brief squeeze before turning back toward her office, her figure fading into the bustling crowd.

Sierra watched her go, her chest tight with unspoken fears. Around her, tourists laughed, vendors called out their wares, and the air buzzed with life. But Sierra could only see the thin threads tying Redstone to its roots—fragile, frayed, and dangerously close to breaking.

Her gaze drifted toward the family near the wildflowers, the parents oblivious to the damage beneath their feet. The knot in her chest pulled tighter.

"We must defend what matters," she said softly.

The breeze stirred, carrying the scent of sunbaked earth and sage. Sierra straightened her shoulders, her resolve firm and unyielding. Whatever came next, she would not turn away.

Chapter 6

Lucas stepped into the Redstone Inn, where the air seemed to hold its breath, steeped in stories and desert quiet. The lobby, though modest, carried a distinct charm—weathered wooden floors creaked softly underfoot, their grain worn smooth by countless travelers. Faded photographs of desert landscapes lined the adobe walls, offering sepia-toned glimpses of a time when the land felt wilder, its keepers fewer. Yellowed mining maps stretched across one wall, their intricate lines drawn like veins over ancient skin.

The air carried a faint tang of sun-warmed clay mixed with varnish from polished banisters and a trace of lemon oil stubbornly clinging to well-loved surfaces. In the corners, paraffin wax from antique lanterns added sharpness to the scent, softened by the faint sweetness of sun-dried mesquite pods tucked into some unseen bowl nearby.

A grand iron chandelier hung overhead, its warm glow pooling soft light into the corners of the room.

At the front desk, Susan—middle-aged, sharp-eyed but kind—stood with an air of practiced hospitality. A silver pendant rested lightly against her collarbone, glinting each time she shifted. Her smile was warm, but her eyes were watchful, cataloging more than they revealed.

Dr. Grant, I presume?" she said.

Lucas adjusted his glasses. "Word travels fast in Redstone, I see."

"Faster than a desert storm." She handed him an old-fashioned brass key attached to a leather fob. Her smile faded just slightly, her voice lowering. "Your arrival has stirred up more than just curiosity, Dr. Grant. Some here think you're here to uncover truth, others… well, let's just say they'd rather keep certain doors closed.

"And what's the general consensus?" Lucas asked. "What's the talk of the town?"

Susan hesitated. "Depends on who you ask. Redstone has its own rhythm, Dr. Grant, and its secrets rarely dance to an outsider's tune."

"I don't dance much, I'm afraid, Susan."

Her smile returned, faint but genuine. "Then just listen. You'll find the town has ways of speaking. Especially at the evening market."

"The market?" Lucas's brow lifted slightly.

"There's more than trinkets and roasted corn there, Dr. Grant. It's a special place. And people talk. Sometimes more freely than they realize."

"Got it." Lucas's voice softened, almost to himself. "Well, I'll do my best to separate fact from fiction."

In his room, Lucas unpacked his bag with slow, methodical movements. When he reached a framed photograph, he paused. The image froze him and Elana in a moment of happiness—smiles unclouded by the fractures that would later splinter them apart. He set it gently on the nightstand, where the glass caught the amber glow of the setting sun.

Sinking into a chair by the window, he opened a leather-bound notebook. Its pages were crisp, blank, expectant. Below, the town murmured with distant voices and the faint strum of a guitar drifting up from the square.

For a long moment, he stared at the empty page. Then, in careful strokes, he wrote a single line:

The truth is a fragile thing, and so is the will to uncover it.

He closed the notebook and exhaled, his gaze settling on the desert stretching endlessly into the horizon. The evening market awaited, and with it, perhaps, the first loose threads of Redstone's tangled truths.

Chapter 7

LUCAS STEPPED INTO MAYOR HELEN JONES' OFFICE, the air cool despite the relentless desert sun outside. The room spoke of history—black-and-white photos lined the walls, their faces gazing out from another era. Leather-bound books crowded wooden shelves, and an old map hung prominently behind the mayor's desk. Its faded ink traced the desert's contours like veins across parchment, etched with both precision and reverence.

Lucas paused, studying the map. "Remarkable detail," he murmured. "Maps like this aren't just geography—they're memory."

Mayor Jones, seated behind her antique desk, nodded. "It was drawn by one of the first cartographers to settle here. He used to say every line was a thread in a tapestry. We have to be careful, Dr. Grant. Tugging too hard at one thread might unravel more than we expect."

She gestured to the chair across from her, and Lucas sat. Beside her, a man in a pressed uniform stood with his hands clasped behind his back.

"This is Chief Martin Vega," the mayor said. "Our chief of police and one of the steadiest voices in Redstone."

Chief Vega extended a hand, his grip firm. "Dr. Grant, good to meet you. This town means a lot to us, and we're at a delicate juncture. Your expertise could be vital."

Lucas returned the handshake, his brow knitting slightly. "I'll help however I can. What exactly do you need from me?"

Mayor Jones leaned forward slightly, her hands folded on the desk. "Redstone's sudden popularity has been… disruptive. What was once quiet reverence has turned into a spectacle. Social media attention brought a wave of tourists, and with them, complications we weren't prepared for."

"Complications?" Lucas asked.

"Damage to protected sites. Conflicts between locals and visitors. And then there's Caldwell." The mayor's lips pressed into a thin line before she continued. "He's a businessman, Lucas. He speaks about investment, about progress. And he's offering generous donations to the community. But I can't shake the feeling there's something more behind his promises."

Lucas adjusted his glasses. "And my role in this?"

Chief Vega answered. "We want you to do what you do best, Dr. Grant—dissect myth with science. Study the ley lines, explain the phenomena with evidence, and dispel the rumors fueling this frenzy."

Mayor Jones nodded. "We believe that if people understand there's a rational explanation for what they think they're experiencing, the hysteria will fade. Things will settle. The town can breathe again."

Lucas considered her words, his thoughts already running ahead. "Spectral analysis, geomagnetic surveys, soil composition studies… I can start with those. But scientific findings don't always sway belief. People hold tightly to what they want to be true."

"We understand," Mayor Jones said, her voice softer now. "But your lectures, your presence—they can help steer the conversation. Show people that there's beauty in understanding, not just in mystery."

Vega's steady gaze met Lucas's. "It won't be easy. People here are divided. Some want Caldwell's money. Others want him gone. And there are those who don't want any answers at all—they want to believe the ley lines are magic."

Lucas nodded slowly. "You're asking me to walk a tightrope, then. Prove a truth that might not be welcome."

"Exactly," Mayor Jones said. "We need a cooling effect, Lucas. Something that eases the temperature on both sides before something breaks."

Lucas leaned back in his chair, letting their request settle in. Outside the window, the golden light of late afternoon spilled across the rooftops of Redstone, painting everything in hues of amber and shadow.

"I'll do what I can," he said. "But you should know—science doesn't always deliver the answers people want to hear."

Mayor Jones smiled faintly. "That's a risk we're willing to take."

Chief Vega extended his hand again, and Lucas shook it.

"Thank you, Dr. Grant," Vega said. "Redstone needs a clear voice right now. We're trusting you to be that."

Lucas stood, his mind already piecing together what came next—field surveys, interviews, and, inevitably, confrontation. But beneath the data points and sensor readings, he felt something else stir: curiosity. The ley lines might not hold magic, but they held something. And Lucas intended to find out what.

Chapter 8

LUCAS STEPPED OUT OF Mayor Helen Jones's office and into the afternoon light. Their conversation echoed in his mind, a series of threads pulling tighter as he began to see the town through a sharper lens. His role was clear now, but so were the fractures running through Redstone.

The main street stretched before him, adobe buildings clustered like sunbaked fossils. Awnings sagged in the dry breeze, bright fabrics fluttering above hand-lettered signs offering pottery, woven blankets, and "authentic desert experiences." Sunlight bleached the edges of everything it touched, casting sharp shadows onto the uneven pavement.

He walked slowly, hands tucked into his pockets, taking in the storefronts and the faces passing by. A shopper squinted at a tourist guide. A shopkeeper rearranged bottles of homemade prickly pear syrup. An elderly woman swept dust from her doorstep in repetitive arcs, her expression carved with quiet determination.

Near a shaded bench, a little girl sat cross-legged, braiding wildflowers into uneven crowns. Her younger brother knelt beside her, both engrossed in their delicate work. Lucas paused for a moment before continuing.

Lucas became aware that conversations hushed slightly as he passed. Glances lingered a second too long. He wasn't being challenged, but he wasn't invisible either. He felt like Redstone was watching him.

From a café patio, sharp laughter cut through the heat. Two men leaned close across a table, shoulders hunched as though sharing a secret. One of them caught Lucas's glance and held it briefly before turning back. Their voices dropped lower.

Lucas paused in front of a general store. A rusted bell chimed faintly as customers shuffled in and out. Through the window, a woman behind the counter wrapped a small trinket in brown paper, her hands quick and efficient. The shelves were lined with dusty souvenirs—tiny bottles of sand art, leather bracelets, postcards painted with desert sunsets.

He hesitated, then stepped inside.

An older man stood near a display of ceramic pots, adjusting a crooked price tag with steady hands. When he noticed Lucas, his expression changed—not quite welcoming, but not hostile either.

"You're the professor, aren't you?"

Lucas nodded. "Yes, sir. I am."

"Careful where you dig, son. Redstone's got layers. Some of 'em don't like being disturbed."

Lucas frowned. "Layers?"

The man shrugged, his attention returning to the display. "People come here looking for answers—to the ley lines, to the desert, to themselves. But answers aren't always kind. Or cheap."

Lucas lingered for a moment, but it was clear the conversation was over.

Back on the street, golden light spilled across the rooftops, and the square began to stir. It was undeniably beautiful—the colors, the warmth, the hum of life threading through every corner. But the cracks were there too, faint but undeniable. The way conversations quieted as he passed. The flicker of suspicion in a shopkeeper's glance.

A child darted past him, chasing a paper airplane as it danced through the air. It landed, skidding across the dusty ground, before coming to a stop. The child hesitated, then turned and ran back to their family, leaving the paper to settle in the dirt.

Lucas stared at the crumpled airplane for a long moment. His thoughts turned to stories—the ones people told themselves and the ones they refused to let die.

Chapter 9

THAT EVENING, at Susan's suggestion, Lucas walked to the Sunset Market, his mind a mix of curiosity and skepticism. Redstone swirled around him. The southwestern sky blazed with hues of orange and crimson and Sunset Market buzzed with energy. Each booth brimmed with handcrafted goods, from pottery painted in earthen tones to jewelry that glittered like shards of desert light. Lucas paused at a booth lined with vivid paintings—scenes of mesas and canyons that seemed to glow with an inner fire.

"Beautiful, aren't they?" a voice said, warm and curious. Lucas turned to see a woman in a linen shirt and jeans streaked with paint. Her dark hair was pulled back, but strands escaped to frame her face, which bore the kind of expression that suggested she could see more than most.

"They're... alive," Lucas replied, surprised by his own words. He gestured to the painting of a sunset cascading over a ridge. "It's as if the desert is breathing."

The woman smiled. "It does, in a way. You just have to listen closely."

Lucas glanced at her skeptically. "So I've been told," he said. "Though I'm here to prove otherwise."

"Prove otherwise?" she asked, her brow arching with interest. "Let me guess—you're the professor."

Lucas nodded. Again he was surprised that anyone at all would know he had come. "Guilty. Lucas Grant. And you are?"

"Sierra Castillo," she said. Her handshake was firm. "Painter, storyteller, and defender of everything you're probably here to disprove."

Her smile was disarming, but there was a challenge in her eyes. Lucas found himself smiling back. "I'm not here to ruin anything. Just looking for the truth."

She tilted her head. "And what will you do if the truth isn't what you expect?" she asked. The question lingered between them like the heat radiating off the sandstone streets.

Lucas hesitated. "I suppose that depends on what I find."

"Or what finds you," Sierra replied. She turned back to her booth. She rearranged a row of necklaces made of turquoise, obsidian and silver. "The desert has a way of revealing things—sometimes what you're looking for, sometimes what you're not ready to see."

Her words hung in the air, unsettling him. Before he could respond, a group of tourists passed by, loudly admiring the paintings and snapping photos. Sierra's smile faltered as she watched them.

"It's not just about art," she said quietly. "It's about connection. I wish more people understood that."

Lucas tracked where she was looking. "Is that why you're so passionate about the ley lines? You think they connect... what, people? Places?"

Turning back to him, her eyes locked onto his with startling intensity. "Everything. They connect everything. And if we lose that connection, we lose ourselves."

The air between them suddenly seemed full of unspoken tension. For a moment, Lucas felt her conviction crackling in the space between them, challenging him.

"I'll admit," Lucas said, breaking the silence, "you've made me curious. If the ley lines really hold the answers you think they do, maybe you can show me."

Sierra's smile returned, softer now. "Meet me at the café behind you in an hour. I'll tell you more."

———

The Sunset Market thrummed with life—a vibrant mosaic of sound, scent, and light. String lights draped over vendor stalls shimmered like suspended stars, their warm glow painting the adobe walls in hues of amber and gold. Lucas moved through the crowd with careful purpose, following the rhythmic hum of conversation and the faint pull of guitar strings carried on the night breeze.

The Desert Rose Café came into view, its patio bustling with clusters of locals and tourists. At a corner table, Sierra Castillo sat beneath the soft glow of a hanging lantern. Her fingers traced the rim of a ceramic mug, her gaze distant as though her thoughts were wandering somewhere far beyond the market square.

When he approached, she looked up. Their eyes met, and for a brief moment, Lucas's world seemed to slow. The crowd's hum dimmed to a murmur. Sierra smiled—small, genuine, contemplative.

"Dr. Grant," she said as he reached the table. "I was starting to wonder if you'd find your way here."

Lucas gestured to the empty chair across from her. "Mind if I join you?"

"Please."

For a moment, neither of them spoke. They watched the buzzing crowd around them—laughter, clinking glasses, the distant wail of a violin. Sierra broke the silence first.

"Have you felt it yet, Lucas? The pulse of this place? The way it holds its breath between each sunset and sunrise? The way that dance comes easy after twilight? You have come to a special place."

"The desert certainly is beautiful." Lucas looked past Sierra to the darkening horizon where the first stars appeared. "It's different this evening. It's like the edges of this place blur when the light fades."

"My teacher, an Elder named Natan, once said, *Long ago, the desert was silent except for the wind and the song of stones. But one day, the earth cracked open, and light poured out—not blinding, but warm, like the glow of a hidden fire. The people who listened carefully said it wasn't just light; it was a promise, and the ley lines are all that remains of that whispered vow.*'"

"What do you see, professor?"

Lucas considered her words, taking his time before replying. "I see a town caught between two stories—one it's telling the world, and one it's trying to tell itself."

Sierra's smile was faint, her eyes sparkling. "That's a good answer. You're observant, even if you don't quite believe what you're observing."

Lucas leaned back slightly, his arms crossing over his chest. "Belief isn't really my specialty, Sierra."

She studied him for a moment. "You think science can explain everything?"

"Not everything," Lucas admitted. "But most things. Eventually."

Sierra tilted her head slightly. "That's the difference between us. You see things like our ley lines as anomalies—data points. I see them as something alive. Not magic, not folklore—just... alive."

Lucas hesitated, choosing his words carefully. "I don't dismiss what you're saying, Sierra. But I also do what I do with just feelings or instincts. I need evidence."

"And what if evidence comes in a form you don't recognize?" she asked. "What if it doesn't fit neatly into your hypothesis?"

He opened his mouth to respond but stopped. For a moment, the only sound between them was the faint melody of the guitar drifting across the square.

Sierra shifted slightly, her voice quieter now. "Yesterday, I saw damage—plants trampled, stones moved, trash scattered across a place that should have been untouched. The energy that I felt there was fractured, chaotic. Like something was bleeding, and no one could stop it."

Lucas frowned. "Energy you felt?"

She nodded. "Yes, Lucas. There was interference. Disruption."

He paused, his fingers tapping lightly against the edge of the table. "And you think the ley lines are… what, sentient?"

"Not sentient. Connected." Her steady and unwavering eyes held his. "And fragile."

Lucas sighed and looked away briefly, his gaze drifting over the glowing lights of the market. "You speak about this place with such certainty. I envy that, in a way."

"It's not certainty, Lucas. It's trust." She smiled softly. "But I suspect that's something you don't give away easily."

"No," he admitted. "I don't."

Sierra took a slow sip from her mug before setting it down with deliberate care. "You know, for someone who claims to rely only on evidence, you've spent an awful lot of time listening to me talk about things you can't measure."

Lucas smiled playfully. "Maybe I'm just good at collecting qualitative data."

She laughed, and it caught Lucas off guard. It felt like something unguarded passing between them—brief, but real.

The market was winding down around them. Vendors packed away their wares; strings of lights overhead dimmed; evening deepened into night. Sierra stood, pushing back her chair, and Lucas rose instinctively with her.

"Lucas," she said, her tone conspiratorial now, her smile returning with a playful edge, "I have a feeling you didn't come all this way to only measure electromagnetic fields and scribble in your notebook."

He raised an eyebrow. "What do you suggest I'm here for, then?"

She hesitated just long enough to let curiosity bloom between them. "Maybe something more. Maybe something you're not quite ready to admit yet."

Lucas let out a breathless laugh. "You know, you're not very good at leaving things on a clear note."

Sierra leaned in closer to Lucas. Her voice took on a conspiratorial tone as she whispered, "Lucas, my new friend. I know we just met," she paused, "but would you like to join me tomorrow evening for some history and maybe a little local color?"

Lucas, his thoughts tossed between anticipation and apprehension, nodded in agreement. "Yes. I think I would."

As Sierra walked away, her silhouette dissolved into the warm glow of lantern light and the drifting haze of desert dust. Lucas remained standing by the table, watching her go.

Chapter 10

THE SUN HAD LONG SLIPPED behind the jagged peaks when Lucas and Sierra arrived at Hank and Marla Jenkins' ranch house. Warm light spilled from the windows, pooling onto the desert floor like molten gold. Faint conversation drifted from inside, carrying with it a current of expectation.

Inside, the room buzzed with quiet tension. Mayor Helen Jones stood near the fireplace, her arms crossed over her chest, her gaze sharp and watchful. Chief Vega leaned against the doorway, his expression unreadable. Members of the Apache County Historical Society filled the space, clustered in small groups, their faces a mix of reverence and unease.

"The man knows how to set a stage," Lucas murmured to Sierra.

Hank stood near the hearth, one hand resting on a battered leather journal displayed on the mantel. He cleared his throat, and the room quieted.

"Thank you all for coming tonight," Hank began, his voice steady but edged with something raw. "Redstone is at a crossroads, and the choices we make now will ripple through generations. This journal belonged to my great-grandfather. It's more than just pages and ink—it's a map, a record, and I believe it's a warning."

He opened the journal carefully, the leather creaking faintly, and began to read aloud. His words painted a picture of ley lines as more than folklore—threads of energy binding the land, the people, and their stories together. Sierra sat rigid beside Lucas, her eyes locked on Hank, her breath measured.

But just as Hank's voice grew softer, carrying a passage about the fragility of those connections, a voice cut through the stillness.

"That's enough."

A man stood near the doorway—a stranger to Lucas. He was middle-aged, his suit sharp but dusty, his boots worn from long walks over rough ground. His face was lean, lined from sun and frown lines, and his sharp eyes scanned the room like a predator assessing prey.

"Folklore, Mr. Jenkins," the man said, his voice calm but biting. "Romantic stories wrapped in superstition. You're wasting everyone's time with fairy tales."

Hank's lips pressed into a thin line. "You are…?"

The stranger smiled faintly. "Randall Greaves. Let's just say I have an interest in seeing Redstone thrive. And nostalgia won't pay the bills, Hank. Progress will."

Sierra stood abruptly. "Tell us about progress, Mr. Greaves. Did you see the damage left behind at the ley line site last week? The crushed plants, the displaced stones, the garbage left to bake under the sun?"

Greaves tilted his head slightly. "I know what growth looks like. And sometimes, it's messy. But growth is survival."

Before Sierra could respond, Lucas spoke up, his voice cutting through the rising tension.

"Mr. Greaves," he said evenly, "stories might not pay the bills, but they anchor a community. They create identity, purpose—even a reason to fight for survival. Ignore them, and you lose something irreplaceable."

Greaves's eyes narrowed. "You're a scientist, aren't you? You should know better than to lean on sentiment."

Lucas didn't flinch. "Science doesn't dismiss cultural value—it contextualizes it. The two don't have to be enemies."

The air in the room felt charged, crackling with something unsaid. Greaves's smile returned, cold and thin.

"Well," he said, spreading his hands. "I suppose time will tell who's right."

He turned and walked out, his boots clicking sharply against the wooden floor. The room stayed silent long after the door swung shut behind him.

Hank exhaled slowly and set the journal back on the mantel. This is about what kind of place we want Redstone to be—what we want to protect, and what we're willing to lose."

Mayor Jones stepped forward, her voice firm but calm. "We need to focus on solutions, not division. Tonight isn't about choosing sides—it's about finding a path forward."

The discussion resumed, hesitant at first but gaining momentum as voices rose and ideas sparked. Lucas listened, his gaze moving from face to face. The divide in the room felt as sharp as the edge of a canyon, but the urgency in the voices around him was undeniable.

Sierra leaned closer to Lucas, her voice low. "Did you notice how he spoke? Like someone who already has a stake in this. Like someone who knows more than he's letting on."

Lucas nodded slowly, his eyes still on the door where Greaves had disappeared.

"Yeah," he said softly. "And I don't think he came here just to argue."

Outside, the night had deepened. Shadows crept along the desert floor, stretching across the horizon like fingers grasping for something unseen.

Chapter 11

THE DIRT ROAD TWISTED alongside the Little Colorado River, its uneven path kicking up clouds of dust as the truck bounced over loose stones and dips in the earth. Sunlight filtered through cottonwoods, dappling the riverbanks in flickering gold. Birds flitted between branches, their bright songs punctuating the low groan of tires against gravel.

Lucas squinted against the glare of the sun reflecting off the water, his voice carrying over the rumble of the truck. "It's strange. Nature often seems random, chaotic even. But here…" His words trailed off as he scanned the vibrant pockets of greenery along the water's edge. "It feels intentional—like the desert itself made a decision to allow this place to exist."

Beside him, Marla Jenkins smiled faintly, her gaze lingering on the river. "This place has always been intentional, Lucas. Survival here doesn't happen by accident—it happens through hard work, patience, and a little faith."

From the driver's seat, Hank Jenkins grunted, his eyes fixed on the sandstone outcrop rising ahead. "We're not here for sightseeing," he said gruffly. "First stop's just up there."

They stopped atop a narrow plateau. Lucas climbed out, boots crunching on gravel as he adjusted his pack. The sandstone formation loomed in front of them, carved with patterns—spirals, lines, and humanoid figures—that shimmered faintly in the harsh light.

Marla stepped forward, her hand brushing against one of the carvings, her voice soft. "These aren't just decorations. They're reminders."

Lucas leaned in closer, tracing the weathered grooves with his eyes. "They're remarkable. Beautiful." He turned to Hank. "But they're just carvings. Stories etched in stone."

"Stories are evidence, Lucas. Evidence of what mattered to people who lived here long before you and I showed up."

Lucas started to reply, but a sudden gust of wind howled through the canyon. Sand spiraled upward, caught in invisible currents. The voice of the wind was deep, resonant, almost melodic.

The group froze.

The wind dissipated almost as quickly as it had begun, leaving behind only the soft rustle of leaves.

"My great-grandfather used to say this canyon speaks when it's ready, not when we are," Marla said

"It's just wind moving through rock formations," Lucas replied. "A natural resonance effect."

But even to himself, the words felt thin.

Hank stepped closer, his boots grinding into the gravel. "Do you honestly believe that, Professor? Or is that just the most convenient answer?"

Lucas hesitated. The canyon stretched out around them—vast, silent, expectant.

Marla's voice cut through the sudden tension. "Maybe that's why you're here, Lucas. Not just to measure. Not just to observe. But to listen."

Far below, the river moved in lazy curls, its surface reflecting slivers of sky. The carvings on the stone spoke their own silent language, one Lucas wasn't sure he could learn.

Marla turned away and started walking. "We should keep moving. There's more to see."

Hank adjusted his hat, muttering something under his breath, before leading the way back to the truck.

Lucas lingered, looking again at the spirals carved into the sandstone.

As they made their way back down the canyon, Hank and Marla's conversation wandered through the history of the ranch. Marla reflected, "It was more than luck that kept this place alive. Divine guidance, perhaps. Those carvings and stories—they're memories of those who showed a resilience that was rooted in something greater than themselves."

Unable to hold back, Lucas countered, his voice clipped. "Isn't it possible they survived because they understood the environment? These glyphs and tales are fascinating, yes, but they're not evidence of anything beyond human ingenuity."

Hank's response was immediate. "Reducing their lives to equations and theories ignores what truly defined them. Their connection to this land wasn't scientific—it was spiritual. That balance was their foundation, their strength."

Hank continued, his voice steady and resolute. "These stories matter, Lucas. Not as relics or quaint traditions, but as a legacy that deserves to be known. I won't let it be forgotten."

Chapter 12

For the second time that day, Lucas took the sightseer's tour of the county. The truck rumbled over the uneven desert path, tires kicking up dust as the horizon shimmered in the afternoon heat. Lucas adjusted the dial on the dashboard—not out of any real need, but to fill the silence stretching between them.

"It might very well be folklore," **Sierra** said, her voice thoughtful as she gazed out the window. Her eyes lingered on the distant mountains, their peaks softened by haze. "But folklore often holds a kind of truth science doesn't know how to measure."

Lucas kept his attention on the winding road ahead. "That's… poetic. But science works in evidence, observation—things we can test and measure."

Sierra turned toward him slightly, her expression curious rather than defensive. "Do you ever wonder if evidence might not be the only way to understand the world? What about the feeling you get in a place like this—the kind you can't measure with instruments?"

Lucas sighed, his hands flexing slightly on the wheel. "I think feelings are important, but they're not what I build conclusions on. What you're calling ley lines might just be magnetic fields or geological oddities. Things we can study and map."

Sierra smiled faintly. "And have those studies ever explained why people across generations are drawn to these places? Why they build stories around them and feel connected to them?"

Lucas hesitated. "No. I guess they haven't."

They drove in companionable silence for a few moments, the hum of the engine filling the space between them. Shadows from scattered clouds stretched across the road, the desert flickering between light and shadow.

Sierra leaned back in her seat, her voice softer now. "When I was twelve, my mom took me to a stone circle deep in the desert. She placed my hands on the ground and told me to listen—not with my ears, but with my heart."

Lucas glanced at her, his brow furrowing slightly. "And did you feel… something?"

Her gaze stayed fixed on the horizon. "Yes. It felt like a vibration, a hum—like the land itself was alive. I can't explain it in a way that would satisfy your research paper, but it was real to me."

The truck jolted over a deep rut, breaking the thread of their conversation. Lucas steadied the wheel, his mind turning over Sierra's words. "I'm not dismissing what you felt, Sierra. But if there's something real there—something measurable—I'd like to understand it."

Sierra smiled, this time warmly. "That's fair, Lucas. I'm not asking you to stop being a scientist. I just hope you'll leave a little room for wonder while you're here."

The wind stirred through the open windows, carrying with it the sharp scent of sagebrush and sunbaked earth. Lucas inhaled deeply, the desert air grounding him in the moment.

"What if I told you I want to believe?" he said, his voice quieter now. "Not in ley lines, exactly—but in something bigger. Something that makes sense of the chaos."

Sierra studied him for a moment, her smile softening into something more genuine. "That's all I ask. To believe there's more to this place than what we can chart on a map."

The truck bumped along the trail, the canyon ahead growing larger with each turn. The weight of their earlier tension had lifted, leaving behind something lighter—an understanding, tentative but real.

Lucas adjusted the rearview mirror absently. "Sierra, what would your abuela say if she were here right now?"

Sierra's smile turned wistful. "She'd tell you that the land doesn't ask to be understood—it asks to be respected. And sometimes, that starts with just listening."

Lucas nodded slightly, his gaze fixed on the approaching canyon. He wasn't ready to admit it aloud, but something about her words lingered, like an echo just out of reach.

The truck crested a hill, and the canyon opened before them—vast, jagged, and ancient. The wind carried a faint whistle as it funneled through the rocks, low and hollow, like the distant note of a string plucked in a cavern.

"We're almost there," Sierra said softly.

Chapter 13

THE NARROW PATH WOUND its way along the ridge, carved into the earth by years of wind, rain, and careful footsteps. Sierra walked ahead, her movements deliberate, her gaze steady on the trail before her. The sun hung low in the sky, casting long, golden shadows across the rocky terrain.

Behind her, Lucas adjusted the strap of his pack, his boots crunching against loose gravel. The air carried a faint chill despite the sunlight, and an expectant stillness seemed to settle around them.

"Lucas," Sierra said softly, her voice clear in the quiet. "These ley lines aren't just coordinates on a map. My mother used to say they're like arteries—pathways carrying something vital through the earth."

Lucas glanced up from his footing, his expression thoughtful. "And what do they carry, Sierra? Energy? Memories?"

She turned slightly, her gaze meeting his. "Connection. Between the sky, the earth, and the people who walk this land. Your instruments might pick up magnetic fields or anomalies, but that's only one layer. Some things you have to feel to understand."

Lucas hesitated, his brow furrowing slightly. "But are those feelings real, Sierra? Or are they just... stories we tell ourselves to make sense of things we can't measure?"

Sierra's smile was patient but firm. "Does it matter if they're stories, if they still guide people to something meaningful?"

The path widened as they crested the ridge, revealing a sweeping view of the valley below. At its center, nestled among scattered brush and stone, stood an ancient stone circle—the whispering stones— weathered and resolute against time's erosion.

"That's it," Sierra said, her voice low with something close to reverence. "The intersection. Where ley lines meet."

Lucas followed her gaze, his eyes narrowing slightly as he took in the formation. His scientific mind began cataloging the scene— stone placement, erosion patterns, potential historical context—but the sheer presence of the site silenced his questions.

Sierra placed a hand lightly on his arm. "Come on," she said, guiding him down the path toward the valley floor.

The silence grew heavier the closer they came to the stones, broken only by the faint rustle of the wind weaving through cracks in the rocks. Lucas hesitated at the edge of the circle, his feet shifting slightly as if stepping over an invisible threshold.

Sierra walked ahead and paused near the largest stone, her posture still, her breaths slow and measured. Her fingertips brushed its surface, the rough texture grounding her in the moment.

"When I was a child," she said, her voice barely above a whisper, "my grandmother brought me here. She didn't tell me what to expect—only to stand still, to listen, and to let myself be present."

Lucas watched her, his own breathing slowing to match the stillness of the scene around them.

"And did you feel something?" he asked after a long pause.

Sierra turned to him, her expression calm but resolute. "I felt like I was part of something much older than myself. It wasn't loud or dramatic—it was quiet, but steady. Like the difference between hearing something and knowing it's there."

Lucas looked down at his boots. "Well, that's hard to quantify."

For a long moment, neither of them spoke. The stone circle stood silent, its edges glowing faintly in the light of the setting sun.

Somewhere nearby, a bird called out—a sharp, clear note that echoed briefly before fading back into the quiet.

Lucas took a slow step forward, crossing into the circle. The air felt subtly different inside its perimeter—cooler, heavier, expectant.

Sierra's gaze stayed on him, her eyes reflecting the deepening twilight.

"Do you feel it?" she asked.

Lucas didn't answer immediately. His gaze moved across the stones, the sky, the horizon stretching endlessly beyond the valley.

"I feel… something," he admitted finally, his voice barely audible.

Sierra's smile was small but genuine, her shoulders relaxing slightly.

The wind stirred again, lifting strands of Sierra's hair as the sun dipped lower, painting the valley in shades of amber and shadow.

"Let's stay a little longer," she said quietly.

Twelve-year-old Sierra crouched behind a gnarled juniper tree, watching her grandmother with wide, curious eyes. The old woman moved with practiced grace, her weathered hands tracing invisible patterns in the air as she walked the perimeter of the stone circle.

"Come, nieta," her grandmother called, her voice as warm and rich as the desert soil. "It's time you learned our family's legacy."

Sierra stepped out from her hiding place, her heart racing with excitement and a touch of fear. As she approached the circle, she felt a strange tingling in her feet, as if the very ground beneath her was alive.

"Do you feel it, Sierra?" her grandmother asked, dark eyes twinkling. "The pulse of the earth?"

Sierra nodded, unable to find words for the sensation coursing through her body. It was like music without sound, a rhythm that resonated in her bones.

"Place your hands on the center stone," her grandmother instructed. "And listen with your heart, not your ears."

With trembling fingers, Sierra touched the ancient rock. Instantly, the world around her exploded into vibrant color. The ley lines, invisible moments before, now glowed with an otherworldly light, crisscrossing the landscape like rivers of pure energy.

"Abuela!" she gasped. "I can see them! The ley lines!"

Her grandmother's smile was radiant. "You have the gift, my dear. Just as I did, and my mother before me. We are the guardians of this sacred knowledge."

As Sierra stood there, hands pressed against the stone, she felt a profound connection to the land, to her ancestors, and to a power greater than herself. Voices whispered in languages long forgotten, sharing secrets of the earth and sky.

"Remember this moment," her grandmother said. "For it is now your duty to protect these lines, to keep their power safe from those who would misuse it."

Sierra nodded solemnly, the magnitude of the responsibility settling over her like an unseen mantle. It was a moment of quiet realization—her path had shifted, her purpose crystallized. Whatever lay ahead, she understood now that her life would never return to what it had been.

Sierra opened her eyes, the memory retreating into the stillness of the evening. The sensation it left behind remained—something steady and grounding, like an anchor within her chest. She smiled faintly, thinking of how that single moment from her past had shaped so many of her choices, leading her here.

She stepped carefully into the center of the stone circle, her movements deliberate. The air felt cooler within the perimeter, as though the stones held onto the last shadows of the day. Sierra closed her eyes and placed her palms lightly against one of the weathered stones, drawing in a slow breath.

"Lucas," she said softly, her voice steady but edged with something close to reverence, "do you feel it? The stillness here— it's… deliberate. Waiting to be understood."

Lucas hesitated on the edge of the circle, his boots scuffing against the rocky ground. Curiosity flickered in his eyes. After a moment, he stepped forward and joined her.

They stood together, side by side, surrounded by the faint glow of twilight. The air shifted subtly, carrying the distant sounds of crickets and the faint hoot of an owl somewhere beyond the ridge.

Sierra's voice was quiet but firm. "Lucas, the Ley lines aren't meant to be measured. They're meant to be experienced—paths of discovery through our lives."

Lucas turned slightly to face her. His brow furrowed, and his voice was quieter now. "And where does this path lead you, Sierra?"

She didn't look away from the stone beneath her fingertips. "To understanding. To stillness. To places where answers aren't spoken aloud, but felt."

Lucas stared at her for a moment, his expression caught between doubt and something softer—an unspoken question he wasn't ready to voice.

Sierra met his gaze, her eyes clear in the fading light. "Don't you ever wonder, Lucas? What might start to make sense if you stopped searching for answers, and, just paused?"

For a moment, Lucas's shoulders seemed to ease. He looked again at the stones around them, then up to the stars beginning to prick through the deepening sky.

Sierra's voice softened. "The first step isn't about believing. It's about being open—to the possibility that there's more here than we know."

Lucas hesitated, his thoughts turning over Sierra's words like stones in his palm. Finally, he gave the faintest nod.

They stood together, surrounded by the quiet expanse of the desert. The world beyond the circle seemed distant, as if this space existed in a slightly different layer of reality—thinner, quieter, more intentional.

Sierra let her hand fall from the stone and stepped back, her expression calm but watchful. Lucas remained still, his focus fixed on the stones as if they might offer him something if he looked long enough.

The stars brightened overhead, scattered across the sky like scattered glass on velvet.

Sierra spoke again, her voice low. "It's enough, Lucas, just to stand here. To not turn away."

He didn't respond, but he didn't step back either.

Chapter 14

The desert was deepening into dusk as Sierra and Lucas made their way back along the narrow trail. The fading light painted the rocks in dusky shades of lavender and burnt orange, shadows pooling in the crevices of the canyon walls.

Ahead, the sound of laughter broke through the stillness—a sharp, jarring note against the evening calm. A group of tourists emerged around a bend in the path, their neon sneakers and bright athletic wear a stark contrast to the muted desert palette.

One woman adjusted an oversized sun hat while angling her phone for a selfie against the fading glow of the rocks. A man posed beside a boulder, flexing for the camera before breaking into a laugh loud enough to echo off the canyon walls.

Sierra slowed her steps, her shoulders stiffening. The light from the woman's phone screen flared against a weathered stone, a harsh rectangle of white that cut through the soft twilight glow.

Lucas paused beside her, following her gaze.

"They don't see it," Sierra said quietly, her voice low.

The tourists bustled past them, oblivious. Someone reset the timer on their smartwatch, glancing down with a frown as if the land owed them efficiency. Another woman tugged at her leggings, muttering about the red dust clinging to the fabric.

Sierra's fingers curled into her palms. These stones—the ones that had stood for centuries, marked by generations of stories—were nothing more than a backdrop for someone's social media post.

Lucas's voice broke through her silence. "They don't know what they're standing on."

Sierra glanced at him, her expression tight. "No, they don't."

Their paths crossed briefly as the tourists chattered and shuffled away, their laughter trailing behind them like fading echoes. Dust swirled in their wake, caught in the dim light of the fading sun.

When the noise of the group finally dissolved into the distance, Sierra exhaled slowly. The stillness returned, but it felt fragile now, like glass that had been tapped too hard.

Lucas watched her carefully, his brow creased in concern. No words passed between them, but something settled in the quiet space—a mutual understanding, heavier than conversation could carry.

Sierra turned back toward the path, her steps steady but her breath tight in her chest. Lucas followed, his gaze flicking briefly back toward the direction the tourists had disappeared.

The canyon stretched out before them, its edges fading into the darkening sky. Somewhere in the distance, the owl called out again— a single note rising and falling before vanishing into the night.

Chapter 15

MARJORIE JOHANSEN'S SEVENTY-TWO YEARS in Redstone were etched into her hands—swollen, stiff, and marked by time. She sat in the corner of Ladawn's Bakery, her fingers wrapped tightly around a steaming mug of chamomile tea. The hum of conversation from the bakery softened as Sierra and Lucas leaned in closer, their attention drawn to the quiet gravity in Marjorie's voice.

"For years, I tried everything," Marjorie began, her voice carrying the weight of old struggles. "Ointments, pills, even a specialist up in Salt Lake. Nothing worked—not for long, anyway. I'd almost given up hope."

She paused, her gaze slipping toward the window as if the memory lived somewhere just beyond the glass. "But then someone told me about the meadow beyond Miller's Creek. They said that's where the ley lines meet."

Sierra nodded slightly, her voice low. "That place is special. My abuela always said it was a place of renewal."

Lucas shifted in his seat. His expression was neutral, but the flicker of scientific curiosity was unmistakable. "What happened there, Marjorie?" he asked cautiously.

"It was just before dawn," Marjorie said, her lips curving into a faint smile. "The air was still, the kind of quiet that feels like the whole world is waiting for something. I knelt in the grass, pressed my hands to the earth, and for the first time in years, the pain in my joints… it eased. It wasn't sudden, and it wasn't dramatic, but it felt… warm. Steady. Like something was moving through me."

Lucas's brow furrowed as he processed her words. He could almost hear the gears turning in his mind—thermal activity, geomagnetic anomalies, placebo effect. But something in Marjorie's tone—steady and clear, yet tinged with awe—left him momentarily silent.

Sierra's gaze flicked toward Lucas, then back to Marjorie. "And the pain? It just… went away?"

Marjorie nodded once, her hands steady around her mug. "Not overnight. It took time. Weeks, actually. But the stiffness eased, and my strength started to come back. There's no scan or test that could explain it."

She leaned forward slightly, her voice dropping to a softer register. "It wasn't about asking for healing, Dr. Grant. It was about being still enough to let it happen."

Lucas's skepticism softened, but it didn't vanish entirely. "And you've never tried to go back? To see if it would happen again?"

Marjorie chuckled, the sound light and warm, like wind moving through dry leaves. "You scientists always want repeatable results, don't you? But the ley lines don't work on demand. They give what's needed, not what's asked."

The table fell silent. The hum of the bakery began to trickle back into focus—the faint rattle of dishes, soft laughter from a nearby table, the hiss of steaming milk behind the counter.

Sierra reached across the table and placed her hand lightly over Marjorie's. "You've been given something rare, Marjorie. A reminder of what's worth protecting."

Marjorie met Sierra's gaze, her smile kind but knowing. "Sometimes reminders are all we get. And they're more than enough."

Lucas sat back slightly, his arms crossing over his chest as his gaze drifted to the mug in Marjorie's hands. "If ley lines really can... connect in ways we don't understand, maybe we're not asking the right questions."

Marjorie's smile grew wider, creases deepening around her eyes. "That's the thing about Redstone, Dr. Grant. It doesn't give you answers until you're ready to hear them."

———

Tommy leaned across the table, his gaze locking onto Lucas with a sharp focus that cut through the dim light of the café. His voice was steady, edged with something between confidence and challenge.

"You probably won't believe me, Dr. Grant," he said. "But I've seen what these ley lines can reveal—if you're open enough to notice."

Lucas's brow lifted slightly, skepticism evident but softened by curiosity. "What exactly did you see?"

Tommy leaned back, his eyes drifting past Lucas, unfocused, as though caught on something far away. "I was twelve, maybe thirteen. I used to sneak out at night, follow the ley lines like they were pulling me somewhere. I didn't know why—I just felt... drawn."

He paused, his fingers tapping lightly on the edge of his coffee cup.

"One night, under a full moon, I followed them deep into the woods. People say there's a place out there—a convergence point. I found it."

Lucas leaned forward slightly, his elbows resting on the table. "And what happened?"

"The air felt different," Tommy said quietly. "Thicker. Charged. Like every sound, every movement, was happening in slow motion.

And then I saw it—Redstone. But not like it is now."

His voice dropped, and Lucas had to strain to hear him.

"It was alive. Not just surviving—thriving. People from every walk of life, connected by something bigger than themselves. They were using the ley lines—if that's even the right word—for healing, for discovery, for building something... better. Tradition and progress weren't fighting each other; they were working together."

Lucas studied him, his skepticism faltering under the weight of Tommy's conviction. "Are you saying it was a vision? A hallucination?"

Tommy shook his head firmly. "No. It wasn't hazy or dreamlike. It felt solid—like I was standing in a place that existed, somewhere, somehow. It wasn't just a glimpse of what could be. It felt like what *should* be."

Lucas tilted his head slightly, considering. "And you've never seen anything like it again?"

Tommy's smile was faint but certain. "The ley lines didn't repeat themselves, Dr. Grant. What they showed me was enough. They give you what you need, when you need it."

———

Old Man Crick leaned back in his creaky wooden chair, the dim light of the pub catching the lines etched deep into his face. His sharp, weathered eyes fixed on Lucas, unblinking.

"You think the ley lines are just some kind of anomaly, don't you?" His gruff voice carried easily over the low murmur of nearby conversations. "Just another set of data points for you to plot on a chart."

Lucas shifted in his seat but said nothing.

Crick pressed on, his gaze steady. "These lines hold power, son. Real power. But power ain't a gift—it's a responsibility. I've seen what happens when people forget that."

He leaned forward, his elbows resting on the scratched surface of the table. His voice dropped, gravelly but sharp. "In my youth, I watched men try to bend the ley lines to their will. Greedy men. Always hunting shortcuts to fortune or control. And you know what happened?"

He paused, letting the question hang in the stale air between them.

"Everything they touched started to break. Crops withered in fields. Machines sputtered and died. People fell sick—sick in ways no doctor could explain. It wasn't revenge. It wasn't punishment. It was balance."

Lucas's brow furrowed, his skepticism clear. "You're suggesting the ley lines... react? That they have some sort of feedback loop?"

Crick let out a low chuckle, dry as sandpaper. "React? Son, the ley lines aren't machines. They don't turn on and off, and they sure don't follow your rules. But they're part of this world's order, and order doesn't like to be messed with."

Lucas's fingers tapped lightly on the rim of his glass, his mind working through Crick's words like pieces of a puzzle. "You're saying people have... experienced consequences from interacting with them?"

Crick's eyes narrowed slightly. "Consequences. That's a good word for it. But let me tell you something, Dr. Grant. You're not gonna find answers in your sensors or your spreadsheets. You'll find them in what you notice when the equipment's off. In what you feel when the air goes still, and the silence gets heavy."

Lucas frowned, his skepticism wavering under the weight of Crick's steady conviction. "But do you have proof? Anything tangible?"

Crick leaned back again, his lips curling into something between a smile and a smirk. "Proof? Boy, proof's in the moments you can't quite explain. When the air shifts and the hair on your neck stands up. When things start breaking for no good reason, and nobody can fix 'em. Proof's in what you see when you stop looking so hard for it."

The old man's eyes stayed locked on Lucas's for an uncomfortable beat before he pushed back from the table with a quiet scrape of wood against tile.

"You keep chasing your answers, Professor. Just don't dig too deep. Some things down there don't like being disturbed."

Crick stood, his movements slow but deliberate, and shuffled toward the door. The bell above it jingled faintly as he stepped out into the night.

———

Ella leaned forward, her hands wrapped tightly around a steaming cup of Brigham tea. The faint curls of steam rose between her and Lucas and Sierra as she spoke, her voice steady but low.

"I didn't always believe in the ley lines," she began. "For years, I thought they were just stories—something people told themselves to feel connected to something bigger. But then… I experienced them for myself."

Lucas tilted his head slightly, his gaze sharpening with curiosity. "What changed your mind?"

Ella's faint smile carried a hint of something distant, her eyes softening as if looking inward. "I'm a writer, and for months, I couldn't write a word. Nothing. It felt like every thought I had hit a wall I couldn't get past. One day, I decided to walk out to the river— the spot where the ley lines are supposed to run close to the water. I wasn't looking for answers. I just needed to clear my head."

Sierra nodded gently, her voice quiet. "And something shifted there?"

"It wasn't anything dramatic," Ella said, shaking her head. "No visions, no flashes of light. Just… quiet. A stillness I hadn't felt in years. I sat there for hours, listening to the river, letting everything else fade away. And then the words came back. Like someone had turned a faucet on inside me, and everything that had been stuck just… started flowing again."

Lucas's brow furrowed as he considered her words. "So you think the ley lines… what? Cleared your mind? Reset something in you?"

Ella shrugged lightly. "I don't know how to explain it. But I left that spot feeling clearer, lighter somehow. Every time I've felt blocked since, I've gone back—and it's worked. Whatever the ley lines are, they're more than just energy or folklore. They're… peace. The kind of peace that lets you hear yourself think."

Sierra reached across the table and placed a hand on Ella's arm, her voice warm with gratitude. "That's exactly why we're fighting for these places. They're not just important—they're necessary."

Lucas tapped his fingers lightly against the side of his cup, his eyes unfocused as if chasing a thought. "Maybe there's something to that. Peace as a kind of energy. Something we haven't figured out how to measure yet."

Ella chuckled softly, breaking the brief silence. "You might be overthinking it, Dr. Grant. Not everything needs to be understood to be valuable. Sometimes it's enough just to sit still long enough to feel it."

———

Bishop Mills adjusted his glasses and studied Lucas and Sierra with a calm steadiness that came from years of guiding others through doubt and conviction. "I'll admit," he said, his voice low but clear, "I didn't always believe in the ley lines. Even as a man of faith, I thought they were just stories—folklore meant to give people something to hold onto when the world felt too big."

Lucas tilted his head slightly, his analytical curiosity surfacing. "But something changed?"

A faint smile tugged at the corner of Mills's mouth. "It did. During a difficult season of my life, I found myself questioning everything—my purpose, my calling, whether I was truly helping anyone. One evening, with no plan and no expectation, I decided to walk the ley lines. I'd heard the stories for years. So I thought, why not see for myself?"

Sierra leaned forward, her expression intent. "And what happened?"

"I wasn't expecting anything," Mills admitted, his hands folding on the table in front of him. "But as I walked, something shifted. It wasn't dramatic—no visions, no voices—but the air felt different, like stepping into a pocket of stillness in the middle of chaos. When I reached what I'd later learn was an intersection of the ley lines, there was a… clarity. A peace that didn't come with answers but with acceptance."

Lucas frowned slightly, his mind turning over the details. "You think that was the ley lines? Not just your own mind finding a way to process things?"

Mills's smile softened, but his eyes remained sharp. "Maybe it was both. Maybe the ley lines aren't magic, Dr. Grant. Maybe they're conduits—threads tying us to the land, to each other, and to something larger than ourselves. You can call it God, or the universe, or even just connection, but it's real. And when you're open to it, you notice it."

Sierra placed her hand flat on the table, her voice steady but threaded with conviction. "That's what we're trying to protect, Lucas. Not just energy, not just history—but connection. To the land, to each other. To something we can't replicate once it's gone."

Lucas's gaze dropped briefly to Sierra's hand, then returned to Bishop Mills. His brow furrowed, his lips pressing together in thought. "Maybe there's more to this than I've been willing to consider," he said quietly.

The bishop gave a slight nod, his smile knowing but not smug. "You'll see, Dr. Grant. These places have a way of showing their significance. It's not about proof—it's about being open to seeing it."

The Stillness that Speaks

The desert, in twilight's last breath, folds into itself—a vast body at rest, its edges blurring into shadow. The cracked earth exhales, the stones still warm from the sun's retreat, and the wind carries the sharp scent of sage and dust like an old hymn sung in the dark. Here, time does not pass; it settles, layer upon layer, seeping into the brittle marrow of this place.

It speaks—not in words, but in stillness, in pauses so deep they feel like waiting. Every ridge and hollow holds the memory of sun and storm, of arrival and departure, of footprints worn thin by wind and time. To listen here is not a matter of ears, but of something older—something that feels more than it understands.

Night gathers, folding over the land, and the world exhales. The air, thin and cool, brushes against skin like the edge of something half-remembered. The desert does not announce itself now; its colors fade into murmurs—ochre bleeding into violet, sandstone etched with quiet light. Here, silence isn't emptiness—it's fullness.

A jackrabbit stirs, its ears thin as blades of grass, catching whispers threaded through the wind. It moves in brief, startling bursts, vanishing before its presence fully registers. A coyote lingers nearby, its shadow a trick of the dim light, moving with the stillness of something that has always been here, watching. Overhead, a hawk cries—a sharp, clean note that splits the dusk wide open. The sound carries hunger and grace, the stark laws of survival written in its flight.

Beneath all of this—the sand, the stone, the fleeting shadows—something runs unseen. The ley lines thread their way below, fine as veins under translucent skin. They hum faintly, a deep resonance pressed into the earth long before words, before people, before stories. They do not move, but they are alive, carrying some ancient intention through rock and root, through all the silent spaces where the wind pauses to listen.

This place does not bend. It does not rush to meet us, nor does it care to explain itself. The desert holds steady, its cracked surface shielding what lies beneath—a patience carved from eternity. Here, progress finds no foothold, no purchase for its hurried intentions. Plans drawn in distant offices falter when met with the unyielding silence of stone and shadow.

But this silence—it isn't absence. It is defiance. It is the refusal to be reduced to lines on a map or figures in a ledger. It is the slow, deliberate breath of something ancient and enduring, something that persists not out of resistance but out of inevitability.

The desert does not belong to us. It does not rise or fall with our ambitions, our failures, or our fragile certainties. It remains. And in its stillness, it speaks—not to the ears, but to the marrow, to the part of us that still remembers what it means to listen.

Chapter 17—Sierra

The valley stretched wide before Sierra, golden light spilling across the jagged horizon that rose above them. The sacred stone circle stood silent in the twilight, its edges softened by shadows. Sierra's bare feet pressed into the cool sand, the texture grounding her in the moment.

Around her, **Tara** and four others stood in stillness, their faces calm but expectant. At the center of the circle, **Natan** moved with deliberate grace, each step measured, each motion intentional. His robe, embroidered with symbols passed down through generations, caught the last light of day. The patterns seemed to shimmer faintly as he passed through the circle. His movements were the measured grace of someone carrying the stories of countless generations.

Sierra exhaled slowly, her hands steadying at her sides. Doubt pressed against the edges of her thoughts, but the stillness of the moment pushed back, holding her steady.

Natan knelt at the center of the circle and began arranging small stones into precise shapes. His voice carried across the still air, low and calm. "Feel the earth beneath you. The sand, the stone, the weight of time pressed into this place."

Smoke rose from the sage bundle in his hand, its scent sharp yet grounding as it curled into the cooling air. Sierra inhaled deeply, letting the sensation settle in her chest.

"How will we know what we're supposed to learn?" she asked, her voice steady but quiet.

Natan looked up, meeting her gaze. His expression was kind but firm.

"You listen, Sierra." His voice was quiet yet commanding. "Not with your ears, but with the part of you that remembers—the part rooted here, like the stones themselves."

Sierra knelt and placed her palms against one of the larger stones. It was still warm from the sun, its surface rough beneath her fingertips. As she closed her eyes and focused, a faint sensation stirred—like a low vibration running just beneath the surface.

She stayed still, her breath even, her thoughts quieting one by one.

Natan's voice broke the silence, clear and steady. "What do you feel?"

Sierra closed her eyes, tuning herself to the land. At first, there was only silence, but then came the rhythm—a low, steady hum. It wasn't sound exactly, but sensation, a connection that tied her to something much larger than herself.

Beside her, Tara spoke softly, her voice barely rising above the breeze. "It feels like threads, woven beneath us. Like… footprints left behind, but still moving forward."

Sierra opened her eyes, her gaze meeting Tara's. There was a flicker of understanding between them, a recognition that they were experiencing something neither of them had words for.

Natan nodded once, his hands steady as he adjusted the stones. "Balance," he said. "That rhythm, those threads—that's balance. It's the connection tying us to each other, to those who came before, and to whatever comes after."

The words settled into Sierra, sinking deeper than simple instruction. Her doubts—the worry that she wasn't enough, that she couldn't carry this responsibility—began to ease.

The wind stirred through the circle, carrying with it the scent of sage and the faint chill of approaching night. Natan lifted an eagle feather fan, moving slowly to each cardinal point of the circle. Smoke followed in a thin, curling line, dissolving softly into the air.

For a long while, no one spoke. The silence felt full—not empty, but expectant.

When the ceremony concluded, the air within the stone circle felt subtly changed, as though something had shifted into place.

Sierra remained still as the others began to step away, her fingers brushing one of the stones again. Its cool texture steadied her, anchoring her in a way she couldn't fully explain.

Natan approached her, his steps slow but certain. His expression was calm, his voice low. "You're beginning to understand, Sierra. Hold on to this stillness. It will guide you when the path feels unclear."

She nodded, her breath steady, her gaze unwavering. "I will."

Natan stepped back, leaving Sierra alone with the stones for a moment longer. The sky above had darkened to deep indigo, the stars beginning to scatter across the horizon.

The shapes of the stones seemed sharper in the faint starlight, their presence resolute against the night.

Sierra closed her eyes briefly, letting herself sink into the quiet. When she opened them again, she felt lighter—not unburdened, but steadier.

"You have begun to understand," he said, his voice resonating with the wisdom of ages. "Hold on to this feeling. It is your guide, your strength."

Sierra met his eyes, her breath even and her heart steady. "I will."

Without a word, she rose to her feet and stepped out of the circle.

Unnoticed by the group, a lone tourist lingered at the edge of the plateau, her phone clutched tightly in her hand. What began as a casual recording for her boyfriend transformed as she became captivated by the ritual's haunting beauty and emotional depth. Through her lens, she captured not just a sacred ceremony but the essence of a culture deeply intertwined with the land.

Weeks later, the video would surface online, its poignant imagery striking a chord with viewers around the world. What started as a quiet moment in Redstone would soon spark a surge of curiosity about the ley lines—and a flood of visitors seeking to experience the mystery for themselves.

Chapter 16

LUCAS RETURNED to the Whispering Stones alone, his pack weighed down with carefully calibrated instruments. The desert stretched wide and unbroken under the evening sky, the last light of day clinging stubbornly to the edges of distant ridges.

He worked methodically, arranging devices across the uneven ground. A magnetometer, a seismograph, and an electromagnetic field meter—all tools designed to strip the mysterious down to raw numbers. Lucas crouched low over one of the devices, his brow furrowed as he adjusted a sensor.

This wasn't about belief. It wasn't about mystery. This was about evidence—patterns, measurable data points, clarity in the face of folklore.

But something unsettled him as he glanced up. The quiet around him felt too still, the fading light too sharp against the stones.

His magnetometer chirped—a sharp, insistent sound. Lucas glanced at the readout, his breath catching slightly. The numbers were erratic, blinking in patterns that made no sense. Nearby, the seismograph etched jagged lines onto its paper scroll, its needle jumping as though reacting to tremors that didn't exist.

"This... this isn't right," Lucas muttered, his voice barely above a whisper.

Then he saw it—a faint glow beneath the sand, flickering like distant lightning trapped underground. It wasn't dramatic, just the faintest pulse, but it moved. It stretched outward in two directions, like a vein branching across the earth.

Lucas stumbled back, his boots scuffing against loose stones. The glow brightened for an instant, accompanied by a vibration that traveled up through his soles, into his chest, and settled somewhere behind his ribs.

The light faded, leaving disturbed sand and faint impressions along the ground. The equipment chirped and whirred, still trying—and failing—to make sense of what had just happened.

Lucas knelt beside one of the devices, adjusting a knob with trembling fingers. His voice was hoarse as he muttered to himself, "There has to be an explanation. There's always an explanation."

Behind him, a faint sound broke through the stillness—a single footstep against loose gravel.

Lucas turned sharply. Natan stood a few paces away, his silhouette etched in faint moonlight. His robe hung still against the cooling breeze, and his expression was calm but unreadable.

"Do you think your machines will find what you're looking for, Lucas?" Natan asked, his voice low but carrying easily across the space between them.

Lucas's pulse slowed slightly, though his mind still raced. "They're tools. Tools are supposed to tell us the truth. And right now... they're not making sense."

Natan stepped closer, his movements deliberate. "And—what then?"

Lucas hesitated. His gaze dropped to the magnetometer, its screen still blinking with nonsense. "Then... I don't know."

Natan knelt beside one of the stones. "You've seen something tonight, haven't you?"

Lucas didn't answer right away. His eyes drifted across the disturbed sand. "I've seen something I can't explain. And I don't like that."

A faint smile touched Natan's lips. "That discomfort—it's the beginning of understanding. Not the end."

Lucas frowned slightly, his hand resting on one of his instruments. "You speak with certainty. How can you be so sure of something you can't prove?"

Natan reached into his robe and withdrew a small, smooth stone, placing it carefully in Lucas's hand. It was cool to the touch, its edges worn soft by time.

"Because some things don't require proof," Natan said. "They require presence. Be still enough to notice what's already there."

Lucas stared at the stone in his palm. Its surface caught the faint moonlight and glowed with a soft, reflected silver.

"This isn't how I work," Lucas said. "I deal in certainties."

Natan stood, his gaze steady. "Certainty is useful, Lucas. But it's not everything."

For a long moment, neither of them spoke.

Natan's voice broke the silence, low and even. "The ley lines don't show themselves to everyone. And when they do—it's because that someone is ready to see them."

Lucas swallowed. "What if I'm not ready?"

Natan's faint smile returned. "You wouldn't be here if you weren't."

He turned and walked away, his silhouette fading into the shadows beyond the circle of stones.

Lucas remained where he was. Still, he clutched the small stone in his hand as his equipment blinking meaningless patterns behind him.

Chapter 17

28 YEARS EARLIER

ON A LATE SUMMER MORNING, Hiram Caldwell stood on the edge of the desert, where the earth cracked open into endless stretches of sunbaked rock and ochre canyons. A tall, lanky teenager with windswept dark hair, he had spent countless weekends exploring these trails, chasing stories etched into stone. But this morning felt different—like the desert itself was holding its breath.

Behind him, his great-grandparents' adobe house blended into the earth, its walls weathered but resolute. This summer tradition—staying in their home, wandering the desert with dusty boots and sunburned shoulders—was ending. Soon, he would return to the city and step into the looming shadow of his father's business empire.

"Hiram!"

The call cut through his thoughts. Mika appeared over the rise, dark hair tousled by the breeze, his smile wide and unguarded.

"Hey, Mika," Hiram said, his own grin breaking through his reverie.

"Ready?" Mika's eyes gleamed with familiar mischief.

"Yeah," Hiram replied. "Let's go."

The two friends set off, their boots kicking up clouds of red dust as they followed narrow trails through sun-bleached rocks and whispering canyons. When they reached a cluster of petroglyphs carved into sandstone, Mika knelt beside them, his fingertips tracing ancient lines with reverence.

"These are stories of my ancestors," he said softly.

Hiram crouched beside him, his gaze fixed on the markings. "What do they say?"

"They tell of our people's journey, the spirits that guide us, and the ley lines that connect us to the earth and to each other." Mika's voice carried a steady rhythm, a cadence that felt older than either of them.

"Ley lines?" Hiram repeated, curiosity sparking in his voice.

"Yes." Mika straightened, his gaze stretching out to the horizon. "They flow beneath us, invisible but alive. They connect plants, animals, people—all part of the same thread. If you're quiet enough, if you listen, you can feel them."

Hiram hesitated, his brow furrowing. "But how do you know they're real?"

Mika's smile was patient. "My people have always known, Hiram. We feel it in our bones, in the stillness of the land, in the way shadows move at dusk." He gestured back to the petroglyphs. "These carvings remind us of that connection. They're not just stories—they're instructions."

For a long moment, Hiram stared at the carvings. The afternoon sun pressed against his back, the silence of the desert settling around them. Something in Mika's words tugged at him—an inkling, a flicker of understanding just beyond reach.

The weekend passed in a golden haze. The boys explored dry riverbeds and climbed rocky outcrops, their voices echoing against canyon walls. At night, they lay under a sky thick with stars, sharing stories—some ancient, some mundane, all of them important in their own way.

One evening, as embers glowed in the campfire, Hiram

remembered his great-grandfather's words—spoken on a similarly still night years ago.

"This land holds secrets older than any of us, Hiram. It's not just rocks and plants. It's stories and connections and energies. Don't forget that, my boy."

The memory settled over him like a blanket, its edges worn but warm.

As summer drew to a close, the desert began its quiet farewell. Hiram stood at the window of his great-grandparents' house on his final evening, watching the sun slip behind distant mesas, painting the sky in deep crimson and gold.

The wind stirred outside, carrying with it the faint scent of sage and dust, and for a brief moment, he thought he could hear the desert breathing.

"Hiram!"

His great-grandfather's voice echoed faintly from another room.

"I'm coming," Hiram said, pulling himself from the window.

The next morning, he boarded the bus back to the city. From his seat, he watched the desert recede, its rock formations fading into the distance, their shadows growing longer with every mile. The ley lines, the stories carved into stone, and the quiet hum of something ancient lingered in his mind.

When the bus pulled into the city terminal, the skyline rose ahead, cold and sharp against the morning sky. Hiram stepped off with a steadiness in his stride. The weight of the desert hadn't disappeared—it had shifted, settled somewhere deep within him.

He would carry it with him, even into the gray monotony of boardrooms and spreadsheets.

Chapter 18

Veronica Miller typed steadily on her laptop, her sharp nails clicking against the keys in a rhythm that matched the tension in Mayor Jones's cluttered office. She sat to the side of the mayor's wide desk, her posture sharp, her charcoal blazer immaculate despite the desert dust that clung to everything in Redstone. A faint sheen of light reflected off her glasses as she glanced briefly at the mayor's drawn expression.

Power isn't just taken—it's understood, watched, and earned.

The thought crossed her mind as a sharp knock shattered the silence.

The door opened and Hiram Caldwell stepped inside. He carried himself like a man who expected the world to yield to him—a polished suit, hair combed to precision, and a faint smile that was at once charming and predatory.

"Mayor Jones," Caldwell said. "I trust I'm not interrupting."

Veronica's fingers stilled briefly over the keyboard before she resumed typing. Her watchful eyes caught Caldwell's quick sweep of the room. His eyes fell on her for half a second—calculating, measuring—and then he returned his focus to the mayor.

Jones didn't rise from her chair. Her pen clicked softly before she set it down atop the stack of papers in front of her. "Caldwell," she said. "We've been expecting you."

Caldwell leaned slightly against the edge of the desk, one hand tucked into his jacket pocket. Veronica noticed the way his eyes scanned the space again, as though cataloging vulnerabilities.

"I wanted to revisit the city planning committee's response to my proposal," he began.

Veronica's fingers moved over the keys. She captured his words with precision, but her focus was divided.

Jones met his gaze squarely. "The committee hasn't been convinced yet, Mr. Caldwell."

Caldwell's face showed an almost imperceptible tightening of his jaw, a flash of impatience in his eyes. Veronica caught it immediately. Her pulse quickened slightly.

"You know that this is my contribution towards Redstone's survival," Caldwell said. "The economy here is stagnant. My proposal is a lifeline to the next generation, to progress."

"Progress?" Jones said. "Or profit?"

The silence that followed felt like a wire pulled too tight.

Veronica picked up her pen from a notepad as she studied Caldwell. His polished exterior was flawless, but beneath it, she could feel something else. He was like a blade wrapped in velvet.

"This isn't about profit," Caldwell said. His voice was carrying an edge now. "It's about opportunity. Jobs. Infrastructure. Hope."

Jones's voice stayed steady. "At what cost, Mr. Caldwell? Redstone's identity isn't something we're prepared to trade away."

Caldwell's grip on the edge of the desk tightened briefly before he let out a slow breath. "You're standing in the way of something inevitable, Mayor. Nostalgia doesn't build futures."

Veronica glanced between them, listening to unspoken threats wrapped in carefully chosen words.

Jones straightened slightly, her shoulders squaring. "You'll have your chance at the committee meeting. Tuesday evening."

Veronica typed the date into her notes, but her gaze lingered on

Caldwell. For a moment, his eyes met hers—an appraising stare that felt as though it could strip away every layer of pretense.

She felt heat creep up her neck and quickly looked back at her laptop, her heart hammering against her ribs.

Caldwell straightened, his smile returning, though it didn't quite reach his eyes. "Very well," he said. "Tuesday, then."

He turned on his heel, the scrape of his shoes cutting sharply through the silence. The door shut behind him with a sound that felt final, almost like the snap of a trap closing.

Veronica let out a slow breath she hadn't realized she'd been holding.

Jones leaned back in her chair, her fingers steepled, her expression unreadable.

"Do you think he'll back down?" Veronica asked.

Jones shook her head, a grim smile flickering across her face. "No. Men like Caldwell don't back down. But neither do we."

Veronica nodded, her gaze dropping briefly to her screen before drifting back to the door Caldwell had exited through.

She didn't trust him. Every instinct she had warned her against him—against the carefully rehearsed charm and that predatory sharpness behind his smile.

And yet... she couldn't ignore the draw she felt. The way he seemed to command the room, the way his words lingered even after he was gone.

Her fingers paused over the keys for a moment before resuming their steady rhythm. The sound filled the room, sharp and methodical. But the unease Caldwell had left behind curled into the corners, refusing to dissipate.

Power isn't just taken—it's understood, watched, and earned.

Veronica kept her head down, but her mind stayed sharp, cataloging his every word, every glance, every pause. She wasn't sure whose side Caldwell was really on—or even if he had a side.

But she knew one thing: he wasn't done yet.

Chapter 19

VOICES DRIFTED through the Redstone Inn's lobby as Lucas Grant stepped into its quiet glow. After hours in the open expanse of the desert, the enclosed space felt small. Every sound was amplified, every shadow deepened. The rustle of papers at the front desk, the sound of steps on the floorboards, even the muted and distant conversation pressed in around him.

Behind the counter, Susan greeted him with a faint smile.

"Dr. Grant," she said warmly. "Mr. Caldwell has been asking about you."

Lucas's jaw tightened. He'd heard enough about Hiram Caldwell—his polished reputation, his grandiose promises, and the shadow of control that seemed to follow him wherever he went.

As if summoned, Hiram Caldwell entered the lobby. His polished shoes tapped softly against the tile floor. His suit was immaculate, his smile sharp and carefully set. Lucas noted the way his eyes scanned the room—assessing, cataloging. Behind him trailed an assistant with a neutral expression but shoulders drawn tight with tension.

"Dr. Grant," Caldwell said. "It's a pleasure to finally meet you in person. I hear you've been out exploring the local wonders. There's certainly potential here, wouldn't you agree?"

Lucas met his gaze directly. "The potential here is undeniable,

Mr. Caldwell. Though I suspect we have very different definitions of the word."

Caldwell's smile held. "Let's not dance around it, Dr. Grant. You do your research and publish. I do my engineering and build. Both are just different attributes of ambition."

Lucas felt his irritation spike at the implication. "There's a difference between seeking understanding and exploitation. The ley lines aren't resources to be mined—they're part of something bigger. Something that deserves respect. Are you here to exploit?"

Elaine shifted uncomfortably behind Caldwell, her eyes darting briefly to Lucas before lowering to the floor. Caldwell stepped closer, his voice dropping just enough to feel deliberate.

"Respect, Dr. Grant, is a word I hold in high regard. You'll see that my plans for Redstone are as much about preservation as they are about progress. But tell me this—are your intentions entirely altruistic? Or do you see the ley lines as a path to cementing your name in academic circles?"

Lucas stiffened, the question striking closer than he expected. "My intentions are to understand this place—not to turn it into a spectacle. Can you say the same, Mr. Caldwell?"

Elaine cleared her throat softly, breaking the tension like a pin against glass. "Mr. Caldwell, we should—"

Caldwell lifted a hand to stop her, his eyes never leaving Lucas. "How about this, Dr. Grant? A friendly debate after your first lecture—science versus business. Two perspectives, one conversation. It would draw interest, give people something to talk about. You want understanding, and I want progress—why not share the stage?"

Lucas considered the offer, his skepticism clear. "As long as the conversation stays respectful. This isn't just about drawing a crowd—it's about something far more important."

Caldwell smiled faintly, but the expression didn't touch his eyes.

"Respect is the cornerstone of all my ventures, Dr. Grant. Elaine, make the arrangements."

Elaine nodded, her voice quiet. "Yes, sir."

Susan cleared her throat softly from behind the desk. "Gentlemen, perhaps some fresh air on the veranda might offer a better view—of everything."

Caldwell glanced at her, his smile returning with practiced ease. "Sound advice, Susan. Dr. Grant, I look forward to our conversation."

He handed Lucas a sleek, minimalist business card—black lettering embossed on cream cardstock. Then, with a small nod, he turned and strode towards the veranda, Elaine trailing behind him like a shadow drawn tight.

Chapter 20

THE BAKERY WAS STILL CLOAKED in predawn quiet, the world outside painted in the deep indigo of fading night. Inside, Ladawn Greer moved through the warm, flour-scented air with the quiet precision of years spent at this counter. Her hands—strong, steady, dusted in white—pressed into soft dough, shaping it with practiced ease.

The bakery had always been more than just her livelihood. It was her inheritance, her sanctuary, and in many ways, her legacy. The wooden beams overhead, worn smooth from decades of desert wind and sun, felt like the ribs of a sheltering backbone—something steadfast in a world that seemed to shift too quickly.

The town had changed. Ladawn could feel it in the hesitant chatter of familiar customers, in the disposable coffee cups tourists left abandoned on her tables, in the polite smiles of strangers whose footsteps faded before the dust settled. Each day brought more visitors, more money, more disruption.

She glanced at the black-and-white photos on the bakery wall, her eyes pausing on an image of her great-grandmother, her face weathered but her smile fierce. The woman's hands, knotted and worn, held a steaming pie—a prickly pear creation, crafted in years when fruit was scarce but hope was stubborn.

"Make do with what you have," her great-grandmother used to say.

"And make something worth remembering."

Ladawn exhaled slowly, her fingers pressing deeper into the dough.

She thought about Jasmine and Eli, about the mornings spent tying shoelaces and packing lunches while the bakery oven warmed the walls around them. Her children had been raised here, their laughter braided into the scent of rising bread and cooling pies. After her husband's death, it was the community that held them steady, their quiet acts of care filling the hollow spaces left behind.

But now… the weight of change pressed against her chest. Tourists came with wide eyes and loud voices, cameras flashing against the ancient stones. They took pieces of Redstone—not just in souvenirs, but in stories stripped of their roots, in moments reduced to captions and hashtags.

She turned her attention to the map of the ley lines pinned to the wall, its inked paths faint but deliberate. Sierra's voice echoed in her memory: *"We're protecting more than history. It's our legacy, the spirit of Redstone."*

Ladawn paused, her hands hovering over the dough. Was she doing enough to protect that spirit? Could she hold the bakery steady while the world outside threatened to erode everything it stood for?

The faint creak of the wooden floor made her glance toward the front window. Outside, the horizon was beginning to blush with the soft glow of dawn, but the shadows lingered—the edges of the buildings stretching long and sharp across the street.

A chill crept across her shoulders, and she pulled her cardigan tighter around herself. There had been talk of trouble recently, murmurs of tempers flaring among locals and tourists alike. She'd seen tensions building, in the sharpness of words exchanged and the sidelong glances cast across her counter.

It wouldn't take much for those tensions to break open.

Her fingers twitched slightly against the dough as her eyes flicked to the small security camera installed in the corner—something she'd never felt the need for until recently.

"It's just the times we're living in," she whispered to herself, though the words felt hollow.

She moved to the oven, pulling out the first tray of golden loaves. The scent of fresh bread filled the air, and for a brief moment, it pushed back the unease curling at the edges of her thoughts.

Each loaf, each pie, each carefully wrapped pastry was more than just food—it was an offering. A reminder of what endurance looked like, of what love felt like when pressed into dough and shaped with intention.

But was it enough?

The faint jingle of the bell above the bakery door made her flinch, though she quickly masked it with a composed breath. A glance told her it was just the wind shifting against the glass.

No, she thought firmly, *this bakery isn't just a place. It's a promise.*

She returned to the counter, her hands steadying over the next ball of dough. Her great-grandmother had held on through droughts and floods, through loss and hunger. She had carved a space in the heart of this town with nothing but determination and stubborn love.

Ladawn couldn't let that legacy fade—not for a tourist's fleeting interest, not for profit margins, and certainly not for Caldwell's glossy promises of progress.

The light outside grew stronger, creeping across the bakery floor in thin, golden streaks. In just an hour or so, the bakery would fill with familiar faces and the soft hum of morning conversations.

She reached up and adjusted the photo of her great-grandmother by the register, letting her fingertips rest against the cool glass for a moment longer than necessary.

"I'll hold the line," she said softly.

The oven timer chimed, sharp and insistent. Ladawn turned back to her work, but the unease stayed with her, curling in the corners of the bakery like smoke caught in still air.

Chapter 21

TARA SAT AT THE OAK DESK in her childhood bedroom, her fingers tracing the leather cover of her journal. The morning light crept in through the window, scattering soft gold across the worn wood and the fragile lace curtains her mother had sewn years ago. Outside, the desert horizon trembled faintly with rising heat.

The carved wooden hawk on the windowsill caught the light, its outstretched wings frozen in mid-flight. Tara's eyes lingered on it, and a familiar ache settled in her chest. This room still carried her mother's presence—woven into the fabric of the curtains, the scent of old paper, the faint memory of laughter in the corners.

Her fingers tightened around her favorite pen, familiar and comforting. She opened the journal to a fresh page. Its emptiness stared back at her like an invitation.

"It's been years, but some mornings still feel like she's here. Mom always found beauty in this desert—in the sharp edges of the cliffs, in the stubborn flowers that bloom where nothing should grow. She made it feel alive, like every shadow had a story to tell."

Her handwriting was careful and deliberate. She turned to the framed photo propped on the desk. Sierra's face beamed back at her—confident, unguarded, joyful. Next to her stood a younger Tara. Her own smile more reserved, her posture slightly turned inward, like she wasn't quite sure where to stand.

Sierra had always seemed so certain—of herself, of her purpose, of her place in Redstone.

"Sierra wears her convictions like armor. She doesn't hesitate, doesn't falter. She believes in things—big, unshakable things. And she loves without caution, without apology. I've spent so long wishing I could do the same."

The pen paused again, trembling slightly.

"I built my life around careful choices. Practical decisions. Logic. But there's a space in me that those things can't fill. A silence I can't explain away. And at the center of it... is her."

The words sat heavy on the page, staring back like a confession she couldn't reclaim. She set the pen down and leaned back in her chair; her hand pressed lightly over her mouth.

Love.

The word echoed in her chest, raw and unsteady. It wasn't just Sierra's confidence Tara envied—it was the way Sierra let herself feel. Fully, fiercely, without apology.

She forced herself to pick up the pen again.

"I've been hiding from this—hiding from myself. But I can't keep living in this in-between space. Not when I know there's something waiting beyond the limits I've drawn. It's time to stop avoiding the question and start searching for the answer."

The quiet in the room felt different now. Tara's hand hovered over the journal before she gently closed it, her fingers brushing over the worn leather cover.

She crossed the room to the window and rested her palms flat against the cool glass. Redstone spread out before her. Its streets were still waking up under the soft glow of morning light. From here, it looked peaceful—timeless. Almost.

Beyond the limits of what she'd allowed herself to believe, there was something waiting for her. A voice, a connection, a truth— something she couldn't quite name but could feel, faint and insistent. It pulled her forward.

"It's time to stop hiding," she whispered.

The words felt like a stone dropping into still water, sending ripples outward into places she couldn't see.

Chapter 22

THE POLICE RADIO CRACKLED in the stillness of the night. "Chief, disturbance reported at the Miller farmstead near the ley line marker," said Dispatcher Ramos, his voice tight with unease.

Chief Martin Vega tightened his grip on the microphone. "Roger that. We're en route."

Beside him, Officer Jenna Marquez shifted in her seat as the cruiser rolled onto the narrow dirt road. The headlights remained off, and the rhythmic crunch of gravel under the tires filled the silence.

Something about this call gnawed at Vega—a slow, persistent knot in his gut.

The farmstead came into view. Bathed in pale moonlight, the obelisk marking the ley line rose from the earth like an ancient sentinel. Shadows pooled at its base, sharp and unmoving.

Vega killed the engine, and the cruiser settled into silence. Neither he nor Jenna spoke as they stepped out. The usual nighttime symphony of crickets and distant coyote howls was absent.

Jenna's flashlight flickered across the ground, catching deep footprints—heavy and uneven. Vega crouched and his gloved fingers felt the edges of a peculiar indentation. His flashlight revealed spiraling symbols etched into the soil intersecting with impossible precision. Their edges glimmered faintly, illuminated by a light that felt neither natural nor artificial.

"Chief…" Jenna's voice was low, almost reverent. "What is this?"

Vega stared at the symbols, his mind racing for logical explanations. "This isn't graffiti. It's too deliberate. Too precise."

Jenna knelt beside him, her flashlight tracing the lines. "It almost looks like a code."

"Or a warning," Vega said softly.

The words settled between them. Vega stood, scanning the perimeter. That knot in his gut tightened, and for the first time in a long while, he felt distinctly *watched*.

A voice broke the silence.

"Chief Vega."

Vega's hand dropped to his holster as he spun toward the sound. Natan emerged from the shadows. His weathered form moved deliberately, blending with the landscape as though he had been carved from it.

"Natan," Vega said, his voice steady but edged with unease. "What are you doing out here?"

Natan stopped a few paces away, his dark eyes reflecting the faint glow of the symbols. "I could ask you the same thing, Chief."

Vega didn't respond, but Jenna shifted uncomfortably.

Natan's gaze drifted to the markings etched into the earth. "The balance here is fragile," he said, his voice calm but heavy with meaning. "When something disrupts it, the earth carries its anger in silence… until it doesn't."

"Warnings," Vega repeated.

"Yes," Natan replied. "These symbols aren't random, and they aren't new. They've been here before, in times of great imbalance. But their appearance always means one thing—something has been disturbed."

Vega crossed his arms. "Disturbed by what? People? Machines? These ley lines—whatever they are—they can't react. They're not *alive.*"

Natan's eyes met his, steady and unblinking. "They don't need to be alive to have power, Chief. You can feel it, can't you? The stillness in the air, the absence of sound, the way the light bends over these symbols. You don't need to believe to recognize when something is *wrong.*"

Jenna took a hesitant step back. "He's not wrong, Chief. It feels... off."

Vega glanced at Jenna, then back at Natan. "What am I supposed to do with this, Natan? I need something I can report. Something I can act on."

Natan's shoulders lifted slightly as he sighed. "Sometimes, Chief, the land doesn't give us answers—it gives us warnings. You must decide whether to listen."

The silence stretched, filled only with the sound of the faint breeze grazing the ley line obelisk.

Vega turned back to the symbols, His flashlight beam was steady but his thoughts anything but. Logic danced in his mind, fighting with the inexplicable sensation that the ground beneath him was *aware.*

"Jenna," Vega said quietly. "Get Ramos on the radio. I want this area marked off. No one comes near it until I say otherwise."

Jenna nodded, retreating a few steps to make the call.

Vega remained, staring at the etchings glowing faintly in the soil. Natan hadn't moved. He stood still, his silhouette blending with the dark ridges beyond.

Before turning back to the cruiser, Vega spoke without looking at Natan. "If there's something more I need to understand about this... you'll let me know."

Natan's voice followed him. "You'll know when it's time, Chief. But listen carefully—because the land doesn't repeat itself."

Vega climbed back into the cruiser, the encounter pressing

against his chest like an unseen hand. The glow of the symbols lingered in the rearview mirror as they pulled away, and despite the engine's growl, the silence stayed with him.

This wasn't over.

It wasn't even close.

Chapter 23

The late afternoon sun hung low over the desert ridge, casting long shadows across the cracked earth. Sierra Castillo stood beneath the sparse shade of a juniper tree, her skirt streaked with faded lines of ochre and turquoise paint. Around her, a small group of teenagers, ranging from thirteen to sixteen, sat scattered in a loose circle. Some clutched sketchpads, others held pieces of charcoal or small jars of pigment.

A short distance away, Lucas stood with his hands tucked into the pockets of his well-worn field jacket. His presence was quiet but intentional. Sierra had asked him to come—to watch, to listen.

She lifted a fragment of sandstone with its surface etched with faint, ancient petroglyphs. She turned it carefully in her hands before holding it up for the teens to see.

"Art isn't about perfection," she said. "It's about memory. About paying attention. Every mark you make, every line you draw, leaves a footprint in time."

The teens were silent and attentive.

Ava, a girl with dark curls and wide eyes, shifted uncomfortably before raising her hand. "But what if we mess it up? What if our lines aren't *right?*"

Sierra knelt and touched the warm surface of the sand. She drew a slow, deliberate spiral with her finger. "See this?" she said. "It isn't perfect. But it carries intention. And that's what matters most."

She brushed the dust from her hands and rose to her feet. "Your art doesn't have to please anyone else. It doesn't have to follow someone else's rules. It just needs to speak to you. The stories etched into this land aren't asking for perfection. They're asking for reverence."

The teenagers slowly began to sketch and paint on recycled paper and smooth stones they'd collected earlier. The silence softened, replaced by the scratch of charcoal against paper, the faint shuffle of feet, and the murmurs of focused effort.

Sierra walked among them, her steps deliberate and unhurried. She paused beside Diego, who was hunched over his sketchpad. Charcoal smudged across his fingertips. The jagged lines he'd drawn stretched across the page symbolized harsh peaks fractured by deep, sharp cracks.

"What are you seeing, Diego?" Sierra asked.

"The mountains," he said slowly. "But they're breaking apart. Like they're cracked inside."

Sierra's looked again at his drawing. The way the stark lines fractured and fell into empty space tugged at something deep in her chest.

"Sometimes art shows us what's fragile before we even realize it's breaking," she said. "Keep going, Diego. You're seeing something important."

Diego nodded. His focus sharpened as he returned to his work.

Sierra glanced over at Lucas, who was observing quietly from the edge of the circle. His expression was thoughtful as he tracked the teens' movements

"Dr. Grant," Sierra called. "Why don't you join us?"

Lucas hesitated for a moment, then stepped forward. Sierra handed him a small, smooth stone and a piece of charcoal.

"Pick a memory," she said. "Something tied to this place—or

something you felt here. Then draw it."

Lucas stared at the stone in his palm. His brow creased in thought. His fingers curled around the charcoal as he settled into a quiet space between two of the teenagers.

For a while, the only sounds were the faint scratch of charcoal, the shuffle of paper, and the occasional sigh of the wind cutting across the ridge. Lucas worked slowly and his lines were hesitant at first, then more deliberate.

Sierra moved quietly among the students again, offering a word here, a nod there. When she returned to Lucas, he was carefully studying the pattern he had drawn.

It was a simple sketch—lines intersecting across the stone's surface, faint but precise.

"What did you see?" she asked him.

Lucas hesitated, his thumb brushing over one of the lines. "Connection," he said. "I think."

Sierra nodded. "Sometimes art shows us what words can't."

One of the older teens, Lina, glanced up from her sketchpad, her charcoal-streaked fingers hovering over her drawing. "You're kind of like… a keeper, aren't you? Like, for the stories and the lines. Why is it important to protect the ley lines?"

Sierra paused, her gaze drifting to the horizon before returning to Lina.

"We're all keepers, Lina. Every one of us who pays attention, who listens to the land, who carries its stories forward. But yes, sometimes it feels like standing at a gate, making sure the way stays open."

"Standing at a gate…" The words struck Lucas.

As the last light of the day began to fade, Sierra clapped her hands gently to gather their attention. "Let's wrap up, everyone. The light's almost gone." She knelt beside a small cloth bag and withdrew a handful of smooth river stones, each one smooth, rounded and worn by time.

"Take these," she said softly. "And remember: every mark you make, every story you tell—it matters."

They began to drift away in pairs and small groups, their quiet laughter and chatter trailing behind them.

But Lina stayed behind. She clutched her sketchpad tightly against her chest, and locked her eyes on Sierra as though searching for something, for words.

Sierra noticed and stepped closer. Her voice was soft but steady: "You feel it, don't you? The pull of something deeper."

Lina nodded. "It feels *important*. Like there's something here I need to understand."

Sierra gently touched Lina's shoulder. "That feeling isn't just in your imagination. You're seeing something real. Something fragile."

The evening air settled around them. "I'll help you learn how to listen to it," Sierra said. "But the path ahead is not easy, Lina. It asks for care, for patience, for courage. Are you ready for that?"

Lina's voice was small but steady. "I think I am."

Sierra smiled, her eyes warm with something close to pride. "Good. Then let's start now."

Chapter 24

LATER, LUCAS GRANT SAT at the small desk in his rented room, the glow of his laptop casting a faint blue haze across scattered printouts and worn maps. Outside, the vast expanse of the desert was cloaked in silence and starlight.

His mind circled back to Sierra's words: *"We're all keepers. Every one of us who pays attention, who listens to the land, who carries its stories forward. But yes… sometimes it feels like standing at a gate, making sure the way stays open."*

Lucas set his pen down. He hadn't known how to respond in that moment, but now, alone with only his thoughts, the truth pressed against him.

Keeper.

Elana had once accused him of dissecting everything beautiful until only fragments remained. She wasn't wrong. Even now, Lucas realized, he was trying to pull the mystery of the ley lines apart and reduce them to the smallest possible rationalizations.

But Sierra hadn't done that. She hadn't tried to *prove* anything. She had simply been *present.*

Lucas walked to the window. The desert sprawled into infinity under the cold shimmer of stars, every ridge and shadow carved into sharp relief.

Closing his eyes briefly, he remembered the faint sensation he'd felt near the ley lines—like something ancient had brushed against him. His instruments had captured anomalies, but no measurement could explain the feeling.

"Maybe it's not about understanding everything," he murmured, his breath fogging faintly against the glass. *"Maybe it's about accepting the parts that can't be explained."*

Those words felt both liberating, and terrifying.

His presentation draft with its neatly written argument sat nearby. He had built it carefully around observable data and empirical results. But looking at it now, the words felt empty, like scaffolding without a foundation.

Sierra's voice returned: *"Sometimes art shows us what's fragile before we even realize it's breaking."*

He sat back down at his desk, but he didn't reach for his pen or his notes. Instead, he folded his hands together and let the silence settle around him.

"What if I'm wrong again?"

But this time, it wasn't sharp with fear. It was soft, edged with something gentler. Hope, maybe, or the beginning of trust.

Chapter 25

Nineteen Years Prior

THE DESERT'S QUIET STRETCHED vast and undisturbed, a silence that had once felt ordinary to Sierra Castillo but now held a depth she was beginning to recognize. The faint rustle of a gentle breeze threaded through the sagebrush, carrying with it the earthy scent of red soil and sunbaked stone.

Sierra's small hand rested in her mother's firm grasp as they walked the narrow trail winding through Redstone's desert expanse. Above them, the sky blazed with deep purples and fiery oranges, as if the setting sun sought to etch this moment into memory.

"Listen, Sierra," her mother said, her voice steady and warm, blending effortlessly with the rhythm of the land. "This earth is alive. If you're still, you can hear its stories. Each stone, each breath of wind, carries the wisdom of those who came before us."

Sierra glanced up at her mother's face, serene and intent, then followed her gaze to a towering saguaro cactus rising like a sentinel against the painted sky. Her mother knelt beside it, her hands pressing gently against its ridged surface. Every movement was deliberate, imbued with reverence.

"This," her mother continued, her tone quiet but certain, "is a keeper of the desert. Like the ley lines, it holds the earth's secrets, connecting all living things."

Curious, Sierra mimicked her mother's actions, placing her small hands on the cactus. Its surface was rough but grounding, the ridges pressing firmly against her palms. She lingered, half expecting to feel something stir beneath her fingers.

"Why can't we see the connections?" Sierra asked, her brow knitting in confusion.

Her mother chuckled softly, the sound rising like a warm note in the cool air. "Some truths aren't meant for our eyes, my heart. They're felt. The ley lines weave through the land and into us, guiding and grounding us if we choose to listen."

The trail brought them to a patch of open ground where the last light of the sun bathed the earth in amber hues. Her mother knelt, scooping a handful of the rich red soil and letting it sift through her fingers like fine sand.

"Our ancestors believed the ley lines were sacred paths," she said, her voice weighted with the solemnity of generations past. "Paths created by spirits to guide and protect us. When I was your age, I thought they were just stories. But now I understand—they're more than myth. They're how we stay connected to our heritage, to the earth, and to those who came before us."

Sierra knelt beside her mother, watching the soil scatter into the breeze. A quiet pull rooted her to the moment, as though the land itself were holding her attention.

"How do we protect them?" she asked earnestly, her voice small but steady.

Her mother looked at her, the tenderness in her gaze deepened by something unspoken. "By honoring the land and its stories. We are its guardians. Like me, and one day, you."

A flicker of something she didn't yet fully understand sparked in Sierra's chest—a promise, unspoken but undeniable.

"What kind of stories?" she asked, her imagination stirring.

Her mother smiled faintly. "The coyote who brought fire to the people. The hawk that watches over us. And the great serpent that guards the ley lines." Her voice softened, her words threading through the evening air like a song waiting to be sung.

The desert seemed to shift around them, as though responding to the stories. Sierra could almost see the coyote, its sleek form darting through shadows; the hawk, its wings slicing through the fading light; and the serpent, unseen but pulsing with energy deep beneath the surface.

They arrived at a circle of stones, their arrangement deliberate, their presence ancient.

"These are called whispering stones," her mother said, stepping into the center. She began to hum—a melody low and resonant, threading through the silence like water carving through rock.

The song rose, the notes both haunting and soothing, weaving into the soft murmur of the breeze. Sierra closed her eyes, the vibrations of her mother's voice blending with the rhythm of the earth beneath her.

When the song faded, her mother placed a gentle hand on Sierra's shoulder. "This is a prayer," she said, her voice quiet but resolute. "A prayer of thanks to the earth, to the spirits, and to the ley lines. It's how we honor their guidance and protection."

Sierra opened her eyes to the vast desert sky, now awash with stars that seemed to shimmer in quiet approval. Her mother's hand remained steady on her shoulder, a grounding presence.

"One day, you'll teach your children these songs and stories," her mother said softly, her words carrying both hope and expectation. "And you'll help them learn to hear the earth's whispers."

Sierra stared out at the stars, their distant light weaving through the night like the stories her mother spoke of. In that moment, she felt a promise take root deep within her—a calling passed down through the generations.

She knelt once more, pressing her small hands against the stones, letting their cool solidity anchor her to the moment.

————

15 YEARS EARLIER

In the dim glow of the University of Oregon's science building, a younger Lucas Grant sat at the edge of his seat, notebook open, pen poised. The lecture hall buzzed with low murmurs as graduate students and faculty filtered in, their voices building a hum of anticipation.

Lucas adjusted his glasses, shifting slightly. This was why he had pursued graduate studies—to confront new ideas, to debate, to push the limits of his understanding. Yet tonight carried an unease he couldn't quite name.

At the podium, Professor Anne Whitmore surveyed the room with sharp, deliberate eyes. Known for her bold challenges to orthodoxy, she had a way of commanding attention that silenced even the most restless students.

"Good evening," Whitmore began, her voice steady and resonant. "Tonight, we examine the boundaries of what science can know—and what might lie beyond."

The murmurs ceased. Lucas straightened as her words settled over the room.

Whitmore's tone sharpened. "We will discuss quantum entanglement and consciousness. These are not theoretical exercises—they force us to confront the assumptions we use to frame reality itself."

Lucas's pen hovered above his notebook. This wasn't the first time Whitmore had steered the class toward the unmeasurable, and while he appreciated her willingness to provoke, part of him bristled at the lack of empirical grounding.

"Skepticism," Whitmore continued, "is the engine of science, but it is not the destination. To question is to seek. To dismiss without inquiry is to abandon the pursuit entirely."

Her gaze swept the room, landing squarely on Lucas.

"Mr. Grant," she said, her tone softening but her eyes sharp, "you've expressed reservations about this topic before. Would you like to begin?"

Lucas felt the weight of every gaze in the room. Inhaling deeply, he steadied himself. "Professor, I value the exploration of new ideas," he said carefully. "But giving scientific weight to something as inherently subjective as consciousness—without measurable evidence—risks crossing into speculation."

Whitmore nodded, her expression thoughtful. "A valid concern. But tell me, Lucas, do you believe all phenomena we study now were once immediately measurable?"

She turned to the blackboard, sketching the double-slit experiment with quick, practiced strokes.

"Consider quantum mechanics," she said, her voice carrying a quiet intensity. "Dismissed for decades as abstract mathematics. And yet, evidence forced us to accept that particles behave differently when observed. Intuition failed us, but evidence transformed speculation into understanding."

Lucas leaned forward despite himself. "Quantum mechanics operates within observable parameters," he countered. "Consciousness lacks such a framework."

"For now," Whitmore agreed. She capped the chalk and turned back to the class. "But what if consciousness interacts with the universe in ways we haven't yet identified? What if it's more than the sum of neural firings—perhaps a field, like electromagnetism, waiting to be discovered?"

The lecture hall fell into a heavy silence, her words hanging in the air like static.

Lucas tapped his pen against the notebook, frustration and admiration warring in his chest. "If that were true," he said finally, "it would upend foundational principles. The implications would be… massive."

Whitmore's expression brightened with conviction. "Precisely. Science evolves by challenging its boundaries. To dismiss the unmeasurable today risks overlooking the undeniable tomorrow."

The room buzzed with quiet energy as students began jotting notes. Lucas stared at his notebook, the pages filling with meticulous outlines and neatly written questions. Yet his usual clarity eluded him. His skepticism, so firmly rooted, now felt entangled with something more elusive—curiosity.

The lecture ended to a smattering of applause, groups of students and faculty gathering in clusters to debate. Lucas stepped outside into the cool night air, the weight of the discussion pressing against him.

He looked up. The stars stretched endlessly overhead, their faint light cold and unchanging, yet somehow alive with potential.

For years, Lucas had sought certainty in dismantling ideas, in reducing the unknown to manageable pieces. But Whitmore's challenge lingered in his mind—not to prove what wasn't, but to explore what might be.

Three Years Earlier

The boardroom of Caldwell Enterprises stood high above Salt Lake City, bathed in the golden light of sunset. The vast expanse of the city stretched below, but Hiram Caldwell turned his back on the glittering view. The room behind him, with its polished mahogany table and attentive executives, buzzed with quiet anticipation.

This wasn't just another meeting. It was the beginning of a transformation—one that Hiram had spent months envisioning.

He turned to face them, his hands resting lightly on the back of his chair. The warm light softened his sharp features, giving him an air of quiet resolve.

"Thank you all for being here," Hiram began, his voice calm but purposeful. "Today marks the start of a new chapter for Caldwell Enterprises. It's time for us to move beyond the shadow of the past and define ourselves not by what we take, but by what we give."

The words drew murmurs of surprise from the executives. Hiram let the reaction settle before continuing.

"For decades, my father built this company with a singular focus: profit. He succeeded—at a cost. His drive was unmatched, but so was his disregard for the communities we touched, for the people whose lives we altered. That's not who I want us to be. That's not who I want to be."

A pause. He met the eyes of each executive in turn, his gaze steady.

"We have the resources, the power, and the opportunity to do more. To become a force for progress—not through exploitation, but through investment, through stewardship. And I propose we begin with places like Redstone."

The room stilled.

James, the oldest member of the board, cleared his throat, leaning forward. "Redstone? That's a small community, isn't it? One with limited returns, I imagine."

Hiram nodded. "Redstone is small, yes. But it sits at the crossroads of tradition and opportunity. Its ley lines have drawn attention, not just from tourists but from researchers and spiritual communities. And yet, its people—its heart—are being overlooked. That's where we come in."

"Forgive me," James said, his voice cautious, "but how does this align with our goals as a company? Profit may not be your only focus, Hiram, but this is still a business. Investments need returns."

Elizabeth, ever the pragmatist, chimed in. "And if we fail? Good intentions don't pay salaries. Philanthropy is admirable, but it comes with risks—financial and reputational."

Hiram leaned forward, his voice steady. "I'm not proposing blind altruism. What I'm proposing is a redefinition of success. We invest in places like Redstone—support their schools, their infrastructure, their heritage—and in doing so, we build something more enduring than short-term profit. We build loyalty. Legacy. Trust."

He paused, letting his words sink in before continuing.

"My father saw power in domination. I see power in partnership. Redstone is a test case, yes—but it's also a statement. We don't have to choose between profit and purpose. We can have both. And if we do this right, Caldwell Enterprises will become a name synonymous with progress *and* integrity."

The room shifted as the executives exchanged glances. James's skepticism softened slightly, though he still looked wary.

Elizabeth folded her arms, her sharp eyes narrowing as she considered his words. "Let's say we back this. What's the first step?"

Hiram smiled faintly, the weight of the moment settling on his shoulders. "We start by listening. Redstone's people know what they need better than we do. We support their priorities—schools, small businesses, sustainable tourism. And we show them that Caldwell Enterprises isn't there to take, but to give."

"And the long-term vision?" Elizabeth pressed.

Hiram's expression turned thoughtful. "The long-term vision is a partnership that benefits everyone. Redstone thrives, and so do we. It's a place where we can prove that investment doesn't have to come at a cost to community or culture."

The murmurs began again, this time tinged with cautious

agreement.

James exhaled, his voice softening. "You make a compelling case, Hiram. But you'll need more than good intentions to pull this off."

Hiram nodded. "I'll need your support. Your expertise. And your belief that we can be better than the legacy we inherited."

Elizabeth leaned back, a faint smile tugging at the corner of her mouth. "Well, I've always believed in calculated risks. You've got my attention, Caldwell."

The tension in the room eased as the executives began to nod. The hum of agreement built slowly, like the tide turning.

Hiram stepped back toward the window as they rose and filed out, their discussions trailing into the hallway. Alone again, he let his gaze sweep over the city, its lights flickering against the encroaching dark.

Chapter 26

As Ladawn Greer turned onto the quiet street leading to her bakery, the sight of its weathered sign offered a fleeting moment of comfort. The soft creak of her car door seemed to echo the tension in her chest.

Caldwell's promises tugged at the edges of her mind—enticing yet uneasy. She wanted to believe Redstone could thrive again, that his plans might bring the town a future worth fighting for. But the shadow of his ambition loomed too large, casting doubt over every word he'd said.

Her hand paused on the bakery door, the wood worn smooth from years of use. This place wasn't just a business; it was a legacy. A sanctuary. Each scuff on the floor, each well-worn stool carried the weight of family, community, and time.

Inside, the familiar warmth wrapped around her. The air was rich with the scent of cinnamon and yeast, but it couldn't touch the unease settling in her chest. Her eyes drifted over the counters and shelves, each one a silent reminder of the life she'd built here. She couldn't lose it.

The bell above the door jingled, and Marjorie Barrett stepped in, her face lined with worry. "Ladawn," she began, her voice low, "I don't mean to alarm you, but folks are saying Caldwell's been sniffing around. Word is he's buying up property debts all over town—even talked about this building."

Ladawn's chest tightened. "My lease still has years on it. He can't just—"

Marjorie's expression softened, but her tone was firm. "Honey, this Caldwell isn't playing fair. If he's set his sights on this place, he'll find a way."

Ladawn's fingers tightened around the edge of the counter. "This bakery's been here longer than Caldwell's known Redstone exists."

Marjorie gave a sad smile. "And that's exactly why he sees it as a prize."

The rest of the morning passed in a haze of strained smiles and distracted conversations. Customers came and went, their warmth a comfort, but Ladawn's thoughts remained clouded. By the time the morning rush eased, her mind was made up.

She hung her apron on its hook, grabbed her purse, and stepped into the bright afternoon sunlight. The walk to Mesa View Law Office felt longer than usual, every step heavy with both fear and determination.

Inside, the cool, sterile quiet of the office felt alien compared to the bakery's warmth. The receptionist greeted her with a polite smile, and soon Ladawn found herself seated across from Jared Harris, the town's most respected attorney.

"Ladawn," Jared began, his voice somber, "I've been following Caldwell's moves. He's buying up debts across Redstone—including your landlord's. If he applies enough pressure, your landlord might have no choice but to sell."

The words hit her like a blow. "Sell? But my lease—it's still good for years. He can't just take it from me."

Jared's gaze softened. "You're right, he can't take it outright. But if your landlord caves, Caldwell will be first in line to take over. He's a strategist, Ladawn. He doesn't leave openings to chance."

Ladawn clenched her fists in her lap. "What can I do?"

Jared leaned forward, his expression grave. "Outbidding him would be the most direct way, but that's no small task. There may be other options—legal or community-driven—but you'll need a plan, and you'll need it quickly."

When Ladawn stepped back into the sunlight, Jared's words followed her like a shadow. She walked the long road back to the bakery, passing the rugged rock formations and the old church bell tower that anchored Redstone in memory.

The thought of losing the bakery gnawed at her, but as her steps slowed in front of the familiar building, a quiet resolve grew within her. Redstone had weathered storms before, and so had she. This wasn't just a business—it was a home. And it was worth fighting for.

Back inside, she called a meeting with her small but fiercely loyal team. They gathered in the kitchen, their faces reflecting a mix of worry and determination.

"We have a challenge ahead," Ladawn began, her voice steady despite the knot in her chest. "Caldwell wants this bakery, but this isn't just a building. It's a home, a haven—for us and for Redstone. We can't let him take it."

Pete, her longest-standing employee, stepped forward. "We're with you, Ladawn. This place means too much to all of us."

The others nodded, their agreement filling the room with quiet strength.

For the first time that day, Ladawn felt the faint stirrings of hope. "Thank you," she said, her voice thick with emotion. "We'll need to be smart and united, but together, we can protect what's ours."

As the meeting broke up, Ladawn lingered, her hand brushing the worn surface of the counter. The bakery wasn't just bricks and mortar; it was the heart of Redstone. And she wasn't about to let anyone take it—not without a fight.

Chapter 27

THE MAKESHIFT FIELD LAB STOOd fragile against the encroaching night, its faint lights flickering like fireflies in the vast emptiness of the desert. Lucas adjusted the calibration on his magnetometer, his movements precise but his thoughts unsettled. Nearby, Sierra sat cross-legged on a threadbare blanket, her posture calm and centered—a quiet counterpoint to Lucas's restless energy.

She wasn't watching him but staring out toward the horizon, where the first stars were beginning to pierce the deep indigo sky.

"You always this twitchy?" Sierra asked, her tone light, though her gaze stayed fixed on the horizon.

Lucas barely looked up, his fingers tapping at his tablet. "When my instruments start behaving like they're possessed? Yeah, I get a little twitchy."

He frowned at the screen. The data didn't add up—erratic spikes in magnetic activity where there should be none.

Sierra tilted her head toward him, amusement threading her voice. "Maybe they're trying to tell you something."

Lucas snorted softly, though the sound lacked conviction. "Machines don't 'try' anything. They measure. Record. Report."

"Maybe they measure too much and feel too little," she countered, her words drifting like the breeze, subtle but sharp.

Lucas finally looked up, his brow furrowed. "You're enjoying this, aren't you?"

"A little," Sierra admitted, her lips curving into a teasing smile. She paused, her tone softening. "But mostly, I'm trying to figure out if you're ready to see what's really out here."

Lucas opened his mouth to retort, but her next words stopped him.

"And, for what it's worth—thank you."

He blinked, caught off guard. "For what?"

Sierra finally turned her gaze to him, her expression earnest. "For standing up for Redstone at the committee meeting. You didn't have to, but you did."

Lucas's jaw tightened briefly, unsure how to respond. "I wasn't trying to take sides," he said after a moment. "I just wanted the process to be honest."

"Well, sometimes honesty is enough," she said, her smile faint but genuine.

Before Lucas could respond, a low hum arose, faint but unmistakable. He froze, his head snapping toward the sound. It wasn't coming from his equipment.

Sierra's smile faded, her expression sharpening. "Do you feel that?" she asked, her voice dropping to a whisper.

Lucas nodded, his fingers tightening around the edge of the camp table. The hum deepened, a low vibration that seemed to travel up through the soles of his boots. He glanced at his instruments—the seismograph remained still, the magnetometer calm. Yet the air felt charged, alive with something he couldn't explain.

A sudden gust of wind swept across the plateau, scattering loose papers and sending a chill through Lucas's spine. Sierra rose smoothly to her feet, her eyes narrowing as she scanned the darkening desert.

"What is this?" Lucas asked, his voice low, more to himself than to her.

"The ley lines," Sierra murmured, stepping toward the edge of the ridge. Her voice was steady, but an undercurrent of awe ran through it. "You're standing at a crossroads, Lucas. Sometimes, the land speaks loud enough for even the skeptics to hear."

Lucas opened his mouth to argue, but the ground pulsed again, stronger this time. The hum thrummed in his chest, making his breath hitch. He grabbed his tablet, his hands trembling as he searched for answers, but the screen remained blank—no anomalies, no readings, nothing to rationalize what he was experiencing.

"This doesn't make sense," he muttered, frustration bubbling over.

"Maybe it's not supposed to," Sierra said, turning back to him. Her face was illuminated faintly by the stars, her expression serene but unreadable.

"That's not how science works," Lucas snapped, though the edge in his voice was softened by his unease.

"Then maybe you're asking the wrong questions," she said simply, her gaze steady on him.

The tension between them hung heavy in the air, but before Lucas could respond, the hum abruptly ceased. The sudden stillness was deafening, the absence of sound pressing against his senses.

He exhaled a shaky breath, his hands falling to his sides. "What just happened?" he asked, his voice barely above a whisper.

Sierra stepped closer, her movements deliberate but calm. "You felt it, didn't you?" she said, her voice low. "The connection. The energy."

Lucas looked back at her, his skepticism tempered by something he couldn't name. "If this is real..." He trailed off, shaking his head.

"It is real," Sierra said softly. "But it's not the kind of real you can measure. It's the kind you feel."

Lucas hesitated, torn between denying what he'd experienced and admitting he couldn't explain it. "I don't know what I felt," he finally said, his voice raw. "But it was... real."

Sierra smiled, the kind of smile that held both reassurance and challenge. "That's a start."

For a moment, they stood in silence, the vastness of the desert stretching out around them. The stars above seemed impossibly bright, their light casting faint shadows on the ground. Lucas felt a strange sense of calm, as if the land itself was waiting for him to catch up.

Sierra broke the silence, her tone lighter. "You're not going to find all the answers tonight, Lucas. But you're asking the right questions now. That's something."

He managed a small smile, though his thoughts still churned. "I don't know what this place is trying to tell me," he admitted.

"Maybe it's not about understanding," Sierra said, her voice quiet. "Maybe it's about listening."

In spite of his puzzlement, Lucas felt grounded by Sierra's presence, her quiet warmth cutting through the storm of his thoughts. The stars above seemed sharper now, their cold light casting the desert in stark clarity, as though the land itself bore witness to something profound.

Lucas turned toward her, his gaze lingering on her profile in the dim glow of the field lab's faint lights. She looked serene, but there was an intensity beneath the calm, a quiet strength that seemed to draw him in.

"I didn't expect this," Lucas admitted softly, his voice carrying the wonder of an unspoken realization. "Being here, with you—it feels… undeniable."

Sierra met his eyes, her expression softening. "It is undeniable," she said, her tone quiet but sure. "You've started to listen. To the ley lines, to this place, and maybe even to yourself."

Lucas hesitated, caught between the logic that had always defined him and the pull of something he couldn't explain. Slowly, he reached out, his fingers brushing her cheek. Her skin was warm, grounding him in the moment. But beneath that touch was something deeper—a connection he couldn't name, as though the pulse of the desert had found its echo in her.

Their breath mingled in the cool night air, the world narrowing until it was just the two of them beneath the vast expanse of stars. When their lips met, the kiss was tentative, a merging of hesitations and possibilities. But as it deepened, a spark ignited—a promise that went beyond words.

Sierra's hands found their way to the back of Lucas's neck, her touch both tender and steady. Lucas responded instinctively, his arms encircling her as though anchoring himself in the moment. He felt her heartbeat against his chest, a rhythm that seemed to align with the faint hum he'd felt earlier—a shared pulse, steady and eternal.

When they broke apart, their foreheads rested together, their breaths still mingling in the space between them. Sierra's voice was barely above a whisper, trembling with emotion. "Lucas, I'm so glad you're here. That you're starting to see what I've always felt."

Lucas nodded, his voice steady despite the quiet storm still churning inside him. "I couldn't do this without you," he said simply, the sincerity in his tone cutting through the night's stillness.

Sierra smiled, her eyes luminous even in the faint starlight. "You don't have to," she murmured. "We'll figure it out together."

Lucas kissed her again, the connection between them deepening in a way that defied explanation. The stars above seemed brighter now, as though the universe itself had shifted, aligning with the moment.

They broke apart once more, their hands finding each other instinctively. Without speaking, they settled onto the blanket, the desert night wrapping around them. Lucas stared up at the sky, the constellations sharper than he had ever noticed before.

For the first time in years, Lucas felt at peace—not because he had found answers, but because he was beginning to accept the questions. The mysteries of the ley lines no longer felt like puzzles to solve; they felt like an invitation, a calling he was ready to answer.

When the first light of dawn brushed the horizon, casting the desert in soft gold, Lucas turned his head to find Sierra resting against his shoulder. He let the moment stretch, the quiet clarity of the dawn settling over him.

"Thank you," Lucas said finally, his voice low but firm. "For showing me how to see this differently."

Sierra stirred, her smile drowsy but radiant. "We're a team," she said, her voice warm and steady. "There's so much more to discover."

Chapter 28

Tara gripped the steering wheel, her knuckles pale against the cracked leather. The wind tugged at her hair through the half-open window, carrying the dry, earthy scent of the Arizona desert. The low hum of the road beneath her tires offered a rhythm she clung to, a fragile anchor as her thoughts churned.

"Just a drive, Tara. Just a drive," she muttered, her voice almost lost in the breeze. But the erratic tap of her fingers against the wheel betrayed her nerves.

Ahead, the jagged cliffs of northern Arizona loomed, their weathered faces carved by time and tempest. Tara's gaze flicked to the rearview mirror—a fleeting glance at the woman she was leaving behind. The reflection met her eyes with quiet determination, though the road ahead still felt like uncharted territory.

She inhaled deeply, letting the cool morning air fill her lungs in an attempt to dispel the tight knot in her stomach. "Why am I so nervous?" she wondered aloud, the words more question than statement. It wasn't just the hike. It was what it represented: opening up, stepping into something unfamiliar, and allowing herself to hope for connection.

As Flagstaff's skyline edged into view, Tara pulled into a truck stop off I-40, seeking a momentary reprieve. The mundane ritual of ordering coffee grounded her.

"Just a coffee, please," she said, her voice steadier than she expected. She clutched the warm cup in her hands, letting its heat seep into her palms as she stepped back into the solitude of her car. The vendor's chatter faded into the background, leaving her alone with her thoughts.

Back on the road, the caffeine cleared her head but offered no easy answers. The closer she drew to Flagstaff, the more her emotions swirled—nerves, doubt, a flicker of cautious hope.

"This could be a disaster," she thought, her fingers tightening briefly on the wheel. But then another thought surfaced, quiet but insistent: *What if it's exactly what I need?*

By the time she pulled into downtown Flagstaff, the city was alive with the bustle of a crisp morning. Tara caught her reflection in the truck's side mirror and paused. She smoothed her hair, adjusted her jacket, and straightened her shoulders. "You can do this," she murmured, the words feeling less like a command now and more like a quiet reassurance.

With her backpack slung over her shoulders, she approached the meeting point beneath the Flagstaff Hiking Club banner. The energy of the group, a mix of eager hikers chatting and adjusting their gear, was infectious, loosening the tension in her chest.

Among the hikers, Ashley Martinez stood out. Her confident posture and easy smile caught Tara's attention immediately. Ashley's fitted blue jacket and scuffed hiking boots balanced practicality with an understated charm that drew Tara in.

"Tara?" Ashley's voice was warm and welcoming. Her handshake was firm but not overbearing, a perfect reflection of her presence.

"That's me," Tara replied, her voice tinged with nervous excitement.

The two exchanged pleasantries as they fell into step with the group. The trail wound upward through towering pines, their branches filtering the sunlight into shifting patterns on the ground.

Ashley's animated storytelling filled the space between them, her laughter light and unguarded.

"You really know your way around," Tara said, impressed by Ashley's ease on the trail.

Ashley grinned, brushing a stray strand of hair from her face. "You'd think so, but I've gotten lost more times than I'd care to admit. That's part of the fun, though—figuring out how to find your way back."

Tara smiled, a quiet warmth blooming in her chest. There was something in Ashley's words that resonated, an acknowledgment of imperfection that felt both freeing and familiar.

When they reached a lookout point, the group paused to take in the view. The valley below stretched wide and endless, a mosaic of greens and browns framed by distant peaks. Tara felt a calm settle over her, as though the land itself were offering its quiet encouragement.

"Beautiful, isn't it?" Ashley's voice was soft, almost reverent.

"It is," Tara agreed, her eyes lingering on the horizon before shifting to Ashley. The warmth in her chest grew, solidifying into something like assurance. For the first time in what felt like years, she knew she was exactly where she needed to be.

Ashley reached out, her hand brushing lightly against Tara's. Tara took it without hesitation, the simple touch grounding her in the moment.

"Thank you for inviting me," Tara said, her voice quiet but steady.

Ashley's smile widened, her grip gentle but sure. "I'm glad you came," she replied.

Later, they sat together at a cozy table in the Pinnacle Ale House, the hum of conversation and clinking glasses filling the space. The easy camaraderie of the trail had shifted into something more uncertain, a quiet tension settling between Tara and Ashley. Tara traced the rim of her glass absentmindedly, half-listening as Ashley recounted another hiking story, her mind wandering through the unspoken possibilities of the night.

The group at their table added a lively energy, contrasting Tara's introspection. Ashley's friend Derek, broad-shouldered with an easy confidence, leaned back in his chair, his arms crossed as he listened to Ashley with a faint smile. His dark hair was tied back, a weathered jacket draped over his chair. He exuded a quiet intensity that hinted at the weight of his experiences.

Beside him, Sarah, petite and animated, chimed in with quick bursts of laughter. Her short-cropped hair and sharp eyes gave her a look of sharp intelligence, though there was a warmth to her that made her approachable. Her hiking boots still bore the dust of the trail, as if she'd just stepped off it and into the pub.

"Okay, okay," Derek interrupted Ashley's story with a grin. "But you didn't tell them about the time you got lost and had to charm the park ranger into giving you a ride back to your car."

Ashley groaned, burying her face in her hands. "I knew you'd bring that up. One time, Derek. One time."

Sarah laughed, nudging Ashley's arm. "Don't let him tease you too much. We all know you can charm your way out of anything."

Ashley threw a mock glare at Sarah before turning back to Tara, her teasing expression softening. "What about you, Tara? Think you're up for another trail next weekend?"

Tara hesitated, her fingers stilling on her glass. "I'm not sure," she said, her smile faltering. "I guess I'll have to see how I'm feeling."

Ashley's brow furrowed slightly, her eyes searching Tara's face. "You seem a little distracted. Is everything okay?"

Before Tara could answer, Derek leaned forward, his voice dropping into a more serious tone. "I don't blame you if you're distracted. A lot's happening out there—especially in places like

Redstone. Places that people like Caldwell are trying to take over."

The shift in tone was palpable. Tara glanced at him, her interest piqued. "You know about Caldwell?"

Derek nodded, his expression tightening. "People like him are all the same—big promises, big profits, and little regard for what they destroy. I've seen it before."

Sarah leaned in, her tone more measured but no less impassioned. "That's why we're planning to head to the protests next month. They're trying to push another project near Flagstaff, and people are organizing to push back. You should come. It's empowering— seeing so many voices come together to fight for something real."

Tara's chest tightened at their words, the idea of action sparking both unease and intrigue. "I'll think about it," she said carefully, though the weight of their conviction lingered.

Ashley reached across the table, brushing her fingers against Tara's hand. "Hey," she said softly, drawing Tara's focus back. "You don't have to decide anything tonight. About the trail, or anything else."

Tara managed a small smile, grateful for Ashley's understanding even as her thoughts swirled.

Later, outside the pub, the cool night air wrapped around them as they stood near Tara's truck. Derek and Sarah lingered by the door, deep in conversation, their words carrying an urgency that Tara couldn't ignore.

Ashley stepped closer, her expression softer now, her voice quiet. "Tara," she began, hesitating just long enough for the moment to stretch. "Do you want to come home with me tonight?"

The question hung between them, laden with possibilities. Tara's pulse quickened as her emotions swirled—wanting to say yes, but held back by her own fears.

"I… I need to think," she said finally, her voice barely above a whisper.

Ashley nodded, her disappointment brief but tempered with understanding. "That's okay. No pressure."

As they lingered, the moment hung heavy with what hadn't been said. On impulse, Ashley leaned in, brushing a soft kiss against Tara's lips. The touch was fleeting but filled with promise, igniting something warm and uncertain within Tara.

Tara leaned into the kiss briefly, but as quickly as it began, she pulled back. Her heart ached with conflicting emotions. "I'm sorry," she murmured, stepping away. "I just... I need time."

Ashley smiled gently, her voice soft. "Take all the time you need. I'll be here."

Tara climbed into her truck and watched Ashley walk back toward the pub. Her feelings were a mix of relief and regret.

In the distance, Derek and Sarah's voices carried, their conversation continuing as if her world didn't just change.

Chapter 29

LUCAS STARED OUT at the desert horizon, its stark beauty amplifying the swirl of questions in his mind. The sharp, dry air anchored him in the present, yet his thoughts drifted back to the previous night. The contrast between the desert's quiet vastness and the energy Sierra had stirred within him left him feeling unmoored, as though he stood at the edge of something he couldn't yet name.

He could still hear her laughter, see her eyes alight with conviction as she spoke of the ley lines. There was a substance to her belief—something unyielding and raw—that had burrowed past his skepticism. He wanted to dismiss it as whimsy or romanticism, but the memory clung to him, challenging his neatly ordered logic.

The ping of his tablet drew him back, and as Elana's face filled the screen, her familiar smile brought a bittersweet pang. "Lucas! Did the desert get its hooks in you yet?" she teased, her voice light but edged with the intimacy of shared history.

Her laughter pulled at him, a tether to a simpler time when the line between belief and doubt felt clearer. He leaned back in his chair, the tablet propped on the makeshift desk in his rented room.

"The desert..." he began, searching for the right words, "it has a way of making you see things differently."

Elana's curiosity deepened, her smile fading into something softer. "Different in a good way or a 'time-to-run' kinda way?"

Lucas managed a faint smile. "Mostly good. The landscapes are mesmerizing," he admitted, though his thoughts were far from the terrain. "But the people here—they're consumed by legends and mysteries. It's like living in a cross between history and myth. It's… overwhelming."

Elana raised an eyebrow, her tone playful. "Oh? Are the mystical ley lines starting to cast their spell on you?"

He chuckled, though the sound felt hollow. "Hardly. Magic and myths don't mix well with science."

"They might not need to," she countered, leaning closer to the screen. "Maybe their faith in something greater isn't harmful, just… different."

Lucas hesitated, the memory of Sierra's words surfacing again: *"You're starting to listen—to the ley lines, to this place, and maybe even to yourself."* His lips pressed into a thin line. "It's about what's real, Elana. And when myths are passed off as truth, that's where things get dangerous."

"But is that what's happening?" she asked gently. "From what you've told me, these people aren't just clinging to myths—they're protecting history, culture, a sense of identity. Maybe there's something worth preserving, even if it's not your area of expertise."

Lucas looked down at his desk, his finger tracing the edge of a notebook filled with diagrams and field notes. He wanted to dismiss her point, to reinforce the clarity of his scientific framework. But instead, he found himself nodding. "Perhaps. Preserving history— that's something I can get behind. Even if it's tangled up in… other things."

Elana smiled, her expression lightening. "See? That's a starting point. Work with them, Lucas. Use your knowledge to protect what they hold dear. You might even discover you're not so far apart."

The words hung in the air, settling over him like the first stars breaking through twilight. He thought of Sierra's unshakable conviction, of the way her connection to the land seemed to defy the boundaries of logic.

"Maybe," he said finally, the word slipping out before he could second-guess it.

"Maybe is a good place to start," Elana said, her voice warm with encouragement. "You've always led with your head, Lucas, but sometimes the heart needs a turn, too."

Their conversation shifted to easier topics, but Lucas's thoughts remained tethered to the desert. As he ended the call, he found himself gazing back out at the horizon, the stars now scattered across the vast sky.

For the first time, the ley lines didn't feel like an academic puzzle or a cultural artifact to be dissected. They felt alive—threads weaving together history, belief, and something more elusive.

The image of Sierra's face lingered, her laughter like an echo in his chest. He wondered what it meant—not just for his work, but for himself. Could he let go of the rigid framework that had defined him for so long?

In the stillness, the desert seemed to answer in its own way, vast and indifferent yet teeming with unseen possibilities. Lucas closed his eyes, allowing the silence to settle over him. The questions weren't gone, but for the first time, they didn't feel like burdens.

Chapter 30

ELANA PACED the small confines of her study, the rhythmic thud of her boots against the worn wood floor echoing her frustration. The laptop screen had dimmed, the video call with Lucas ended, but his words clung to her thoughts like burrs.

"Maybe," he had said. Such a small, noncommittal word, but one that carried a weight she wasn't used to hearing from him. Lucas, the eternal skeptic, had let something slip—something unguarded. There were cracks forming in his logic, spaces where doubt and wonder might coexist.

She paused by the window, looking out at the blurred glow of Seattle's streetlights against the night sky. Their cool, structured precision mirrored her life—orderly, predictable, and secure. Yet for the first time in years, it felt like a façade, a world too neatly confined compared to the raw, open desert Lucas had described.

The ley lines. Sierra. Redstone.

Lucas hadn't spoken much about Sierra, just enough to mention her conviction in the ley lines and her connection to the land. But Elana couldn't ignore the way he'd said her name—softer, almost reverent. A pang of something—jealousy? Curiosity?—tightened in her chest.

Her gaze drifted to the desk where her notebook sat, a well-worn companion to years of research and careful planning. She picked it up, flipping to a blank page. With her pen poised, she began mapping the fragments Lucas had shared: ley lines, the desert's mysteries, Sierra's name. The lines she drew crisscrossed the page, but none of them connected the way she needed them to.

The desert, Lucas had said, *"makes you see things differently."*

What had he meant by that? Was it the ley lines themselves? Or Sierra? Was she simply overthinking this, or was Lucas truly beginning to change? The Lucas she had known would have dismissed Sierra's beliefs outright, reducing them to cultural myths or pseudoscience. But now... he seemed drawn to them, as though he were letting go of the rigid framework that had once defined him.

And perhaps that was what unsettled her most.

The study's clean lines and meticulously arranged shelves, once a comfort, now felt suffocating. Her life was structured to avoid risks and uncertainty. Yet, as she sat in her perfectly curated world, Elana realized how stifling that safety had become. She could almost feel the desert wind Lucas had described, hear its vast silence.

Sierra's image lingered in her mind, unbidden. Elana wasn't one to jump to conclusions, but the woman had clearly made an impression on Lucas. Was she a guide? A muse? A threat?

Elana shook her head, frustrated with her own spiral of thoughts. *Why does it matter so much?* Lucas was free to make his own choices. Yet she couldn't shake the feeling that whatever he was experiencing in Redstone would ripple far beyond himself.

She leaned back in her chair, staring at the ceiling. "Maybe," Lucas had said. A single word, but it meant so much more. He was hesitating, questioning—not just the desert or the ley lines, but himself. And wasn't that worth exploring? If Lucas, the man who thrived on certainty, was finding space for doubt, shouldn't she do the same?

Her eyes flicked to the calendar pinned beside her desk. Flagstaff.

Flagstaff wasn't far from Redstone, just a quick flight from

Seattle. She could see the desert for herself, confront the ley lines and the stories Lucas was navigating. And yes, meet Sierra.

The name lingered like a question she hadn't yet answered.

Elana took a deep breath. If Lucas was stepping into uncharted territory, she wouldn't let him face it alone—not entirely. But more than that, she needed to understand what had captured him so profoundly. The desert, the ley lines, the woman who spoke of them with unshakable belief—whatever it was, it had drawn Lucas out of himself.

And now, it was pulling her, too.

She leaned forward, closing her notebook with quiet resolve. The city hummed faintly in the background, but Elana was already imagining the silence of the desert, its vastness waiting to be explored.

She stood, her pulse steadying as the decision rooted itself firmly in her mind. She would go.

Chapter 31

HIRAM CALDWELL ADJUSTED the phone against his ear, his voice steadier than he felt. "Mika, it's me. Can you meet me tonight? At the ridge."

A pause, heavy with unspoken history. "You sure about that?" Mika finally asked, his tone cautious.

"I need your perspective," Hiram admitted. "You always had a way of seeing things clearer than me."

Another pause, then Mika sighed. "Alright. I'll be there."

The desert unfolded before Hiram, the ridge stretching into the distance like an unbroken promise. The sun had dipped below the horizon, leaving the landscape drenched in shadow and streaks of fiery orange. The quiet pressed against him, wrapping around the questions he couldn't answer.

He heard Mika's footsteps crunching against the loose dirt behind him. Hiram didn't turn. "I wasn't sure you'd come," he said, his voice carrying on the breeze.

"You called," Mika replied simply. "Figured it must mean something."

Mika stepped up beside him, his silhouette solid and familiar, carved from the same rugged land that surrounded them. For a moment, neither spoke. The desert stretched out before them, vast and silent, as though waiting for the conversation to begin.

"You ever wonder," Hiram said finally, his tone quieter now, "if we were wrong? Back then, when we thought we'd fix everything?"

Mika tilted his head, his expression hidden in shadow but his voice steady. "I don't think the land's changed, Hiram. Just us."

The words settled heavily between them, sharper than Hiram had anticipated. He exhaled slowly, his shoulders sagging. "You think I've forgotten, don't you? What this place means?"

Mika's gaze shifted to the horizon, his hands shoved deep into the pockets of his jacket. "I think you remember it, Hiram. But remembering isn't the same as fighting for it."

Hiram's jaw tightened as the truth of Mika's words pierced through his defenses. He turned slightly, his eyes searching his friend's face. "Do you know how hard it is? To carry the weight of everyone else's expectations? To balance what they want with what I thought I'd be?"

Mika finally looked at him, his voice calm but unyielding. "You think I don't know what it's like to make hard choices? You're not the only one carrying things, Hiram. But the land doesn't care about board meetings or bottom lines. It'll be here long after those things are gone—if we let it."

Hiram let out a bitter chuckle, though the sound lacked humor. "You make it sound so simple. Like I can just walk away."

Mika stepped closer, his tone softening but losing none of its conviction. "You can't change everything, Hiram. But you can choose where to draw the line. And if you're calling me, standing out here, asking these questions... I think you already know what that line is."

The stars emerged one by one, their cold light glinting off the jagged peaks in the distance. Hiram turned his gaze to the horizon, the vastness of the desert pulling at something deep within him.

"They're breaking ground next week," he said after a long silence.

"Contracts signed, money flowing, the whole machine in motion."

Mika nodded slowly, his expression unreadable. "And yet here you are, calling me out to this ridge. Looking for... what? Permission? Absolution? You won't find it in me, Hiram. But maybe you'll find it out there." He gestured to the expanse before them, his hand steady and deliberate.

Hiram closed his eyes briefly, the wind brushing against his face. "I wanted to believe this plan was about saving Redstone. About giving it a future."

"Maybe it was," Mika said quietly. "But whose future are you saving, Hiram? Redstone's, or yours?"

The question cut through the air like a knife, leaving Hiram with nothing to hold onto but the echoes of his own doubts.

Mika stepped back, his boots crunching against the dirt as he turned to leave. "You always saw the big picture," he said over his shoulder. "But sometimes, you've got to look closer. See what's right in front of you."

Hiram didn't respond, his gaze fixed on the stars that now dotted the night sky, their light stark and indifferent. He stayed rooted in place as Mika's footsteps faded into the distance, leaving him alone on the ridge.

For a fleeting moment, he felt the faintest stirrings of something—memory, regret, hope? He wasn't sure. The echoes of childhood laughter flickered in his mind, mingling with the distant hum of promises he'd once believed in.

The desert stretched out before him, vast and unmoving, its silence as heavy as the choices pressing against his chest.

Chapter 32

Sierra sat cross-legged on the floor of her studio, surrounded by scattered photographs and the brittle pages of old letters. The air was thick with the scent of sage from the bundle smoldering nearby, the faint smoke curling like tendrils of memory. Her grandmother's leather-bound journal rested in her lap, its cracked spine and worn cover evidence of generations of hands that had turned its pages.

The flickering light of a single candle danced across the room, casting shifting shadows on the journal's words. She turned the fragile pages carefully, her fingers brushing against the faintly inked lines of her grandmother's handwriting.

Her eyes landed on a passage she had read before but now carried new weight:

"The Castillo family has guarded the secret of the ley lines since time immemorial. Our blood is tied to this land, our spirits to its energy. Should the lines fade, so too will our connection to our ancestors, our power, our very essence."

Sierra's breath caught. She pressed her hand lightly against the yellowed paper, as though to steady herself against the enormity of those words. She had always carried pieces of her grandmother's wisdom in her heart, but this—this felt different. This was not just history or folklore. It was a responsibility that demanded acknowledgment.

Beside her lay a carefully preserved Edward Curtis photograph, sepia tones lending the image a timeless quality. Sierra picked it up, her fingers trembling slightly. It showed her great-grandmother, posed by Curtis for his lens, standing before the ancient stone circle. Her dress, chosen to evoke a romanticized idea of the "noble savage," was foreign to her lived reality, yet her strength radiated through the artifice.

Her back was straight, her eyes fierce and unyielding, as though staring straight into Sierra's soul across the decades. The photograph was a paradox—both artifact and distortion—but her great-grandmother's essence, her defiance, could not be masked by Curtis's framing.

"You knew," Sierra whispered into the stillness, her voice catching. Her thumb brushed over the edges of the photograph, tracing the figure's resolute outline. "You carried this. And now it's mine to carry, too."

The weight of those words settled heavily on her chest. This wasn't just about her or Redstone—it was about a connection stretching back through time, through bloodlines and stories, through whispered prayers beneath the stars.

Setting the photograph back down, she turned her gaze to the scattered relics around her: letters worn with age, small trinkets, fragments of a legacy she was only now beginning to fully grasp. These weren't just keepsakes. They were evidence of a lineage that refused to be forgotten, threads woven into a tapestry that spanned generations.

Her fingers returned to the journal, tracing the words again as a quiet determination began to take root. Her great-grandmother's gaze stayed with her, a silent call to action.

Sierra closed her eyes and inhaled deeply, the scent of sage grounding her. Generations of responsibility pressed against her, but beneath that weight was a clarity she hadn't felt before—quiet, steady, unshakable.

"I won't let this die with me," she said softly, her voice growing firmer. "I won't let them take this from us."

She began carefully organizing the photos and documents, her movements deliberate and reverent. With each item she handled, a fragile resolve crystallized into something stronger. This was more than Redstone or the ley lines—it was her family's essence, their unbroken connection to the land, and something ancient and irreplaceable that thrummed beneath her feet.

The flickering candlelight caught the edges of the Curtis photograph again. Her great-grandmother's eyes seemed to watch her still, a reminder that strength was not in avoiding the burden but in carrying it forward.

Sierra placed the journal and photograph together on her desk, standing and brushing the dust from her hands. Her heritage wasn't just stories or relics. They were a heartbeat, a legacy, a reminder of who she was and where she came from.

And she would fight to protect them.

————

Lucas leaned against the hood of his truck, arms crossed tightly over his chest. The desert sky deepened into velvet blue, stars piercing the darkness like silver pinpricks scattered across an endless expanse. The air was cooling now, the day's heat retreating into the cracked earth, but Lucas felt the weight of it linger in his chest.

Elana's voice crackled through his phone's speaker, steady and familiar. "You sound far away," she said.

"I guess I am," Lucas replied, his breath escaping in a long sigh. "Physically, mentally... all of it."

Elana paused, the silence filled with an intimacy only years of knowing each other could carry. "This place is getting to you, isn't it?"

Lucas kept his eyes on the horizon, where the desert stretched endlessly, stubborn and unyielding. "It's not just the place, Elana. It's everything. The people. The stories. The depth of what we're messing with out here."

"Sierra?" she asked gently, her tone probing but kind.

Closing his eyes briefly, Lucas nodded to himself. "She's... remarkable. Committed, brave, passionate. It's like she's carrying this entire place on her shoulders. And I—I don't know if I'm helping her or making things worse."

Elana's voice softened. "Lucas, you always do this. You take on every fracture, every problem, as if fixing them is solely your responsibility. But you can't hold everything together by yourself."

Lucas barked a tired laugh, shaking his head. "You always know exactly what to say, don't you?"

There was a pause, and when Elana spoke again, her voice carried a firmness that cut through the distance. "No, Lucas. I just know you. You've got this big heart, but you're stuck between trying to fix everything and being terrified of what happens if you fail."

He rubbed the back of his neck, guilt and responsibility pressing down on him like the weight of the sky. "It's not that simple, Elana. There's more at play here than just ley lines and fragile agreements. People are drawing lines in the sand. And I don't even know where I stand."

"You stand where you've always stood," she replied, her voice calm but unyielding. "Right where people need you. But you can't let fear stop you from moving forward."

A gust of wind swept across the truck, carrying the faint scent of distant rain. Lucas let the silence settle, drawing strength from the steadiness of her voice, even across the miles.

Then, suddenly, he asked, "Do you regret it?"

"Regret what?" Elana sounded puzzled, though her tone shifted, tentative.

"Us. The way things ended. The way I walked away."

Her hesitation felt like an eternity. Lucas braced himself, his pulse quickening in the still night.

"Sometimes," she admitted quietly. "But I also know we did the best we could with what we had. And Lucas… you didn't walk away because you didn't care. You walked away because you cared too much, and it scared you."

Lucas swallowed hard, his throat tightening. "I—I don't know what I'm supposed to do here, Elana. With Sierra. With this town. With… everything."

Her voice was clear, her conviction unshakable. "Then start with what you know. Trust your gut. Trust Sierra. And Lucas, for once, trust yourself."

He nodded, even though she couldn't see him, his gaze fixed on the faint lights of Redstone flickering in the distance. "You're right," he murmured.

"I usually am," Elana teased, her warmth cutting through the weight of the conversation.

Lucas let out a slow breath. "Thanks, Elana. For this. For… everything."

"You're welcome," she said. "But Lucas, promise me something."

"Anything."

"Don't let this place break you. Whatever happens out there, whatever you uncover—don't lose yourself in it. Promise me."

Lucas hesitated, the words catching in his throat before he finally said, "I promise."

The call ended, and the silence of the desert returned, pressing against him like a heavy blanket. He slipped his phone into his pocket and looked up at the stars. They burned brighter now, cold and unblinking, ancient witnesses to a world he was only beginning to grasp.

He pushed off the hood of the truck, his steps deliberate as he began walking toward the distant lights of Redstone. For the first time, he held the faintest glimmer of hope—that maybe, just maybe, he could start to find a way forward.

Chapter 33

THE VELVET CACTUS WAS QUIETER than usual, the low hum of conversation merging with the faint clink of glasses. The bar's dim lighting cast long shadows over the worn wooden floor, giving the space an intimacy that felt calculated. Veronica Miller stepped inside, her heels striking sharp, deliberate notes with every step. Her tailored black blazer and silk blouse gave her an air of precision, but the glint in her eyes betrayed her purpose.

In the far corner, Hiram Caldwell waited, a figure half-draped in shadow. The flickering wall sconce above him accentuated the sharp angles of his jaw, the deliberate set of his shoulders. He nursed his drink, his gaze steady and unreadable as it locked onto Veronica's approaching form.

"Ms. Miller," he greeted, his voice low and deliberate. "I wasn't sure you'd come."

Veronica slid into the seat across from him, her spine straight, her chin lifted in defiance of his subtle challenge. "You knew I'd come, Hiram. The question is whether you'll make it worth my while."

A faint smirk curved his lips as he reached for the bottle on the table, pouring another glass of deep amber liquid. "To alliances," he said, his tone rich with amusement. "Or at least... to negotiations."

She accepted the glass but didn't drink, holding it between her fingers like a weapon. "You have ambition, Hiram. Grand plans for Redstone. Plans that, without the right leverage, will crumble before they even reach the blueprint stage."

He swirled his drink, his gaze never leaving hers. "And you think you're the leverage?"

"I know I am," she replied smoothly, her voice a blade cloaked in silk. "You need someone who can move where you can't. Someone with access to things you can only speculate about. My position with the sheriff's office isn't ceremonial, Hiram—it's influence. Information. The key to doors you don't even know exist."

Hiram leaned back in his chair, his fingers drumming against the side of his glass. "And in return?"

Veronica leaned forward, her voice dropping to a murmur. "A stake. Not scraps from your table—a real stake. Partnership, not patronage."

Her words hung in the air, taut as a drawn bowstring.

Hiram's smirk faded into something colder, more measured. He studied her, his eyes narrowing with an intensity that felt like being stripped bare, dissected, and cataloged. "You have a knack for bold demands," he said, his voice cutting through the tension like a scalpel.

"And you have a knack for underestimating the people you need," she countered, a faint smile tugging at her lips.

He chuckled, his fingers tightening around his glass. "Ambition suits you, Veronica. But it's a dangerous thing. People with ambition often outgrow their usefulness."

She leaned back. "Then let's make sure I never outgrow mine. You talk about rebuilding Redstone—about preserving its legacy. But I see through you, Hiram. Underneath all the talk of 'the greater good,' you're already calculating the profit margins."

His expression darkened slightly, but he said nothing.

"That's not a weakness," she pressed. "It's who you are. And it's what makes you good at this. So stop fighting it. Lean into it. Build your empire, Hiram. Make it as big, as bold, and as profitable as you can."

"And you expect to be part of it," he said, his voice flat.

"Not just part of it," she corrected. "Essential to it. You know as well as I do—empires aren't built alone. You need people who can get their hands dirty, who can handle the shadows while you stay in the spotlight."

Hiram's grip on his glass loosened, but his gaze remained steady. For a moment, silence stretched between them. The hum of the bar faded into the background.

"Let's say I indulge this proposition," he said finally. "What's to stop you from turning those shadows against me when the time comes?"

Veronica took a slow sip of her drink, her eyes never leaving his. "Because I know where my best interests lie. And I know how to stay useful."

Hiram tipped back his glass, finishing his drink in one smooth motion. The deliberate click of the empty glass against the table echoed between them. He stood, smoothed the front of his jacket, and extended a hand toward her.

"Come with me," he said, his voice a quiet command.

Veronica rose, her steps unhurried as she fell into stride beside him. The shadows of the Velvet Cactus stretched long behind them as they left, the night outside crisp and full of unspoken promises.

As they walked, Hiram glanced at her out of the corner of his eye. "If we're doing this, Veronica, it won't be without risk. The people in Redstone are watching. They're not going to make this easy."

"Good. Anything worth building is worth a fight." Beside him, Veronica walked with the poise of someone who knew exactly how to collect.

The following morning, the hum of the private jet's engines filled the cabin with a low, constant vibration as Veronica Miller adjusted the cuff of her blazer. Sunlight streamed through the small oval windows, casting thin golden beams across the leather seats and polished mahogany trim. Across from her, Hiram Caldwell reclined in his seat, one hand wrapped around a crystal glass of whiskey—too early for most, but Hiram operated on his own timeline.

Veronica's tablet rested on her lap, a spreadsheet flickering across the screen. But her attention wasn't on numbers or projections. It was on Hiram, on the way he watched her over the rim of his glass—calculated, appraising, yet softened by something unspoken.

"You've been quiet this morning," he said, breaking the silence. His voice carried easily over the hum of the engines.

She glanced out the window briefly before turning back to him. "I'm thinking, Hiram. About what happens when we land. Your board isn't going to roll over just because you flash them a confident smile and a stack of projections."

He smirked faintly, setting his glass down on the side table. "Confidence and numbers open more doors than you think, Veronica. But you're right. This meeting isn't about charm—it's about control."

She leaned back in her seat, crossing one leg over the other. "You brought me along for a reason, didn't you? You're not planning to face them alone."

His smirk faltered for half a second before returning sharper, more deliberate. "I brought you because you understand leverage. You know how to read people, how to spot fractures in alliances. I need that today."

She studied him. "You mean you need me. That's different."

Hiram didn't answer immediately. He reached for the glass again, but this time, he simply turned it in his hand.

"Last night wasn't just strategy, Hiram," Veronica said. Her voice was steady, but there was an edge of vulnerability threaded through it. "Whatever this… alliance is, it's fragile. If we're going to move forward, we need to decide what this really is."

For a moment, neither spoke. The jet lurched as it hit a pocket of turbulence, but Veronica didn't flinch. Hiram kept his eyes on her, his expression unreadable, like a mask carefully set in place.

"I'm not a man who makes decisions lightly, Veronica," he said finally. "You're right. Last night was more than just strategy. But this—what we're building—it's bigger than you or me. We can't afford to let sentiment distract us."

She nodded, but her jaw tightened. "Sentiment isn't the problem, Hiram. The problem is whether we trust each other enough to see this through. You have the vision, but I have the reach. You need me, and I need to know that won't change the second it becomes inconvenient for you."

The engines droned on as silence settled between them again. Hiram's smirk was gone now, replaced by something heavier—a weariness he rarely let slip.

"Trust isn't given freely, Veronica. But you've earned enough of it to be sitting here."

She accepted that answer for now, though it wasn't the full truth. But then, nothing with Hiram Caldwell ever was.

The intercom crackled, and the pilot's voice came through. "We'll be descending into Salt Lake City shortly. Please prepare for landing."

Hiram straightened in his seat, adjusting his cufflinks as if donning armor. Veronica turned off her tablet and placed it in her bag. The plane banked gently to the right and the city came into view below—a sprawling grid of opportunity and conflict.

Before the descent could fully pull them into their next battle,

Hiram spoke again. "Whatever happens in that room today, Veronica, you're at my side. We present a united front. No hesitation."

She didn't waver. "Then let's make sure we don't fall."

The wheels touched down with a gentle jolt, and the hum of the engines began to fade. But the tension between them remained—unspoken, electric, and deeply entwined with whatever fragile alliance they had forged in the dark hours of the night before.

Chapter 34

Hiram Caldwell stepped into the sleek conference room of Caldwell Enterprises' Salt Lake City headquarters. The room was a monument to corporate precision, with stretched wide with floor-to-ceiling windows offering a panoramic view of the city. The skyline glimmered against the early morning light, a fitting backdrop for Hiram's renewed sense of purpose.

Veronica Miller followed him. She was a quiet force in tailored navy, her hair pulled into a no-nonsense chignon. She carried herself with the poise of someone who knew the power of presence. It was unspoken but unmistakable; she wasn't just there as an aide—she had Hiram's trust

The board members—James, Elizabeth, and three others with decades of Caldwell corporate history etched into their features—exchanged wary glances as Hiram took his seat at the head of the polished mahogany table. Veronica sat a few paces behind him. She folded her hands folded in her lap and sat calm and unreadable.

"Good morning," Hiram began. "I've asked you all here today because it's time to reevaluate the scope and direction of our efforts in Redstone."

Elizabeth leaned forward. "I thought the planning committee vote already gave us a green light. What's changed, Hiram?"

"What's changed," Hiram said, "is our understanding of

Redstone's potential. Up until now, we've treated it like a passion project—a way to pay lip service to heritage while eking out modest returns. That's not enough. Not for the investment we're making."

James, the eldest and most conservative member of the board, frowned. "Are you suggesting we abandon the preservation angle entirely? That was the cornerstone of the proposal."

Hiram's jaw tightened. "I'm suggesting we stop pretending preservation is the endgame. Redstone isn't just a quaint little town clinging to its past—it's an untapped resource. The land, the tourism, the story we can shape—there's profit there. Significant profit."

The room fell silent. Hiram leaned forward and his voice gained momentum. "My father understood something that I've resisted for years. Sentiment doesn't pay the bills. It doesn't build legacies. Profit does. And if Redstone is going to thrive—if Caldwell Heritage Partners is going to thrive—we need to think bigger."

Elizabeth crossed her arms. "And what exactly does 'bigger' mean, Hiram? Turning Redstone into a theme park? Selling off parcels of sacred land to the highest bidder?"

Hiram held her gaze. "It means leveraging every asset we have. The ley lines, the stories, the history—it's all part of a brand we can sell. Redstone isn't just a town; it's an experience. And experiences are profitable."

Veronica's voice cut through the growing murmurs. "If I may," she said, drawing every eye in the room. "What Hiram is proposing isn't a betrayal of the preservation angle—it's an evolution. By creating a sustainable profit model, we ensure the resources to protect Redstone's heritage. Without funding, preservation is nothing more than a pipe dream."

James turned his gaze to her. "And who are you exactly? An advisor? A consultant?"

Veronica smiled, "I'm someone who believes in the vision Hiram is building. Someone who understands that to preserve anything, you first need the power and influence to protect it."

Elizabeth's eyes flicked between Hiram and Veronica. "Vision is all well and good, but what about the people in Redstone? They're already wary of us. How do you propose we sell this to them?"

Hiram stood. "We don't sell it to them. We sell it in spite of them. The community will come around when they see the jobs, the infrastructure, the opportunities we're bringing. Resistance is inevitable, but it's temporary. Once the benefits become tangible, even the most vocal critics will fall in line."

James rubbed his temples. "And if they don't?"

Hiram gripped the back of his chair. "Then we move forward anyway. Progress doesn't wait for permission. And if we succeed—when we succeed—the naysayers will have no choice but to acknowledge the good we've done."

The room erupted into muted debate. Voices overlapped as the board weighed Hiram's proposal. Veronica remained seated, and calm. She glanced at Hiram, offering him a small, approving nod when their eyes met.

Elizabeth's voice finally cut through the noise. "Hiram, this is a drastic shift. You're asking us to risk the reputation of Caldwell Heritage Partners on a gamble that could alienate an entire community."

Hiram's confidence was unshaken. "I'm not asking you to gamble. I'm asking you to trust me. Redstone is an opportunity we can't afford to squander. And I won't let us fail."

The board exchanged uncertain glances. Hiram's words settled over them. Slowly, James leaned back in his chair, his frown deepening but his resistance softening. Elizabeth, though clearly skeptical, nodded curtly.

"We'll review the details," James said finally. "But if this backfires, Hiram, the blame will fall squarely on you."

"I wouldn't have it any other way," Hiram replied.

As the meeting adjourned, Veronica fell into step beside Hiram. "You handled that well," she whispered.

Hiram adjusted his cuffs. "I learned from the best."

As they exited the boardroom, her eyes turned back to the towering windows and the sprawling city below. Whatever empire Hiram intended to build, she intended to ensure her place within it—and to keep him tethered to her vision as much as his own.

Chapter 35

THE NEXT EVENING, Marla Jenkins stood at the head of the long oak table in her ranch house, her hands gripping its worn edge. The flickering candlelight cast warm halos around the gathered faces—Tom from the hardware store, Paula from the diner, and a few others she had painstakingly persuaded to join Redstone's pro-growth cause. Voices settled as Marla cleared her throat. Her presence was commanding but underpinned by a restless energy.

"We cannot let fear of change paralyze us," she began. "This town is dying a slow death, and if we don't act now—if we don't trust Hiram Caldwell's vision—there won't be anything left to save."

Marla turned to look towards the head of the table where Hiram had sat the last time he visited. She could still picture him there, sleeves rolled up, his deep voice resonating with authority. Her chest tightened at the thought; her words took on a sharper edge.

Around the table, heads nodded—Tom leaned forward with quiet intensity; Paula's hands fidgeted nervously in her lap. Veronica Miller stood to the side, arms crossed. Her sharp blazer unwrinkled and immaculate, a portrait of confidence. Marla felt the woman's watchful eyes settle on her. Why did Veronica always seem to carry the air of someone with the upper hand?

"Marla," Tom said, "We believe in what Hiram's building, but people are scared. They don't understand the stakes like we do. And the opposition—they're loud."

Marla's lips pressed into a thin line. "Then we'll be louder," she declared. "We'll show them results, not just promises. The Celestial Ranch Sanctuary and all of Hiram's plans aren't just a business plan—they are our town's future."

Paula hesitated before chiming in. "But what about the ley lines? If something happens to them…"

Marla stiffened, her polish cracking for half a second before she caught Veronica's smirk from across the table. That smirk—a cool, knowing thing—ignited a flare of irritation deep in her chest.

"The ley lines are stories, legends," Marla snapped. "They can coexist with progress, and they will. Hiram's been clear about that."

"Stories don't keep the lights on," Veronica interjected. Her voice carried the calm authority of someone used to being right. "Our message needs to be about jobs, about prosperity, about keeping our children here. If we let the conversation drift into mysticism, we'll lose control of the narrative."

Marla nodded briskly. "You're right—on paper," she admitted. Yet Veronica's smooth certainty grated on her. Marla couldn't shake the feeling that Hiram was directing Veronica's every move and word.

After the meeting wrapped up, the attendees filed out with murmurs of agreement and promises to spread the word. Marla stayed behind, her gaze lingering on the empty chair Hiram had once occupied. The room was silent now, save for the faint creak of the ranch house settling against the cooling desert air.

On the porch, Veronica leaned against the railing. A coffee cup steamed faintly in her hands. Marla joined her.

"Tonight went well," Veronica said. "But you'll need to keep the momentum up. Hiram's counting on you."

That edge. That faint suggestion she spoke for Hiram in ways that Marla never could. she refused to let emotion show.

"I know what's at stake," Marla replied.

Veronica's eyes glittered with unspoken challenge. "Do you? Because it feels like you're getting distracted."

Marla froze with her coffee cup halfway to her lips. "What exactly are you implying, Veronica?"

"Oh, nothing," Veronica said lightly. "It's just that some of us are keeping our eyes on the project, while others seem to be looking elsewhere."

Marla's pulse quickened. She thought of the way Hiram had lingered in her doorway after their last meeting. She thought of how her heart had fluttered, the softness in her voice whenever he was near.

"You should watch your tone," Marla said coolly. "I've been advocating for this project long before you took your interest."

"And yet," Veronica said, "here we are."

Veronica's calm only deepened Marla's frustration. Each pointed word cut closer to truths she wasn't ready to confront.

Finally, Veronica pushed off the railing. "Good night, Marla. Don't lose focus."

Marla stayed rooted in place. Her coffee had long gone cold in her hands. She turned her gaze toward the dark horizon where the boundaries of the Jenkins' land stretched. Hiram's voice echoed in her mind, and she wondered, just briefly, if she was fighting for Redstone's future or for something else entirely.

Chapter 36

LUCAS ADJUSTED the tripod. His hands were steady but his thoughts restless. The sensor array blinked to life with a faint blue glow, casting shadows over the weathered Whispering Stones. He checked his notes again, cross-referencing the landmarks etched into his memory. The alignment had to be perfect.

The thin red beam of his handheld scanner swept across the carvings, catching in the grooves and markings on the surface. The air around him was cool and dry. A breeze carried the desert's endless quiet. But tonight, the vast silence of the desert felt different, as though the stones themselves were watching.

He jotted down the initial readings,. His eyes narrowing to look at the screen. Irregular spikes appeared, erratic but persistent. His equipment wasn't malfunctioning, but the data didn't follow any known pattern. The scanner beeped faintly, then flatlined.

Lucas sighed, crouching beside the nearest stone. His fingers brushed the surface absently, and then he felt it. A vibration. Faint at first, like tremors of machinery buried deep beneath the earth.

His breath stilled.

He pressed his palm flat against the stone. The vibration grew stronger, resonating through his hand, up his arm, and into his chest. It wasn't sound. It was texture, movement, something alive. The instruments on the ground seemed crude now, laughable in their inability to capture what his body was registering.

It deepened, filling his ears, his mind, his very skin. Lucas staggered back, glancing at his gear. The readings were gone, replaced by flat lines and static. But the sensation wasn't gone. If anything, it was amplifying.

Then came the voices.

They started as faint murmurs at the edges. Fragments slipping through his comprehension. At first, they were indistinct—alien syllables dissolving before he could hold onto them. But soon they sharpened, weaving into something deliberate and rhythmic:

Vrïna, šo'na, kes'ri mæ qena ivæl māshînes. Zēra tilā si'nsa kılla fi'lun.

The words filled his mind, not heard but felt. They vibrated against his skull as though they were meant to awaken something buried deep within him. He gasped, clutching the edge of the stone. Then, the desert around him changed.

The ground gleamed. Faint lines of light appeared like veins coursing through the earth. The stones pulsed in unison in a rhythm that he could feel in his chest. The sky seemed alive. Faint ribbons rippled between stars as if the heavens were answering the earth.

He reached out toward a glowing line on the stone. His fingertips brushed its surface, and energy surged into him like a bolt of lightning. It felt as if fire was racing through his veins, not burning but illuminating. He felt filled with blinding, overwhelming clarity.

His body snapped upright and his head flung back as the vision took him.

He was standing elsewhere. Whether it was past, future, or some liminal space, he couldn't tell. Around him, vast ley lines stretched into infinity, like glowing rivers of light that flowed both beneath and above the earth. Shadowy figures moved along them, their forms human yet indistinct, their faces painted.

He saw ceremonies—rituals under ancient moons, hands raised to skies burning with unfamiliar constellations. The earth and its energy were one, connected through the lines that pulsed with life.

The vision shifted.

Glass and steel towers rose from the ground, their bases trembling under the same tremors he had felt moments ago. Machines spun and clicked, their gears glowing with ley line energy, humming in harmony with the earth. It was a both ancient and modern, a precarious balance that felt impossibly fragile.

Then the balance tipped.

The lines frayed at their edges and their glow dimmed. Shadows spread across the towers and the ground, consuming the light. The hum in his head twisted into a scream, a piercing sound of destruction.

Lucas felt the tear—like something vital being ripped apart. The air itself seemed to collapse, to evaporate. He tried to speak, to stop it. But his voice was swallowed by the void.

"No!" He fell to his knees.

The vision shattered.

He was back in the desert, gasping for breath. His knees were digging into the gravel. He braced his hands against the stone, trembling as the vibrations ebbed into silence. The lines of light faded back into the earth, leaving only the cold, indifferent night.

Lucas knelt with his forehead pressed to the stone. His body was wracked with aftershocks. His mind struggled to process what he had seen. What he had felt. His rational framework was unable to contain the enormity of what had just passed through him.

Lucas sat back on his heels, staring at his useless instruments. The scattered papers now felt laughably inadequate. The desert was quiet again, but it wasn't the same. And neither was he.

He rose slowly on unsteady legs. His focus turned to the stones one last time. The lines were gone, but their memory had burned into his mind as surely as the vision itself.

Chapter 37

THE CITY COUNCIL CHAMBER was filled to capacity, the air humming with an electric anticipation. Residents, business owners, and civic leaders packed the room, their whispered conversations creating a low murmur that reverberated against the old wooden beams. Mayor Helen Jones, clad in her trademark navy suit, stepped up to the podium. The mural behind her, a proud depiction of Redstone's pioneer history, seemed to loom over the gathering like a silent witness.

"Ladies and gentlemen," she began, her voice carrying both warmth and authority, "Redstone stands at a pivotal moment in its history. This land, rich in stories and resilience, is drawing attention from far beyond our borders. With that attention comes opportunity—and challenge. Tonight, we come together to discuss two perspectives on what our future could look like."

The room fell silent, all eyes fixed on the mayor as she gestured toward the table to her left. "First, we will hear from Mr. Hiram Caldwell, a man whose family roots run deep in Redstone and whose vision seeks to bridge our town's heritage with a sustainable future. Following Mr. Caldwell, Dr. Lucas Grant, a distinguished geophysicist, will provide us with a scientific perspective on the ley lines that have so captivated our imaginations. These discussions will help us navigate the complex balance between preservation and progress."

Polite applause followed as the mayor stepped aside, her gaze steady as she invited Hiram Caldwell to the podium.

Hiram adjusted the microphone, letting his gaze sweep across the room. The faint crackle of the sound system quieted the audience, their collective attention falling on him like a spotlight. He exuded a calm confidence as he began.

"Good evening, everyone," he said, his voice smooth and measured. "Thank you for taking the time to be here tonight. Redstone's future is not just my concern; it's all of ours. What I share with you this evening is more than a development plan. It's a vision for how our community can thrive."

Behind him, glossy renderings of the Celestial Ranch Sanctuary were displayed on easels, their sleek designs juxtaposed with the rustic charm of the chamber. Hiram gestured toward the images.

"Caldwell Heritage Partners is dedicated to preserving what makes Redstone unique. This isn't about erasing our past but building on it. Sustainable tourism, revitalized infrastructure, and opportunities for local businesses—this is how we ensure that Redstone remains a place where our children can stay, build their lives, and contribute to a thriving community."

He paused, scanning the room. Some faces bore skeptical frowns, while others nodded in cautious approval. His tone remained steady, laced with a quiet urgency.

"Imagine a Redstone where heritage and innovation coexist," he continued. "Where the beauty of our land is celebrated, and our economy is strengthened. Together, we can build a future that honors our past while embracing the possibilities ahead."

The applause that followed was polite but subdued, the tension in the room palpable. Hiram offered a small nod of gratitude before stepping aside, his polished demeanor betraying none of the unease

Mika's earlier words had stirred within him.

Mayor Jones returned to the podium, her voice calm and steady. "Thank you, Mr. Caldwell, for your thoughtful presentation. Now, let us turn to Dr. Lucas Grant, whose work bridges the gap between folklore and science. Dr. Grant will help us better understand the ley lines and their significance to our land and history. Dr. Grant, the floor is yours."

Lucas rose, his movements deliberate as he approached the podium. The scattered applause faded into an expectant silence. He adjusted the microphone and gripped the edges of the podium, his fingers brushing the stack of notes he knew he wouldn't need.

"Thank you, Mayor Jones," he began, his voice steady but tinged with apprehension. "And thank you all for giving me the opportunity to speak tonight. As the mayor mentioned, my work focuses on the intersection of myth and measurable phenomena. And the ley lines—as fascinating as their stories are—fall firmly within the realm of measurable science."

The screen behind him lit up with a satellite map of the region, glowing lines crisscrossing the landscape like veins beneath skin. "What you see here are the ley lines as they've been mapped through centuries of lore. But tonight, I'd like to overlay that with data—data that reveals the underlying truth."

The map transitioned to a heat map, vivid reds and yellows marking areas of heightened activity. Lucas gestured to the screen. "These lines correspond to natural geophysical anomalies. Specifically, they align with measurable pathways of magnetic energy within the Earth's geomagnetic field. What we're seeing here isn't magic or myth. It's the Earth itself."

A faint murmur rippled through the crowd. Lucas took a breath, his confidence growing. "These anomalies are amplified by factors unique to certain locations—mineral deposits, subterranean water movement, even fault lines. And when these elements converge, they create what we call nodes: points of heightened electromagnetic activity."

He clicked again, revealing a close-up of a fault map overlaid with ley lines. The intersecting points glowed faintly on the screen. "For centuries, humans have instinctively responded to these nodes. We've built monuments, temples, and settlements on them without fully understanding why. Here in Redstone, we see that same pattern—a convergence of history, culture, and natural phenomena."

Lucas paused, scanning the room. Some faces remained inscrutable, but others leaned forward, their expressions shifting from skepticism to intrigue.

"This is a place where science and history intersect," he continued, his tone earnest. "The ley lines aren't just stories. They're part of a much larger narrative—one that connects us to the Earth in ways we're only beginning to understand."

He advanced to the next slide, a graph showing fluctuations in electromagnetic activity recorded near the Whispering Stones. "This data was collected right here in Redstone. The spikes you see correspond to times when the ley lines intersect most strongly with geological factors. These are natural processes, but their impact on us—on our senses, our perceptions—can feel profound."

Lucas hesitated, then stepped out from behind the podium, meeting the crowd on their level. "I know this might challenge deeply held beliefs. It might feel like science is stripping away the mystery. But I'd argue that understanding the ley lines doesn't diminish their significance. If anything, it amplifies it.

He caught Sierra's eye, her subtle nod bolstering him. "The choices you make now will shape not just your future, but the way you honor your past. Understanding the ley lines as they truly are doesn't erase their importance. It grounds them in reality, giving you a foundation to protect and preserve what makes this place unique."

"For most of my life, I've believed every answer could be found in data—explained, measured, and cataloged." His voice softened. "But Redstone has shown me something different. Sierra Castillo showed me something different."

He turned to Sierra, who nodded almost imperceptibly.

"Science tells me these ley lines are geophysical anomalies—mineral conductivity, magnetic fields, water pathways. And that's true. But standing on those lines, feeling them... it's more than data points on a graph. There's something alive there. Something resonant."

Lucas hesitated, but only for a moment. "Last night, I revisited one of these intersections at the Whispering Stones. I was ready to measure, to analyze, to explain it away. But instead, I felt something. A stillness. A hum, deep and low, like the earth itself was breathing. And in that moment, I realized my instruments could only show me part of the story. The rest—well, the rest requires humility and an open mind."

The audience was silent now, every eye locked on him.

"We can't dismiss what we don't fully understand. Not anymore. The Caldwell project threatens something rare and irreplaceable— not just an anomaly to be studied, but a connection to something greater than ourselves."

He took a step closer to the podium, his voice steady and clear.

"I'm asking you to vote against the Caldwell proposal. Not out of fear, but out of respect. Respect for the science. Respect for the history. And respect for the intangible but undeniable force that runs beneath our feet. Turning these sacred sites into tourist traps, into profit margins for a corporation, will strip away the very essence of what makes this place extraordinary."

"The planning committee will now enter executive session to

deliberate," Mayor Jones announced, her voice firm as she tapped the gavel lightly against the table. She rose from her seat, her expression composed, and led the committee members into the adjoining chamber, leaving the room buzzing with hushed conversations and anxious glances.

When the committee returned after several tense minutes, Mayor Jones resumed her seat and addressed the room, her tone measured. "By a vote of three to two, the planning committee approves the development application of Caldwell Heritage Partners as proposed."

Chapter 38

THE NIGHT OUTSIDE the community hall pressed in, thick and damp against Lucas's skin. Voices from the vote still clung to the air—scattered applause, murmured debates, and unspoken tension humming in the quiet. Overhead, stars gleamed indifferent in the black expanse, their light faint against the looming shadows of the distant mesas.

A figure shifted just beyond the glow of the adobe columns. Caldwell stepped forward, his tailored suit too stiff for the desert breeze that teased at his polished appearance. His smile was thin, sharp as the edge of a blade.

"Well," Caldwell said, his voice smooth, measured, "you certainly know how to turn a quiet evening into a spectacle, Lucas. Almost impressive."

Lucas's shoulders tensed, the stiffness lingering from the council meeting. "I wasn't trying to make a scene, Caldwell. Just speaking the truth."

Caldwell's chuckle was low, clipped of humor. "Ah, yes. Truth. Convenient when it aligns with one's beliefs. Dangerous when it doesn't." He stepped closer, the crunch of gravel underfoot deliberate, controlled. "Tell me, Lucas—do you honestly think tonight changed anything?"

Lucas held his ground, his voice steady despite the simmer of frustration beneath his calm. "I think it made people stop and think. That's a start."

"Questions," Caldwell repeated, the word slipping from his mouth like an afterthought. He tilted his head, his smile curving into something harder. "Questions don't halt progress, Lucas. At best, they delay it. And tonight, you've delayed it admirably."

Lucas's jaw tightened. He straightened slightly, the words rising from somewhere deeper. "If 'progress' means gutting this land and selling its soul for profit, then yeah, Caldwell—I'll delay it as long as I can."

For a moment, silence stretched between them. A car engine growled faintly in the distance before fading into the stillness. Caldwell's expression shifted, his easy veneer cracking just enough to reveal a shadow of irritation.

"You're an idealist, Lucas," he said, his voice cool. "But ideals don't win battles. Resources do. Influence does. And I have both. What do you have? A handful of nervous allies and a dusty collection of theories?"

Lucas took a step forward, his movements deliberate. "I have people who believe this place matters. And no amount of money or influence can buy that."

For a flicker of a second, Caldwell's composure wavered. His eyes narrowed, something sharp and fleeting flashing across them. "Let me make this simple for you, Lucas. You're either with me, helping guide this transition, or you're in my way. And standing in my way isn't safe."

Lucas thought he saw it then—a faint sheen of sweat above Caldwell's brow, the line of his jaw tightening. But the crack was gone as quickly as it had appeared, replaced by the unyielding mask Caldwell wore so well.

"I won't let you hollow this place out," Lucas said firmly. "I won't let you strip it of what makes it whole."

Caldwell stepped back, his smile fading entirely now. "Suit yourself," he said, his voice sharp, clipped. "But remember—momentum doesn't stop for one man standing still. It rolls right over him."

With that, he turned sharply and disappeared into the night. The faint crunch of his footsteps dissolved into the quiet.

Lucas remained where he was, his gaze fixed on the spot where Caldwell had vanished. Somewhere in the distance, a night bird's call trilled briefly before the silence reclaimed the moment. His pulse thudded heavy in his ears, and a sudden gust of wind stirred the stillness around him.

Tonight wasn't the end. It was only a beginning. Caldwell had power, but Lucas had something he knew the man underestimated. He turned back toward the community hall, where light and voices still spilled faintly through the windows.

The fight for Redstone was far from over.

Chapter 39

CALDWELL LINGERED in the Jenkins' living room. His polished shoes stood out against the weathered floorboards, which had borne the weight of family life for decades. The candlelight flickered unevenly, illuminating faces filled with unease. Eyes shifted between Caldwell and the roll of blueprints unfurled on the dining table. The room felt thick with tension, as though Redstone itself waited for the outcome of this moment.

"This isn't just a development plan—it's a lifeline," Caldwell said. His voice was precise, each word deliberate. He placed his hand over the map, steady and deliberate, as if claiming control of its sprawling lines. "This isn't about erasing what's here. It's about preserving your heritage while building something sustainable. The profit Heritage stands to make is incidental."

Marla sat at the far end of the table. Her back was straight, and her hands were tightly folded in her lap. She felt the practiced persuasion in his words but couldn't shake a sense of unease. Hank, seated beside her, drummed his fingers on the edge of the table. The rhythm was slow, deliberate. His silence hinted at thoughts running deeper than he would show.

He leaned forward and spoke. "Plans look good on paper, Mr. Caldwell. Promises sound good in meetings. But this land isn't just dirt to be reshaped. It holds history. Sacred history. What happens when your lifeline cuts through that?"

Caldwell didn't hesitate. His tone remained steady. "That's exactly why we've brought in the Thierry team. They've set the standard for integrating preservation with development. Their work speaks for itself."

Near the fireplace, Janice Thierry adjusted her blazer. She smoothed the lapel, though it was already flawless. Her sharp gaze moved briefly to Marla before focusing on Hank. "In Sedona, we worked with the land, not against it," she said. "The trails were designed to respect the environment. Visitor centers focused on education rather than exploitation. Local crafts were given priority over mass production. This isn't just construction—it's stewardship."

Veronica's voice cut through the conversation with practiced precision. "It's a remarkable plan, Hiram. The kind of vision this town has needed for decades."

Marla's lips tightened. Veronica's tone was too polished, too knowing. She noticed how Caldwell's attention shifted slightly toward Veronica as she spoke. It sent an unfamiliar chill through her.

Hank squinted at the blueprints. The neat lines and annotations felt foreign to him, disconnected from the rugged terrain outside. "Visitor centers. Parking lots. Curated trails," he murmured. He shook his head. "You can't put a desert behind glass and call it preservation."

Marla broke her silence, her voice steady despite the tension in the room. "But Hank... isn't it better than letting it fall apart? Better than debt swallowing it whole?"

Caldwell seized the moment, his focus shifting back to her. "Exactly, Marla. This isn't about replacing Redstone—it's about giving it a chance to survive. Without this plan, the town's decline is inevitable."

"Progress doesn't mean erasure," Veronica added. Her tone was cool and decisive. "But progress doesn't wait for endless debates either. Decisions need to be made, and soon."

Marla glanced at Veronica. There was something in her voice—a quiet dismissal hidden beneath the polished delivery. Caldwell stepped back from the table, his movements measured and deliberate. His gaze shifted between Hank, Marla, and Veronica, pausing on each of them.

"Hank," Caldwell said. His tone lowered slightly, almost intimate. "This isn't just another business venture for me. It's a responsibility. But standing still isn't an option. If we don't act, others will—and they won't care about your history."

Marla clasped her hands in her lap, tightening her grip as she listened. His words seemed convincing, but there was something off. His polished exterior no longer felt seamless. For the first time, she sensed a strain beneath the surface.

Hank's jaw tightened. "We can't afford to get this wrong," he said.

Marla turned her eyes back to the map. The lines and markings intersected the rugged reality of the land she knew so well. "But what if this is our only chance to get it right?"

Later that night, Marla walked down the hallway of the Jenkins' home beside Hiram. The antique sconces cast faint light against the walls, creating flickering shadows. The silence between them was weighted with the unresolved tension from earlier.

Each of her steps echoed faintly in the narrow space. "What you said earlier," she began, her voice quiet. "About the land. About listening. It's been turning over in my mind."

Hiram stopped and turned toward her. His hand rested lightly against the wall as he spoke. "It's not just land, Marla. It's memory. It's story. And it'll speak if people bother to listen."

They stopped at the door to his guest room. The space between them felt close, as though the air itself had thickened. Marla reached for the brass doorknob but hesitated, her breath catching for a moment. The faint trace of his scent lingered in the air—something sun-warmed and herbal, distinctly him.

"Thank you," she said softly. Her voice carried an edge of vulnerability. "For what you said tonight. For not letting us get swept away."

Hiram's smile came slowly, one side tugging higher than the other. "You carry this place in you, Marla. You just needed to remember it."

The words struck her with clarity. They carved through the doubt that had weighed on her throughout the evening. Hiram reached out and placed a hand on her shoulder. His touch was warm, steady.

"Good night, Marla," he said.

"Good night, Hiram."

He stepped into the room, closing the door behind him. Marla stayed in the hallway, her hand brushing the edge of the wall where his had rested moments before. She leaned back lightly against the cool plaster and let herself breathe. The ache of the evening lingered in her chest, undefined but undeniable.

Chapter 40

THE DESERT SUN HUNG LOW, casting long shadows that stretched over Sierra's adobe home, brushing the courtyard with a quiet golden haze. Lucas sat on a stone bench, his elbows braced against his knees, his gaze fixed on the far-off horizon. Sierra stood a short distance away, her arms folded tightly, her expression veiled but tense.

"So you are done. And you are just going to leave?" she asked. Her voice was low, edged with a restraint that threatened to break.

Lucas exhaled slowly, dragging a hand through his hair. "I don't know, Sierra. After everything—everything I've seen, everything I've felt—it still doesn't add up. It still doesn't make sense to me."

"Why does it have to?" she shot back, her tone sharpening. "Not everything fits into neat boxes, Lucas. Not everything can be measured."

He glanced at her, his expression caught between guilt and frustration. "I can't just... believe," he said. "That's not how I work."

The quiet of the courtyard pressed against them until the scrape of boots broke it. Chief Vega rounded the corner of the house, his shoulders slumped with weariness, his coat fringed with desert dust.

"I went to the stones," Vega said, his voice quiet but carrying the weight of what he had seen. "I had to see it myself."

Sierra took a step closer, her brow furrowing. "And?"

Vega looked at Lucas, then back to Sierra. "They were warm, alive. The stones—they glowed, not brightly, but like they held something beneath the surface. And there was... a hum. Not sound exactly, but a pulse. You could feel it, here." He pressed a hand flat against his chest.

Lucas straightened, the words hooking onto his logical mind and refusing to let go. "A magnetic anomaly? A trick of the light?"

"It wasn't a trick," Vega replied firmly, his tone almost reverent. "It was the lines."

Sierra stepped closer to Vega, her eyes wide but steady. "If Caldwell digs out there..."

Vega's jaw tightened. "He'll destroy something we can't replace."

Lucas crossed the courtyard, his steps hesitant but firm. "You're certain? This isn't confirmation bias or... or folklore clouding judgment?"

Vega's eyes locked onto Lucas, unflinching. "You felt it too. Out there, when your instruments failed, when the air shifted. You know what I'm talking about."

Lucas swallowed hard, the words stirring a memory he didn't want to name.

Sierra moved between them, her voice calm but insistent. "So what do we do?"

Vega looked at both of them, his face lined with exhaustion but resolve. "We make them see it. Feel it. This isn't a fight we win with numbers or logic. People need to believe."

"And if they don't?" Lucas asked, his voice low.

Sierra turned to him, her voice soft but sure. "Then we show them. We use your data, my stories, Vega's truth. Together, we'll make them listen."

At that moment, Lucas's phone rang. "Hello Chief."

Chapter 41

LUCAS SHIFTED IN HIS CHAIR, the cracked leather protesting beneath him. The blinds cast thin stripes of light and shadow across the mayor's desk, the patterns cutting through the room's stillness. Framed photographs lined the walls, their subjects frozen in time—generations of Redstone's history etched in faces that seemed to silently demand something of him.

The door opened. Chief Vega stepped in first, his boots striking the floor with deliberate force. Deputy Martinez followed, holding a tablet close to her chest, her shoulders tight. Veronica Miller entered last, closing the door with a careful, soundless click. Her gaze swept the room, resting briefly on Lucas. He caught the momentary shift in her expression, fleeting but sharp enough to stir unease.

Mayor Helen Jones adjusted her glasses, her voice breaking the tension. "Caldwell isn't here to build. He's here to strip this town down, and he's moving faster now. Piece by piece, he's taking control."

Martinez stepped forward, gripping the edge of her tablet tightly. "We've traced the money. Properties are changing hands under shell companies, all leading back to Caldwell. His confidence is growing. He isn't even trying to hide it anymore."

Vega leaned against the edge of the desk, his tone calm but grim. "I've seen this pattern before. First, it's the land. Then it's the businesses. By the time people notice, it's too late. Caldwell isn't just buying property—he's buying silence."

Lucas straightened, his hands braced on his knees.

Mayor Jones nodded, leaning forward. "That's where you come in, Lucas. We need you to stay. Make them see it. Use the science, the stories—whatever it takes."

Veronica shifted in her seat, her tone cutting through Lucas's growing intensity. "Stories won't stop Caldwell. Neither will data. Martinez, dig deeper into the financials. Vega, make sure the town stays steady. And Helen," she added, her gaze locking on the mayor, "you need to speak to the people. Directly. Start now."

Her delivery was precise, almost rehearsed, but there was something behind it—something Lucas couldn't name. He noticed the way her attention lingered on Martinez's tablet for just a moment too long before snapping back.

Mayor Jones straightened, nodding. "No room for missteps. We do this together, or we lose everything."

The meeting dissolved into motion. Chairs scraped against the floor as the group began to move. Lucas rose slowly, watching as Veronica headed toward the door. He stepped into her path.

"Veronica," he said quietly.

She turned, her expression composed, her smile faint and detached. "Yes, Lucas?"

"There's something off," he said, his voice barely above a whisper. "With you. With this."

She didn't flinch. Her smile widened, but her eyes remained distant. "You're tired, Lucas. This kind of fight—it can get into your head. Be careful where your imagination takes you."

She stepped around him and left without waiting for a response.

Lucas stayed where he was, his hands tightening into fists at his sides. He turned back to the wall of photographs, their faces fixed in silent observation. He studied them, searching for something he couldn't name.

The silence of the room seemed to carry an unspoken message. Watch closely.

Chapter 42

THE RIVER MIRRORED the sky's reflection in its glassy surface, broken only by the faint ripple of wind moving across the water. Sierra stood ankle-deep in the sand, her toes pressing into the cool, damp earth. Above her, the cottonwood tree swayed faintly, its leaves stirring with the faint rustle of the breeze. A loose circle of people from Redstone surrounded her, uneven and quiet. Some leaned on walking sticks, others kept their children close, their expressions drawn with concern and quiet anticipation.

At the front, Mr. Martinez stood firm, his cane planted in the sand as though anchoring him in place. Beside him, Mrs. Ortega clasped her grandson's small hand tightly. On the edges of the group, teenagers lingered, shifting uncertainly like birds unsure whether to join or retreat.

Sierra inhaled deeply, her shoulders rising and falling in a controlled rhythm. When she spoke, her voice was calm but purposeful, reaching everyone without effort.

"You feel it, don't you?" she asked, her tone steady. "Something is moving beneath us."

The crowd murmured, their bodies shifting in quiet acknowledgment. A shuffle of feet against stone broke the stillness, but no one answered. They didn't need to.

"They're coming," Sierra said, her words clear and deliberate.

"People like Caldwell. They don't see what we see. They don't feel what we feel. To them, this land is nothing more than numbers on a ledger."

The silence that followed was sharp. A child coughed once, then fell quiet, the sound disappearing into the still air.

A woman near the center stepped forward. Her daughter clutched a fabric doll tightly, her knuckles pale against its worn dress. "But what can we do?" she asked, her voice trembling but audible. "They have power. Lawyers... everything."

Sierra met the woman's gaze, her own unwavering. "They don't have us," she said. "They don't have our stories. They don't have roots in this place. They don't know what it means to belong here. And they can't drown us out—not if we stand together."

At the edges of the group, the teenagers began to shift closer. Their arms lowered, their eyes focusing, their feet inching forward. One boy, his shaggy hair falling into his uncertain expression, spoke up. "But what if they don't listen?"

Sierra turned toward him, her voice firm. "Then we'll make them listen."

The sound of Mr. Martinez lifting his cane broke the momentary silence. He drove it into the ground, the impact solid and deliberate. The sound carried across the circle, sharp and commanding.

"This land speaks," he said, his voice worn but resolute. "It's spoken to us for generations. And now it's calling on us to answer."

The crowd seemed to hold its collective breath, bodies stilling as they absorbed his words. Sierra saw it settle in their postures—a shared readiness, quiet but determined.

"Tomorrow," she said, her voice softer but no less firm, "we begin. Letters, calls, meetings. We'll show up. We'll make ourselves impossible to ignore."

There was no applause, no cheering. Instead, the group nodded. Quiet affirmations rippled through the crowd. A teenager leaned toward a friend and whispered, "I'll help," loud enough for Sierra to hear.

As the gathering began to dissolve, small groups formed to exchange plans. Hands clasped in agreement, quick words were shared before people turned to leave. Mrs. Ortega bent to speak softly to her grandson, her voice too quiet for Sierra to catch. Mr. Martinez gave Sierra a brief nod before stepping away.

When the others were gone, Sierra remained. The sand beneath her feet cooled as the evening deepened. She walked to the cottonwood tree and placed her hand on its bark. Her palm rested there, taking in its rough texture, the steady strength of its presence.

The ground beneath her feet seemed alive, steady and vibrant. A faint vibration hummed through the earth, a quiet energy that moved upward, reaching her ribs, her throat, her thoughts.

It wasn't everything. But it was enough to begin.

Across the river, Lucas sat in silence, hidden by the shadows of the boulders. He stayed still, unseen, watching the scene unfold.

Chapter 43

THE NEXT DAY, TARA STOOD behind the counter at Ladawn's, watching Lucas. He sat at a central table, leaning forward slightly as he spoke to two local men about the coming rainstorm. His words carried an easy confidence, each point measured and deliberate, drawing nods of agreement from his companions. The men listened intently, their brows furrowed, their hands resting on coffee cups that had long since cooled.

Tara watched the exchange, her focus sharpening on Lucas. His gestures punctuated his words, precise and purposeful. The room hummed with the quiet din of Ladawn's regulars, but the subtle energy around Lucas seemed to pull his audience closer. His voice, though calm, carried a sincerity that made every word feel vital.

Tara inhaled slowly, letting her thoughts settle into clarity. She wiped her hands on her jeans and stepped out from behind the counter, crossing the room with deliberate steps. Lucas glanced up as she approached, his expression softening into a warm smile. He gestured toward an empty chair at the table.

"Hey, Tara," he said. "Join us?"

She hesitated for a moment before taking the seat, her fingers brushing the edge of the table as she settled in. "Am I interrupting?" she asked, her tone light but curious.

"Not at all," Lucas replied, leaning back slightly as his attention shifted to include her. "We were just talking about Caldwell's next moves—and what comes next for us."

At the mention of Caldwell, the atmosphere at the table shifted. The easy rhythm of their conversation gave way to a quiet tension. Tara straightened in her seat, her voice firm when she spoke.

"I want to help," she said. "I've been listening, watching—and it's clear this isn't just about the land. It's about who we are. What we're willing to fight for."

Lucas regarded her carefully, his gaze steady. A faint tilt of his head suggested he was weighing her words. Then, he nodded, his expression serious. "We need more voices. The protests are gaining traction, but we can't make a dent without visibility."

Tara leaned forward, her resolve gathering strength. "I know people who'd stand with us. My friend Ashley has a group back in Flagstaff—they're passionate, and they care about protecting places like this. If I call her, they'll come."

Lucas's eyebrows lifted slightly, a flicker of surprise breaking through his thoughtful demeanor. Then his smile widened, a genuine lightness touching his features. "That's exactly what we need, Tara."

Across the table, one of the ranchers, a wiry man with sun-creased skin, raised his coffee mug in a quiet gesture of approval. The motion carried a silent solidarity that rippled through the group.

Behind the counter, Ladawn paused in her work. She glanced toward Tara, noting the quiet determination in her voice and the new steadiness in her posture. A small smile tugged at Ladawn's lips before she returned to slicing loaves.

Tara met Lucas's gaze, her voice clear and confident. "I'll call Ashley tonight. This is too important to let slide."

Lucas placed a hand lightly on her arm, his tone warm but resolute. "Thank you, Tara. It means more than you know—to all of us."

Chapter 44

THE SUN HUNG LOW, casting long shadows across the desert as Hiram followed Mika along a narrow, winding path. It was their first conversation since the heated town meeting. Mika had initiated it, calling Hiram early that morning with the request.

Now, the air around them felt dense, charged with the weight of unspoken words and unresolved tension. Rain hung in the distance, its faint scent mingling with the dry tang of sagebrush. Hiram kept pace with Mika, his thoughts a restless churn. The echoes of the meeting lingered in his mind, tangled with doubt and frustration.

"Not much further," Mika said, glancing back briefly. His voice carried the calm certainty of someone who had walked this path countless times. His stride was steady, confident, while Hiram's faltered on the uneven terrain. The narrow trail forced Hiram's focus outward, his boots crunching against brittle earth.

The landscape opened gradually, a mosaic of ochres and muted greens stretching into the horizon. Hiram had walked these trails before, but they felt different now—unfamiliar, as though the land itself had shifted. A faint vibration seemed to hum through the air, more sensed than heard, brushing the edges of his awareness.

Mika stopped at a rocky outcropping overlooking a shallow valley. He gestured for Hiram to join him. Below, the land dipped into a natural basin encircled by jagged rocks. At its center stood a ring of ancient stones, weathered and solid, their arrangement deliberate, unyielding to time.

"This is where the ley lines converge," Mika said quietly. He stood still, his focus on the stones. "Our ancestors came here for guidance, for healing. It's a place of power."

Hiram's gaze shifted to the circle. The stones seemed to anchor the valley, standing sentinel against the desert's shifting seasons. He could see the marks of time on their surfaces—erosion's delicate scars—but the energy they radiated felt immutable.

"I remember when you brought me here years ago," Hiram said. His voice was subdued, almost reluctant. "But I didn't understand it then."

Mika nodded, his eyes never leaving the stones. "You can't understand it by just looking. You have to feel it, listen to the land. It speaks, if you're willing to hear."

Hiram crossed his arms, his posture tightening. "Mika, I respect what you're saying, but we both know development is inevitable. Progress always means change."

Mika turned to face him, his calm exterior giving way to a flash of urgency. "Progress doesn't have to mean destruction, Hiram. It's not about stopping change—it's about respecting what you're building on. This land isn't just dirt and stone. It's history. It's connection. Bulldozing it would sever something irreplaceable."

Hiram shifted uneasily, glancing toward the horizon as if searching for an answer in the distance. "It's just one site," he said, though his voice lacked its usual conviction. "There's plenty of land to build on. People adjust."

Mika's expression hardened, his voice gaining an edge. "It's never just one site. These places are like roots. Cut one, and the damage spreads. You might not see it immediately, but it's there—in the land, in the people. Once it's gone, you can't bring it back."

Hiram let his gaze drift back to the stones. He imagined the bulldozers, the survey markers, the neatly drawn plans that promised modernity and convenience. Yet, standing here, he felt a gnawing unease. The stones seemed to radiate something he couldn't name, something that resisted the cold logic of progress.

"You really believe that," he said softly, though it wasn't quite a question.

"I don't just believe it," Mika replied. His tone was calm but unyielding. "I know it. This place has survived because generations before us understood its value. They knew when to take and when to protect. If we forget that—if we treat this land like it's disposable—we lose more than a patch of dirt. We lose part of ourselves."

Hiram swallowed, Mika's words settling into the silence that stretched between them. He wanted to argue, to insist that his project wouldn't destroy what mattered, but the words caught in his throat. Instead, he found himself studying the stones—their unassuming strength, their silent endurance. They stood as they had for centuries, witnesses to a history Hiram was only beginning to grasp.

Mika turned his attention back to the stones, his voice soft but firm. "It's not too late, Hiram. Not yet."

Hiram said nothing.

Chapter 45

THE PARK FELT RESTLESS, the late evening wind stirring leaves and whispering through the cottonwoods. Sierra stood beneath a large, weathered tree at the center of the clearing, her presence commanding despite the scattered seating of the crowd. The makeshift gathering had been hastily organized after the planning committee's vote, and frustration hung in the air, heavy and palpable.

Tara lingered at the edge of the group, her arms folded tightly as she watched Sierra. The rows of mismatched folding chairs and upturned crates gave the meeting a raw, impromptu energy, as if the ground itself had demanded this gathering. A circle of lanterns cast shifting light across the group, shadows playing on anxious faces.

Sierra's voice rose above the murmurs, clear and steady, but edged with fire. "The vote doesn't end this. Caldwell and his investors think they've won, but this land isn't theirs to take. It's not just property—it's part of us. The ley lines, the stories, the history that's in the earth beneath our feet—it's worth more than any promise of prosperity."

Tara felt the pull of Sierra's words, the way they seemed to strip away the clutter of doubt and cut to the heart of things. Around her, the crowd began to shift, some leaning forward on their seats, others standing with arms crossed, expressions hardening into resolve.

Marla Jenkins stepped forward, her voice breaking the momentary silence. "Sierra's right. This fight isn't over, not by a long shot. But we have to act now. We can't wait for someone else to come along and save this town. It's up to us."

Tara's chest tightened as she moved closer to the group. She caught Sierra's eye briefly before turning to face the gathering. The words came unbidden, her voice carrying a strength she hadn't expected.

"She's right. We can't just make speeches and hope for the best. Caldwell isn't going to back down, and we shouldn't expect him to. We need a plan—a real one. Protests, rallies, letters—whatever it takes to make them hear us."

The crowd turned to her, and for a moment, Tara's pulse quickened under the weight of their attention. But she pressed on, grounding herself in the urgency of the moment.

"This isn't just Sierra's fight, or Marla's, or mine. It's all of ours. If we don't act, we'll lose more than land. We'll lose the heart of this town."

Sierra stepped forward, her expression softening into a smile. "You're absolutely right, Tara. Tonight, we organize. Tomorrow, we fight."

Agreement rippled through the group, a current of determination replacing the unease. Small knots of people began forming, voices rising and overlapping as they discussed plans. The park seemed to shift with the mood, the scattered lantern light illuminating faces that no longer looked uncertain, but resolute.

Tara turned away briefly, moving toward the edge of the clearing. The cool night air steadied her, brushing against her skin and carrying the faint scent of sage and pine. She pulled her phone from her pocket and saw Ashley's name flashing on the screen. She answered without hesitation.

"Hey," she said, her voice quieter now but no less firm.

Ashley's voice crackled through the line, bright and purposeful. "Tara! I wanted to call you earlier, but it took time to round everyone up. We're coming. Me, Derek, Sarah—the whole crew. We'll be there for the protests."

Tara exhaled sharply, relief flooding her. "You're really coming?"

"Of course," Ashley replied without hesitation. "You care about this place, and that's all I need to know. We'll bring signs, supplies—whatever you need. Just tell me."

For a moment, Tara couldn't speak. Ashley's words settled into her chest, steadying her in a way nothing else had. "Thank you, Ash. That means more than I can say."

"You don't have to thank me," Ashley said gently. "Just promise me you'll stay safe. And if you need anything else—anything at all—let me know."

"I will," Tara replied, her voice soft but resolute. "I should go. There's someone I need to talk to."

Chapter 46

THE TWILIGHT SKY DEEPENED into indigo, the first stars faint against the horizon. Natan's adobe home perched on the rocky outcrop, its rough walls blending seamlessly with the earth, as though shaped by the land rather than built upon it. Smoke rose in a thin, curling column from the chimney, dispersing into the cool desert air. Lucas stood at the weathered wooden door, his hand hovering mid-knock.

The memory of the Whispering Stones returned unbidden—the hum, the light, the impossible vision. It pressed on his chest, sharp and unresolved, as if asking a question he didn't know how to answer.

The door opened before his knuckles touched it.

Natan stood in the threshold, wrapped in a thick wool blanket patterned with geometric designs that seemed alive in the firelight behind him. His sharp eyes locked on Lucas, reading more than Lucas intended to reveal.

"Come in," Natan said softly, stepping aside.

The scent of woodsmoke greeted Lucas as he entered. The small room radiated warmth, its earthen hues bathed in flickering firelight.

Shelves lined with pottery and drying herbs hugged the walls, and a low wooden table held bundles of paper and ink-stained brushes, scattered as though abandoned mid-thought. A kettle hissed softly over the fire, adding to the room's quiet rhythm.

"Sit," Natan said, gesturing toward a cushion near the hearth.

Lucas sank down stiffly, his backpack slipping from his shoulder onto the floor. His gaze flitted around the space, landing on a chipped clay mug Natan had picked up. Steam rose as Natan poured tea into it from the kettle.

"You've forgotten to eat since yesterday," Natan said, placing the mug in front of him. It wasn't a question.

Lucas opened his mouth to protest, but Natan raised a hand, his weathered palm halting the words.

"Drink," Natan instructed.

The tea was bitter, its spices unfamiliar. It warmed Lucas from the inside, a heat that melted the tension he hadn't realized had settled into his shoulders. Natan lowered himself onto a cushion opposite Lucas, his movements unhurried and precise.

The fire crackled between them. For a while, neither spoke. Outside, the wind whispered through the desert, carrying with it secrets Lucas couldn't decipher.

Finally, Natan's voice broke the silence. "You've seen something."

Lucas's fingers tightened around the clay mug, his throat constricting. He nodded but kept his gaze fixed on the fire.

"The Stones spoke to you," Natan said. His tone was calm, but the certainty in his words was unyielding. "Did they frighten you?"

Lucas exhaled sharply, the sound uneven. "I don't know if it was fear," he admitted, his voice strained. "It felt... too big. Too impossible. I couldn't make sense of it."

"And yet, you felt it," Natan replied.

Lucas looked up, frustration clouding his expression. "How am I supposed to accept this?" he demanded. "I've spent my life with instruments, data, and measurements—things I can quantify. What I felt out there doesn't fit into any of that. It doesn't belong in the world I know."

Natan studied him, the firelight reflecting in his deep-set eyes. "Lucas," he said after a pause, his voice low but resonant, "let me tell you a story."

He leaned forward slightly, his hands resting on his knees. "Once, there was a man who found a spider's web stretched between two branches at dawn. The dew clung to the threads, turning it into a glistening map of impossible precision. The man, curious and clever, brought out his magnifying glass and his measuring tools. He noted every angle, every thread, every droplet of water. But in his effort to understand, he missed the web's true purpose. It wasn't built to be measured; it was built to hold. To connect."

Natan's gaze held Lucas's. "The ley lines are like that web. You can study them with your instruments, map their paths, and write papers about them. But their truth isn't in the data. It's in the holding. The connection. To understand that, Lucas, you don't need sharper tools—you need stillness."

Lucas let out a ragged breath, his hands falling into his lap. "But what do I do with this, Natan? I can't just unsee it. When I close my eyes, it's there—the light, the lines, the... everything."

"No," Natan said. "You can't unsee it. And you shouldn't. What you saw was truth—not the kind taught in schools or plotted on charts, but truth all the same. You came here because part of you already knows that. You're afraid, not because it doesn't make sense, but because it does."

Lucas dropped his head into his hands, his voice barely audible. "I don't know if I can carry this."

Natan rose, his knees creaking softly, and moved to a small wooden box on a nearby shelf. From within, he lifted a turquoise stone strung on a simple leather cord. The stone shimmered faintly in the firelight, veins of black cutting through its sky-blue surface like rivers on a map.

"This is more than a stone," Natan said, pressing it into Lucas's hand. "It's a thread, like the ones you saw out there. When the burden feels too great, hold it. Let it remind you that you're not alone, and that the connections you feel are real."

Lucas turned the stone over in his palm, the smooth surface cool against his skin. It felt impossibly ancient, as though it carried the memory of the earth itself.

Natan reached over and tied the cord around Lucas's neck. "This land doesn't ask for answers. It asks for stillness. For listening. Let it remind you that you are part of something older and grander than yourself."

The fire crackled softly as Lucas sat back, the tension in his chest easing just enough to let a faint sense of clarity in. His eyes met Natan's, and for the first time since he'd entered, he allowed himself to believe the elder's words.

"I don't know where to begin," Lucas said, his voice steady but quiet.

Natan's faint smile deepened the lines around his eyes. "You've already begun, Lucas. You came. You listened."

Outside, the wind brushed against the adobe walls, carrying whispers across the desert. Lucas exhaled slowly, the weight he'd carried loosening into something he could bear.

For now, it was enough.

Chapter 47

EVENING SPILLED across the room, the fading light casting Lucas's reflection onto the window—a faint, distorted shadow of the man he thought he was. Sierra's words from earlier rang in his mind, their weight hard to shake: *We're allies in this cause.* Meant as reassurance, the phrase only deepened the void within him. His voice broke the stillness, quiet and resigned. "Why does it feel like I'm chasing ghosts?"

He dragged a hand through his hair, the motion offering no clarity. Redstone pressed on him in ways he couldn't explain, its ley lines a force that seemed both ancient and alive. They defied his logic, unraveling the certainties he had built his life upon. Every encounter left him unmoored, his foundation crumbling under truths he couldn't quantify.

A knock on the door shattered his thoughts. Visitors were rare at this hour. Lucas hesitated, then crossed the room and opened it.

Tara stood in the dim hallway, her eyes sharp with urgency. Yet beneath the determination, there was something else—hesitation, rare and uncharacteristic.

"Tara," Lucas said, surprised. "What's going on?"

She stepped inside without waiting for an invitation, her words spilling out. "Ashley agreed to join the protest. And she's not coming alone. She's bringing friends—people who've organized environmental campaigns, pipeline blockades, real high-stakes stuff. These aren't just idealists with signs; they're people who know how to disrupt systems when it matters."

Lucas gestured for her to sit, his curiosity overtaking his exhaustion. Tara hesitated, then sank into a chair near the window.

"That's not all," she added, her voice softer now. "I've been thinking about you. About everything you've been dealing with—Sierra, Caldwell, the ley lines. It's too much for one person, Lucas. And I think you're trying to carry all of it alone."

Lucas sighed, leaning against the edge of his desk. "What choice do I have? Someone has to understand what's happening before Caldwell turns this place into something unrecognizable. But if this goes wrong—if we fail—I'll lose everything. My reputation, my work, the trust I've spent years building in my field... it could all disappear. The university won't stand by a professor tied up in protests, let alone one talking about mystical energy lines. I could lose everything I've built. And yet..." He paused, his voice softening. "None of that matters if we don't stop this."

Tara stood and crossed the room, her gaze steady and unrelenting. "That's why I'm here. You're brilliant, Lucas, but you're also human. No one can carry this alone."

She knelt in front of him, her hand resting lightly on his arm. Lucas froze at the unexpected contact, her words—and her presence—rooting him in place. Tara's usual confidence had shifted, replaced by a quiet vulnerability.

"Lucas," she said, her voice barely above a whisper, "you don't have to carry this alone."

Her words lingered in the charged air between them. Tara's hand slipped away, but her gaze didn't waver. "If I stayed... if we talked... if we just stopped thinking about all of this for one night..." Her voice trailed off, her meaning clear even in the quiet.

Lucas looked away, his breath uneven. "Tara, I—"

She cut him off, shaking her head as though pulling herself back. "I'm sorry. That was unfair of me."

"No," Lucas said quickly. "It's not that. It's just... everything feels so fragile right now."

The tension between them broke, but its imprint lingered. Tara straightened, folding her arms and retreating to the edge of the room. Her expression shifted back to practicality.

"Listen," she said, her tone firm again. "Ashley's group changes the game. Caldwell's going to accelerate his plans the moment he senses real resistance. We have to be ready."

Lucas nodded, pushing himself upright. "You're right. We can't afford to hesitate."

Tara's voice softened again as she turned to the door. "But Lucas, whatever happens, don't lose yourself in all of this. Whether it's science, mysticism, or something in between—you have to stay centered. Don't let this break you."

Lucas exhaled, the tension in his shoulders easing slightly. "Thank you, Tara. For everything."

Tara paused in the doorway, her hand resting on the frame. Her eyes met his, steady but filled with something unresolved. "Lucas... you don't have to be alone tonight. Just let me stay. No expectations, no strings—just someone here with you. You shouldn't have to face this by yourself."

Lucas's breath caught as the words hung in the air. Their eyes met, and for a moment, the room felt impossibly small, the rest of the world receding.

"Tara..." he began, his voice low, but the rest of the sentence failed him.

She smiled faintly, stepping back into the hallway. "It's okay, Lucas. I understand."

The door clicked shut behind her, leaving Lucas alone in the room. He stood motionless, the echo of her presence still tangible.

Her words lingered, wrapping around the unspoken tension she had left behind.

Chapter 48

THE MORNING SUN FILTERED through the warped slats of the abandoned storage shed, casting fractured beams of light over dust-laden shelves and rusted tools. The air inside was heavy, carrying the faint scent of oil and neglect. Five figures stood in a loose circle, their faces etched with exhaustion and the unspoken weight of what lay ahead.

Derek was the last to enter, gripping the hand of someone unfamiliar. "This is Jenna," he said, his voice tight. "She works for the Sheriff."

A ripple of unease passed through the group. Tara Castillo, standing near the door, stiffened, her arms crossing more tightly over her chest. Ashley Martinez, crouched beside her overstuffed backpack, paused mid-check, her sharp eyes flicking to Jenna. Tom Young, his faded cap pulled low, gave a curt nod but said nothing. Sarah lingered at the edge of the circle, her arms crossed, studying Jenna like a hawk assessing a threat.

Jenna stepped forward, holding out a crumpled sheet of paper smudged with ink and sweat. "I've got the delivery schedules," she said, her voice trembling. "The equipment's moving soon."

"Let her speak," Derek pressed, his tone brooking no argument.

Tom turned back to the rusted workbench, his hands braced on its edge. "This is it," he muttered, his gravelly voice carrying the finality of a gavel. "No more stalling. No more second-guessing."

Ashley rose from her crouch, slinging her pack over one shoulder. "We'll join the march in town, keep the crowd focused and visible. But..." She hesitated, her fingers tightening on the strap. "The real work happens when we break away. We can't lose sight of that."

Jenna's voice broke the silence. "The equipment leaves in less than an hour. If we're fast, we can intercept it on the access road before it moves out." She swallowed hard. "It's a tight window, but it's doable."

Derek paced near the door, his boots grinding against the sandy floor. "Stopping them isn't enough. They'll regroup tomorrow and start again. The equipment needs to be taken out of play. For good."

Tom's head snapped up, his jaw tightening. "Damn it, Derek, that's a line we can't cross. If we get caught messing with that machinery, it's not just fines—it's prison. Do you understand that?"

Ashley pressed her lips into a thin line, her gaze darting between Derek and Tom. The tension in the shed thickened, palpable in the narrowing distance between decisions.

Tara's voice was barely audible, but it carried. "I don't like this," she said, her arms hugging herself like a shield. "But if we back out now, everything we've done—all of this—will have been for nothing."

Ashley exhaled sharply, her shoulders sagging before she straightened again. "Fine. But if it feels wrong—if we're about to cross a line—I'm pulling back. No arguments."

A heavy silence settled over them. Outside, the distant hum of construction equipment crept closer, its mechanical cadence ticking away their resolve.

Tom straightened, his voice steadier now, as if the weight of the moment had clarified his purpose. "This isn't about grand gestures. It's about buying time. Enough time for people to see the truth. Enough time to stop Caldwell."

Jenna nodded, her fingers clutching the crumpled paper as if it anchored her courage. "I'm in. I can't stand by and let them destroy everything."

Tara's eyes darted to the cracked window, the sunlight growing harsher as the seconds ticked by. She took a deep breath, her words almost pleading. "Alright. But... let's be careful. Please."

Ashley adjusted her backpack, the trembling in her hands easing as her grip steadied. "We stay focused. We stay calm. And whatever happens—we stay together."

The shed seemed to hold its breath as they moved to the door, the golden light streaming through the cracks in the walls illuminating faces marked by fear, determination, and resignation. Outside, the construction hum grew louder, a relentless reminder of what they were up against.

The protest in town would serve as a diversion, drawing Caldwell's attention elsewhere. But here—on the narrow access road—the fight would truly begin.

No one spoke as they filed out of the shed, their footsteps muffled by the sandy ground. In the distance, the machinery droned on, unmoved by their plans.

Ladawn moved briskly down the cobbled street, her coat pulled tight against the sharp night wind. The rally's echoes still resonated in her chest—the chants of defiance, the glow of lanterns casting halos against the darkness. It had been a night of unity, a moment where fear had sharpened into resolve. But now, as the streets emptied and the energy began to dissipate, another sound pierced the quiet.

"Working late again, Ladawn?"

The voice came from the shadows, smooth but carrying an edge like steel drawn across stone. Veronica Miller stepped into view from beneath the bakery's awning, her arms crossed over her chest. Her stance was casual, but the deliberate tension in her movements betrayed intent.

Ladawn halted, her keys biting into her palm, the cold metal anchoring her. She steadied her breath before answering. "Veronica. Out for an evening stroll?"

Veronica's smile was polished, yet there was no warmth behind it. "Oh, you know me. Always keeping an ear to the ground. Especially after such... spirited gatherings."

The words lingered like smoke. Ladawn felt her pulse quicken. The rally had been peaceful, but it had crackled with something undeniable—something raw. The fear that change was coming too slowly, or not at all, had mingled with the anger bubbling beneath the surface. It was a fragile mix, potent enough to spill over if mishandled.

"People have a right to be heard," Ladawn said firmly. "You can't expect them to stay silent while Caldwell redraws this town without so much as asking who lives here."

Veronica's heels clicked against the cobblestones as she stepped closer, her movements measured and precise. "And yet, Ladawn, you must wonder—how far can righteous anger stretch before it snaps? Before it spills into something no one can control?"

The question landed heavily between them. Ladawn thought of the rally's undercurrent of desperation. People had gathered with hope, but also with the knowledge that hope alone might not be enough.

"Control isn't the goal," Ladawn replied, her voice steady. "Awareness is. Choice is. If Caldwell gets his way without anyone understanding what it'll cost, then we've already lost."

Veronica's smile thinned, her eyes narrowing as she studied

Ladawn. "And if your stirring words light a fire no one can put out? When the ashes settle, who will you blame?"

Ladawn squared her shoulders, the weight of Veronica's question settling like a stone in her chest. "If that fire burns, it won't be because people were told the truth. It'll be because those in power refused to listen."

The two women stood in silence, the dim light of the streetlamp casting shifting shadows over their faces. For an instant, Veronica's polished exterior faltered. Ladawn caught a glimpse of something behind the mask—doubt, maybe, or fear. Or was it something closer to understanding?

"You care about this town, Veronica," Ladawn said, her tone softer but no less resolute. "I know you do. You don't have to stand with Caldwell. You can still choose to be on the right side of this."

Veronica's lips pressed into a tight line, the flicker of vulnerability replaced by something harder. "Careful, Ladawn," she said, her voice low. "You're walking a fine edge."

"We all are," Ladawn replied evenly.

The silence between them grew taut, like a string pulled too tight. Then Veronica stepped back into the shadows, her silhouette fading into the darkness. Her parting words drifted after her, light as ash on the wind.

"Take care, Ladawn. The weather's turning."

Ladawn didn't move until the sound of Veronica's heels had disappeared into the night. Only then did she let out a slow, measured breath. The keys in her hand felt heavy, their sharp edges digging into her palm. The ley lines seemed to hum faintly beneath her feet, a quiet vibration that steadied her.

The rally had been a spark. Veronica's warning was the smoke.

But Ladawn knew she couldn't stop now. The town was waking up, its people beginning to see the threads being woven—and pulled apart. The lines of conflict were becoming clearer, both visible and unseen.

Chapter 49

THE HILLSIDE CLEARING GLOWED in the golden wash of the setting sun. The wide expanse of the desert stretched beyond, its ridges and plateaus bathed in amber light. Sierra Castillo stood at the edge of a rocky outcrop, framed by the open sky and the silhouettes of cottonwoods swaying gently in the breeze. She had chosen this spot deliberately—a place where the land itself would speak louder than any room ever could. Below her, a small group gathered, the wind carrying murmurs as anticipation built.

She wore a woven shawl draped across her shoulders, turquoise earrings glinting softly, and her dark braid resting neatly over one shoulder. Each detail felt intentional, not as vanity but as a statement of identity. The press was here—two cameras perched on tripods, reporters with microphones and notepads poised. Sierra knew every photo, every quote would carry the story far beyond Redstone's borders.

Behind the group, Tara stood with Derek, Sarah, Ashley, and Tom, clustered near the natural curve of the hillside. Ashley leaned closer to Tara, her voice low but urgent. "You remember Derek and Sarah, right? From Flagstaff?"

Tara nodded, her stomach tightening at the memory of her first meeting—and rejection—of Ashley. Derek, broad-shouldered and steady, reached out a hand. "Good to see you again, Tara. We're here to help however we can."

Sarah smiled faintly, her sharp eyes scanning the gathering. "Flagstaff feels like another world. But Ashley called, and when she says jump, we don't ask how high—we're already in the air."

Tom, standing a step behind, smirked. "We drove through the night for this. Caldwell's got his claws in deep, huh?"

Tara relaxed slightly, letting out a breath she hadn't realized she was holding. "Thank you. All of you. I didn't realize how much I needed to see familiar faces."

Ashley placed a reassuring hand on Tara's arm. "We're not just here to watch. We're here to fight."

At the front, Sierra's voice rose above the shifting wind. "Thank you for coming," she began, her tone clear and deliberate. The crowd stilled, their attention locking onto her. "This isn't just a fight about ley lines or land. This is about our legacy. About what we leave behind for those who come after us."

She gestured behind her to the vast expanse of land below. "The Caldwell project threatens more than this earth. It threatens our identity, our connection to something far older and deeper than we can measure. These ley lines are not superstition. They are pathways—energy that connects us to this land and to each other."

The reporters shifted closer, cameras clicking. One microphone extended toward her, and Sierra let the silence hold for a moment before continuing.

"Caldwell wants us to believe that progress comes at the cost of destruction. That bulldozers and profit margins are worth more than what this land gives us. But we know better. We feel it beneath our feet every day. And we will not let it be erased."

At the edge of the group, Tara felt a flicker of hope. Derek's phone recorded every word, while Sarah stood with her arms crossed, her stance unwavering. Ashley leaned closer to Tara, her voice soft. "She's not just speaking for herself."

Tara nodded, her voice quiet. "She's speaking for all of us."

From the periphery, Marla Jenkins and Veronica Miller lingered under the shadow of a cottonwood tree. They exchanged a brief glance, their expressions tight. Veronica's sharp blazer caught the light, her lips pressed into a thin line as she surveyed the gathering. Marla looked away, her jaw tightening, her hands shoved into her coat pockets. Neither woman spoke, but their stillness radiated tension—an unspoken current that hinted at their brewing frustration.

Sierra continued, her voice steady and unyielding. "We are not rejecting growth. We are demanding respect. Respect for the land, for its history, and for its power. If Caldwell's machines continue, they will destabilize more than the earth—they will unravel the connection that has kept this town alive for generations."

A skeptical voice rang out from the crowd. "What evidence do you have that these ley lines are anything more than superstition?"

Sierra turned, her expression unflinching. "I have walked these lines. I have felt their pulse. And while science can measure the electromagnetic fields, it cannot measure their meaning. But this isn't just about belief—it's about responsibility. Caldwell's machines are destabilizing something we don't fully understand. If we don't stop it now, the damage will be irreversible."

A murmur spread through the group, and Tara felt the resolve in the air deepen. Sierra wasn't just giving them facts—she was giving them purpose.

Another reporter spoke up, their tone sharper. "What happens if Caldwell proceeds anyway? What's your next move?"

Sierra's shoulders squared. "We will not let this happen quietly. We will shine every light we can on what's happening here. We will resist, peacefully but forcefully, and we will not back down."

The applause that followed started hesitantly but grew in momentum. Cameras flashed, voices rose, and reporters crowded forward to ask more questions. Sierra answered each one with deliberate poise, her presence commanding the moment.

Near the tree, Veronica and Marla exchanged another glance. Veronica's eyes narrowed, her gaze flicking briefly to the reporters, then back to Sierra. Marla muttered something under her breath, her hands tightening into fists. Without a word, they turned and walked toward the slope, their retreat unnoticed by the gathered crowd.

Tara watched their departure, unease prickling at the back of her mind. Ashley touched her arm gently. "What's wrong?"

"Nothing," Tara murmured. But her gaze lingered on the shadows where Marla and Veronica had disappeared.

As the crowd began to disperse, Sierra stood at the edge of the rocky outcrop, her silhouette framed by the fiery hues of the setting sun. The desert wind picked up, carrying with it the faint hum of the ley lines beneath her feet. For the first time, Sierra allowed herself to believe that the world beyond Redstone was starting to hear them.

But she also knew that not everyone listening would hear the same call.

Chapter 50

THE WIDE WINDOWS of Mayor Helen Jones's office framed a panoramic view of Redstone, the sprawling desert town cast in the amber glow of late afternoon. The glass reflected the tense conversation inside, each participant a study in controlled emotion. Veronica Miller stood by the bookshelf, arms crossed, her sharp gaze fixed on Helen, who sat behind the heavy oak desk. Chief Vega stood near the window, his squared shoulders backlit by the fading sunlight, his crisp uniform contrasting with the exhaustion carved into his face.

Helen's brow furrowed deeply as she read the report Vega had handed her moments before. Veronica already knew what it said—the shattered windows of Henley's general store, overturned shelves, a crimson smear streaked across the front steps. It wasn't the first incident tied to Caldwell's development, but it was the boldest.

"They aren't just applying pressure anymore," Helen said, breaking the silence. Her voice was tight, simmering with restrained anger. "This is escalation."

Vega's voice was measured but edged with steel. "It's not just Henley's. People are talking about veiled threats, subcontractors showing up uninvited on private property. This isn't intimidation anymore—it's provocation."

Veronica tilted her head slightly, her tone smooth, almost

dismissive. "Or it's frustration spilling over. These subcontractors aren't trained enforcers—they're workers, Helen. Tempers flare, someone makes a bad decision, and things get out of hand. It happens."

Helen's sharp response cut through the room like a blade. "You don't believe that. You've seen the way Caldwell operates, Veronica. This isn't random. It feels calculated."

Vega nodded, his expression grave. "They're testing boundaries, seeing how far they can push before someone pushes back."

Veronica sighed, letting a trace of concern soften her features. "Helen, if we accuse Caldwell without solid evidence, we'll lose leverage. Chaos doesn't serve him—it destabilizes his plans. I'm not saying we ignore this, but if we react emotionally, we'll only strengthen his hand."

Helen leaned back in her chair, her fingers tapping a restless rhythm against the armrest. "Carefully? Carefully hasn't worked. Someone's going to get hurt—or worse—if this keeps escalating."

A heavy silence fell over the room. Veronica's posture remained composed, but her thoughts raced. Helen was getting too close to the truth, and Vega's quiet pragmatism wasn't helping. Caldwell's moves were becoming bolder, sloppier, harder to defend. And Veronica knew her carefully curated role between these forces was beginning to unravel.

Vega broke the silence. "One of Caldwell's subcontractors had a confrontation near the Jenkins property this morning. It turned physical before my team intervened. We're lucky it didn't escalate further."

Helen rose from her chair, her tone firm and unyielding. "We need to be seen—out there. All three of us. The town needs to know we're not turning a blind eye to this."

Veronica's mask didn't slip. Her expression remained unreadable. "Visibility does matter. You're right."

Vega nodded. "I'll coordinate with my team. We'll ensure there's a strong presence."

Helen's gaze moved between the two of them. "This stops now. Caldwell doesn't own this town, no matter how much he wants to act like he does."

The words landed heavily in the room, the weight of the mayor's conviction clear. The meeting ended abruptly, Helen leading the way out with Vega close behind, his quiet resolve evident in every step. Veronica followed a pace behind, her face calm but her thoughts churning.

As they descended the stairs, Helen spoke briefly with a staffer, her voice low but purposeful. Vega scanned the street below, his sharp eyes cataloging everything, his stance already preparing for the next confrontation. Veronica's steps remained measured, but inside, a storm brewed.

Caldwell was running out of patience. The incidents were no longer easy to deflect, no longer subtle enough to smooth over. And Helen—relentless, sharp—was pushing harder, her suspicion growing with every passing day. Vega was echoing her concerns with precision, adding weight to every accusation. The careful balance Veronica had maintained for so long was beginning to crack.

But there was still time. If she could manage the fallout from Henley's, redirect Helen's focus, and feed Caldwell just enough to keep him from tipping the scales too far, she might hold that fragile balance a little longer.

Outside the office, the fading sun painted long shadows across the town, the jagged lines cutting through the streets like fault lines. Veronica's gaze lingered on the horizon, where Caldwell's development loomed ever closer. For now, she could still play both sides, still keep the peace between forces that were destined to collide.

Chapter 51

Chief Vega's Jeep rumbled off the paved road, the gravel crackling beneath the tires as the vehicle jolted onto the desert's uneven surface. The engine's hum faded into the vast expanse around him as he brought the Jeep to a halt. Ahead, a sandstone monolith loomed, its weathered surface bathed in the soft indigo light of dusk. It rose from the earth like an ancient sentinel, silent and resolute.

Vega lingered in the driver's seat, his hand resting on the key, as if reluctant to sever the faint connection the engine offered. Through the half-open window, the cool desert breeze drifted in, carrying with it the faint, earthy scent of sagebrush and the distant sound of a restless wind. For a moment, the stillness of the land felt heavier than the vastness itself, pressing against his chest.

He stepped out, his boots sinking into the loose sand, the crunch of his steps punctuating the silence. Each movement felt deliberate, as though the desert itself were watching, listening. The air around him was alive with an energy he couldn't name, a hum that seemed to rise from the ground and flow into the darkening sky.

Stopping just before the monolith, Vega tilted his head back, taking in its towering form. Its edges were softened by centuries of wind, its surface carved with cracks and crevices that seemed like the lines of an ancient map. He pressed his hand to its cool surface, grounding himself as his voice broke the stillness.

"Abuelo Eduardo," he said, his words soft but steady. "They say you understood this land better than anyone—the ley lines, their power, their paths. I need your guidance. How do I protect something I barely understand?"

The wind stirred, carrying whispers through the sagebrush. Vega closed his eyes and inhaled deeply, the question lingering in the quiet. "The people are counting on me," he continued, his voice rough with doubt. "But I'm not sure I can do this. How can I guard something I can't even explain? How can I carry a burden I don't know how to hold?"

The silence pressed in, heavy and expectant. Frustration rippled through him, and he leaned his forehead against the monolith's surface. The stone felt cool beneath his skin, unyielding and ancient. For a moment, he let the weight of his doubt settle there. But then, from somewhere deep within—a place he rarely let himself go—his grandfather's voice surfaced, steady and clear.

Martín, naciste para este momento. Mantente erguido y acepta los dones que se te han dado. (Martin, you were born for this moment. Stand tall and accept the gifts that have been given to you.)

The words unfurled in his chest, not as a command, but as a truth he had always known but had refused to acknowledge. He opened his eyes, lifting his head from the rock. The monolith seemed different now, its warmth faint but present beneath his palm. The desert no longer felt vast and indifferent. It felt alive—watching, waiting.

"Alright, Abuelo," Vega murmured, his voice steadier now. "I'll stand tall. I'll accept the gifts I've been given. And I'll protect these lands—not just as Chief, but as their guardian. As you were. As I'm meant to be."

He stepped back, the quiet of the desert settling around him once more. The hum beneath his feet seemed to echo his resolve, a vibration that wasn't sound but something deeper—a connection.

As Vega climbed back into the Jeep, the weight that had pressed against him all evening began to lift. The drive back to Redstone felt different. The road stretched long and dark before him, but the vastness of the desert no longer felt empty. The ley lines, the land, the people—they were his to protect, and the desert's quiet energy reminded him he had never truly been alone.

Above, the stars emerged, scattered and brilliant, like a map stretching endlessly into the night. Vega tightened his grip on the wheel, his shoulders straightening as the Jeep rumbled forward.

Chapter 52

MORNING LIGHT STREAMED through the bakery's wide windows, painting the worn wooden tables in soft gold. The air smelled of fresh bread and roasted coffee, but the tension hanging over Sierra and Lucas muted the usual warmth of the space. Maps, papers, and documents were strewn across the table, chaotic but purposeful. Sierra, her dark braid woven with turquoise beads, leaned over a faded map, her finger tracing a ley line with focused intensity. Across from her, Lucas adjusted his glasses, flipping through a thick sheaf of notes, his jaw tight with concentration.

The bell above the door jingled, breaking the quiet. Ladawn stepped in, clutching a leather-bound folder to her chest. Her face was pale, her posture hesitant. For a moment, she lingered by the door, her eyes darting to the table and then to the counter, as though she were unsure where to place herself.

"Ladawn," Sierra said, her voice softening as she rose from her seat. "Come, sit."

Lucas quickly cleared a space at the cluttered table, brushing aside stacks of maps and handwritten notes. "What's wrong?" he asked, his voice calm but edged with urgency.

Ladawn hesitated before lowering herself into the chair. Her knuckles whitened around the folder, and when she finally spoke, her voice wavered. "I talked to Jared—the lawyer. Caldwell's not just buying up property. He's consolidating debts, targeting businesses like mine. He waits until we're desperate, then swoops in with 'offers' that seem like lifelines but are really nooses. It's not just my bakery he's after. It's Redstone."

Sierra's jaw tightened, her hand pressing flat against the map. "Caldwell doesn't see Redstone as a community. He sees it as a carcass he can pick clean. He'll hollow this place out and leave nothing behind but ruins dressed up as progress."

Lucas pushed back his chair abruptly, standing to pace the length of the bakery floor. His steps were quick, his agitation clear. "This isn't just business," he said, his tone sharp. "It's predatory. He's counting on fear to paralyze everyone—fear of losing what little they have left."

Ladawn's voice cracked as she spoke. "But what can I do? I'm not a lawyer or a politician. I'm just—"

"No," Sierra interrupted, her voice firm but laced with empathy. "You're not 'just' anything, Ladawn. You're the heart of this place. Your bakery isn't just about bread or coffee. It's about connection. It's where people come to feel like they belong."

Lucas stopped pacing and turned to face her, planting both hands on the table. "Caldwell can buy buildings and debts, but he can't buy what you have—trust. The people here trust you. That's worth more than any contract or bank account."

Ladawn's grip on the folder loosened, and she looked between them, her breath coming a little steadier now. "Then we can't wait. We have to act now. We can't let him win."

Sierra leaned forward, reaching across the table to clasp Ladawn's hand. "We'll rally the town. We'll remind everyone what Redstone stands for—what it means to fight for something real."

The bakery door jingled again, and Mr. Thompson strolled in, tipping his hat with a familiar grin. "Morning, Ladawn. The usual, if you've got it."

Ladawn managed a small smile as she stood. "Of course, Mr. Thompson. And how's that dog of yours?"

"Still losing his battle against that lawn flamingo," he said with a chuckle.

Lucas watched the exchange, his gaze sweeping over the room. The baskets of fresh bread on the counter, the mismatched chairs worn from years of conversation, the mural Sierra had painted on the far wall depicting the desert's vibrant hues and ley lines—it all told a story. It wasn't just a business. It was Redstone's heartbeat.

"This bakery isn't just a place to eat," Lucas said quietly. "It's where this town remembers itself. Caldwell will never understand that."

Ladawn turned back to them, her shoulders straightening as her voice found its strength. "Then let's make sure he never gets the chance to take it."

Sierra and Lucas began gathering their papers as Ladawn moved behind the counter, the sunlight spilling across her face. She glanced out at the street, where her loyal customers wandered in and out, unaware of the storm gathering around them. Determination settled in her chest—not just a fleeting emotion, but something solid, rooted. She would protect what was hers.

No matter the cost.

Chapter 53

LADAWN SLAMMED the bakery's ledger shut, her hands trembling as the final numbers blurred before her eyes. The street outside was quiet, shrouded in shadows as the last traces of dusk gave way to night. The bakery was empty now, its warmth faded into an eerie stillness broken only by the rhythmic ticking of the wall clock and the faint hum of cooling ovens. Ladawn leaned heavily against the counter, her breath uneven, her phone trembling in her hand.

She stared at the dim glow of the screen, willing herself to act. Her fingers hesitated before dialing, and when the voice on the other end picked up, Ladawn's words faltered.

"Mom, it's me," she said, her voice thin and strained.

Her mother-in-law's familiar warmth came through the line, tinged with concern. "Ladawn? It's late. What's wrong?"

Ladawn swallowed hard, pressing her palm against the counter as though it might steady her. Memories of the past few weeks clawed at her—foreclosure notices folded tightly in her purse, veiled threats from Caldwell's representatives, the pit in her stomach every time she looked at her children.

"I need to send the kids to you for the rest of the summer," she said, the words spilling out in a rush. "It's not safe here anymore. I can't let them see this—see me like this. I won't."

The silence that followed felt like a chasm. When her mother-in-law finally spoke, her voice was steady, layered with love and quiet understanding. "You're carrying too much, sweetheart. But are you sure? They'll miss you—and you'll miss them."

Ladawn's breath hitched. "I'm sure," she whispered, though her voice cracked. "I just need time to figure this out. The bakery's barely holding on, and Caldwell... he's not backing down."

A deep sigh came through the line, filled with compassion and resignation. "Alright. Send them to me. But, Ladawn, promise me something. Don't let this place—or that man—take everything from you."

Tears burned in Ladawn's eyes as she nodded, though no one could see her. "I won't. I promise."

She hung up carefully, her hands shaking as she placed the phone on the counter. Her gaze drifted to the framed photo by the register—her late husband, Robbie, caught mid-laugh on a sunlit day long gone. His belief in the bakery, in this dream, had carried her through so much. But dreams weren't enough to fend off men like Caldwell.

A sudden sound outside made her flinch. Her breath caught, and she whipped her head toward the window. A shadow flickered at the edge of the property line, half-obscured by the dim streetlights. Just a drifter? Or something worse—someone sent to watch, to intimidate? Her pulse hammered as she backed away from the window, her chest tight with fear.

She stood frozen for a moment, gripping the counter as she fought to breathe. Then, with deliberate effort, she turned to the ledger. Her fingers flipped through the pages, smudging the ink with flour-dusted fingertips. Every dollar, every choice mattered now. If she couldn't hold onto the bakery, Redstone wouldn't just lose its bread and coffee. It would lose its anchor—its heart.

A tear slipped down her cheek as she forced herself to focus. The distant hum of the ovens pressed gently against her back, a small warmth in the growing chill. Ladawn wiped her face with the back of her hand and reached for the dough resting under its cloth. She kneaded, her hands moving with automatic precision.

Morning pastries needed preparing. Her children needed her to fight—not just for the lights and the bills, but for the soul of this place.

Tomorrow, she would face Caldwell's men. Tomorrow, she would find the strength to rally her neighbors. But tonight, she worked. Flour dusted the counters, and the clock ticked steadily on, each second reminding her that time was running out.

Ladawn's hands stilled for a moment as she looked toward the darkened window. Her fear was a constant presence, pressing against her like a shadow she couldn't escape. But beneath it, fragile and flickering, burned a resolve that refused to be snuffed out.

The bakery's ovens warmed the space around her, a reminder of what she still had left to protect. And so, she kept moving—because stopping meant losing everything.

Chapter 54

ELANA'S RENTAL CAR cut through the desert, the endless horizon stretching like an unwritten story before her. The urgency that had brought her here pulsed beneath her ribs, sharp and relentless. Every passing mile brought her closer to Redstone—and closer to the truth she had been avoiding for months. Lucas wasn't just another voice from her past. He was the unresolved question that had haunted her in the quiet moments of her carefully ordered life. Whatever had drawn him to this place, whatever had been important enough for him to leave everything behind—it was enough to bring her here now.

The sun dipped low as she neared the town limits, casting the sandstone cliffs in fiery hues of amber and red. Redstone emerged from the desert like a half-forgotten memory, its quiet streets exuding a stillness that felt anything but peaceful. The air seemed to vibrate faintly, charged with something she couldn't name but couldn't ignore. Her grip tightened on the steering wheel, Lucas's voice echoing in her mind.

The last time they'd spoken, he had insisted everything was fine, his words carefully controlled. But there had been a crack in his voice, a hesitation that had slipped past his usual composure. That crack had shattered her resolve to stay away.

The Redstone Inn greeted her with a quiet warmth, its worn rugs and faint scent of wood smoke wrapping around her like an old quilt. She stepped inside, her heels clicking softly against the wooden floor. From somewhere deeper in the inn, laughter bubbled, distant and faint. But the weight in her chest didn't lift. Elana pulled out her phone, her fingers trembling slightly as she dialed.

"Lucas," she said when he answered, her voice catching. "I'm here."

His reply was quick, subdued. "I'll be right down."

She ended the call, her heart thudding in the silence that followed. Her hand trembled as she poured herself a glass of lemon water from a nearby dispenser. The cold sting on her throat did little to calm her. Each passing second felt fragile, stretched thin under the weight of her questions.

When Lucas finally appeared at the top of the staircase, the air seemed to shift. Elana's breath caught as she took him in. He looked older, more worn—lines etched into his face, his shoulders heavier than she remembered. But in the way he held her gaze, there was something unchanged: the sharp mind, the quiet intensity that had always drawn her to him.

For a long moment, neither of them moved. Then, slowly, Lucas descended the stairs. When they met, their embrace was tentative, careful, as if they were both testing the fragile ground beneath them. Elana pulled back, searching his face for answers, but his expression revealed nothing.

"I have room 312," she said, her voice quiet.

Lucas nodded. "Let's grab your bags."

They walked to her car together, their conversation light and hollow. Elana talked about her drive, Lucas asked about her work, and their words hung in the air like placeholders for confessions they weren't ready to make. But beneath the small talk, Elana felt the urgency rising, pressing against her ribs like a tide that wouldn't recede.

It wasn't just about Lucas anymore. It was about what had drawn him here—what had been powerful enough to break the trajectory of his life and leave her questions unanswered. The ley lines he'd mentioned in passing, the energy he'd described as "thrumming" beneath the desert floor, the way his voice had cracked when he'd tried to explain. Whatever this was, it was bigger than either of them, and Elana needed to know why.

In her room, Lucas set down her bag and turned toward the door, but Elana's voice stopped him.

"Lucas," she said, her tone sharper now. "I didn't drive all this way to dance around whatever's happening here. You need to tell me what's going on."

Lucas hesitated, his shoulders tensing as he turned halfway back to face her. "It's not that I don't want to tell you," he said, his voice low, almost pleading. "It's that I can't. Not yet. What's happening here... it's bigger than us, Elana. Bigger than anything I've ever dealt with. And it's not just about discovery or science—it's dangerous. There are people watching, listening. If I say the wrong thing, if I tell you too much, we could both end up making things worse. I need you to trust me."

Elana's chest tightened at his words. His warning felt less like an excuse and more like a lifeline tossed across a chasm. For a brief moment, his mask slipped, and she caught a glimpse of the fear behind his composed facade. It was raw, unguarded, and it scared her more than his words.

"We'll talk," Lucas said, his voice firmer now. "But not here. Not yet."

Elana nodded slowly, though every fiber of her being resisted the patience he was asking of her. She had come to Redstone for answers—not just about the ley lines or whatever strange forces had lured him here, but about Lucas himself. About why he had left her, why he had chosen this place over the life they had almost built together. His words, cautious as they were, left her no closer to those answers.

"Okay," she said finally. But her voice carried the weight of her resolve. She wouldn't let him hide for long.

Lucas left the room, and Elana stood by the window, staring out at the darkened town. The desert stretched beyond, vast and quiet, but alive with a presence she could almost feel. Whatever Lucas was caught up in, it had its claws in him deeply. And now it had drawn her here, too.

Chapter 55

THE NEXT MORNING, Sierra stepped into the bustling lobby of the Redstone Inn. The hum of conversation mixed with the inviting aroma of coffee and freshly baked pastries. The warmth of the space seemed to wrap around the guests, but for Sierra, it might as well have been ice. Her chest tightened as her eyes swept the room, searching for the one person she both needed and dreaded to see.

"Sierra!" Susan Andrews's cheerful voice cut through the air, drawing attention from a nearby table. "Good morning! What brings you here so early?"

Sierra forced a small smile, though it felt brittle. "Morning, Susan. I'm looking for Lucas. Is he here?"

Susan's face softened, her expression hinting at understanding. "He's in the breakfast nook. I can grab him for you if you'd like."

"No, that's okay. I'll go." Sierra's voice steadied as she turned toward the hallway leading to the nook. Her footsteps echoed faintly, their rhythm matching the pounding of her heart.

The cheerful hum of voices grew louder as she approached. Lucas's voice drifted toward her, followed by Elana's light, melodic laughter. Sierra stopped short, her breath catching in her throat. Shielded by the leaves of a potted plant, she caught sight of them seated together.

Lucas leaned forward as he spoke, his body language open,

relaxed. Elana listened intently, her lips curving into an easy smile, her eyes fixed on him. It wasn't just their conversation—it was the rhythm of it, the intimacy in the way they spoke without hesitation, without walls.

A sharp pang lanced through Sierra's chest, followed by a tide of doubt that left her breathless. Had she misread everything? Had Lucas's quiet encouragement, his shared moments of reflection, meant more to her than to him? Had her sacrifices for Redstone—her unwavering dedication—been nothing more than her duty, invisible and unvalued?

Lucas laughed then, the sound clear and familiar, but it cut through Sierra like shattered glass. It was the laugh she had come to treasure in their quiet moments, a piece of him she thought she understood. But here, it felt hollow, as though it belonged to someone else entirely.

"Foolish," she whispered, the word trembling in the stillness of her thoughts. She turned sharply, her feet moving on instinct, her chest tightening with the weight of words she couldn't say.

She was almost at the door when fate intervened. Lucas glanced up, his eyes landing on her. Their gazes locked across the room, and Sierra froze. His expression shifted—surprise, concern, and something else that made her pulse race. He leaned toward Elana, murmuring something, then stood and began weaving his way toward Sierra.

Panic surged through her veins. She turned on her heel, quickening her pace until she reached the glass doors. The crisp morning air hit her like a wave as she pushed through, her lungs burning as she gulped it in.

Sierra didn't stop moving. The streets of Redstone blurred around her as she walked, the tightness in her chest refusing to ease. Every doubt she had tried to suppress clawed its way forward, relentless and loud. What was she fighting for if the people closest to her didn't see her? If Lucas didn't see her?

Inside, Lucas stopped at the threshold, his hand brushing against the doorframe. He stared out at the street, watching Sierra's retreating form until she disappeared around the corner.

"Lucas?" Elana's voice drew him back, soft but probing. She tilted her head, her gaze steady. "Is everything okay?"

He returned to the table and sank into his chair, his coffee still untouched. His fingers traced the edge of the cup as he let out a breath he hadn't realized he was holding. "I don't know," he admitted. "I really don't."

Elana studied him, her curiosity quiet but insistent. "You don't have to figure it all out today," she said, her tone careful. "Maybe it's enough to sit with it for now."

Lucas's lips pressed into a thin line, but he nodded. The weight in his chest remained, an unspoken tension tethering him to a thousand unanswered questions. The silence between them grew, heavy with what neither was ready to say.

Chapter 56

Lucas wasn't sure if bringing Elana to Sierra's rally was a mistake. But he had promised Sierra he would be there, and promises to Sierra were not something he broke lightly. The gravel shifted under their feet as they walked, the red rocks rising around them like silent sentinels. The sharp scent of desert sage mingled with the faint hum of voices ahead, and the open expanse seemed to carry their silence further than Lucas liked.

Elana matched his pace, her gaze fixed on the horizon. "You didn't say it would be this… organized," she said, her voice quiet but laced with curiosity.

"It wasn't, at first," Lucas replied, his voice clipped. "Sierra makes people believe."

When they reached the clearing, the hum of gathered voices transformed into a palpable current of energy. The rally site—set against a natural amphitheater of sandstone formations—was alive with activity. Folding chairs were scattered across the uneven ground, where locals, young and old, had gathered. Some leaned forward in rapt attention, others stood with their arms crossed, their expressions tense but focused.

Elana lingered at the edge, her gaze sweeping across the scene. "This is… something else," she murmured, her tone caught between awe and skepticism.

Lucas didn't answer. His eyes were on Sierra, standing on a makeshift platform built from crates and wooden planks. She was speaking to the crowd, her voice clear and resonant as it carried through the natural acoustics of the site.

"Today," Sierra said, her posture commanding, "we stand together to protect what is sacred—not just to us, but to the generations that will follow. This land isn't just scenery. It holds our stories, our roots, our connection to everything that has come before us. It's alive—and it's ours to protect."

Lucas felt the familiar pull of her words, her ability to weave purpose into every syllable. He stole a glance at Elana, who was watching intently. Her brow furrowed, her hands fidgeting with the edge of her jacket, but she didn't look away.

At the edge of the crowd, Tara stood near a cluster of locals, her arms folded as she observed the rally. When her eyes met Lucas's, the connection was instantaneous—and unsettling. Her gaze carried an intensity that felt like a question, unspoken but unavoidable. Lucas hesitated, unsure of what to make of it, before her attention shifted to Elana, standing at his side. The moment dissolved, leaving a lingering discomfort in its place.

Sierra's words drew Lucas back. "We are not standing against progress. We are standing against destruction. Against greed. Against those who would hollow this land for their gain and leave us with nothing but scars."

The crowd's murmurs grew louder, their energy shifting toward solidarity. Lucas felt a flicker of hope—brief but present. Sierra had always been able to channel the emotions of others into action. But then came the sound that shattered the moment.

Engines roared from the ridge above the site.

The crowd turned as four motorcycles barreled into the clearing, kicking up clouds of dust and gravel. The machines snarled as the bikers maneuvered through the gathered chairs, parents pulling children back, folding chairs tipping over in the chaos.

Lucas stepped instinctively in front of Elana, his body tense as he scanned the scene. Sierra stood her ground on the platform, but her grip on the edge of the crate was tight, her knuckles pale. The lead biker, a broad man with a scar running across his cheek, twisted his throttle and skidded close to the stage, sending gravel flying.

"Big talk," the biker called out, his voice sharp. He leaned forward, the mirrored lenses of his sunglasses reflecting Sierra's resolute stance.

Another biker cut sharply through the crowd, his tires spitting gravel as he weaved between the scattered chairs. Sierra flinched as the platform rocked beneath her, and her foot caught on the uneven planks. She fell, the back of her head striking the edge of the crate with a sickening crack.

Lucas's breath stalled. "Sierra!" He ran to her side, dropping to his knees as blood trickled from a cut on her temple. Her eyes fluttered, unfocused, as she tried to sit up.

"Stay down," Lucas said firmly, his hands hovering near her shoulders. "You hit your head. Don't move."

The lead biker laughed, the sound jagged and cruel. "This is what happens when you don't know your place."

"Get out of here!" Lucas shouted, his voice cutting through the panic.

The biker sneered but twisted his throttle, and the group sped away in a spray of dust and gravel. As the noise of their engines faded, the crowd began to move closer, fear and confusion giving way to purpose.

Elana knelt beside Lucas, her voice trembling as she called for help. "We need a medic—now!"

A man rushed forward with a first-aid kit, others scattered to find assistance. Tara appeared beside them, her expression sharp but focused. "Sierra," she said softly, her voice heavy with concern. "Can you hear me?"

Sierra's eyelids fluttered open, her voice weak but resolute. "They… want us to give up," she murmured. "But we won't."

"No," Lucas said, his voice steady now. "We won't."

The crowd began to organize, their fear hardening into determination. Sierra was lifted onto a stretcher, the cut on her head bandaged but still seeping through. Lucas watched as she was carried toward a waiting car, her hand briefly gripping his wrist as she passed.

"You'll see this through," Sierra whispered.

"I will," Lucas replied.

As the crowd dispersed, their faces carried a new intensity. Redstone's fight wasn't just about words anymore—it had drawn blood.

Chapter 57

THE STREET IN FRONT of Mayor Helen Jones's office was anything but quiet. What had begun as a small gathering of concerned citizens had grown into a restless crowd. Voices rose and fell, fractured by sharp whispers and heated exchanges. The glow of the old streetlights spilled unevenly across tense faces, their expressions a mix of fear and simmering anger. Above them, the desert sky stretched vast and unbroken, but the air below felt charged, brittle.

Mayor Jones stepped onto the cracked steps of her office, her tailored jacket tugged by the evening breeze. The crowd stilled as her sharp gaze swept over them, her presence steadying but not soothing. The murmurs softened, but the tension remained palpable, like an unstrung bow poised to snap.

"Friends," Helen began, her voice carrying the authority of someone used to commanding a room, "I hear you. I see your concerns, and I feel the strain this town is under. I know what's happening out there—the threats, the intimidation, the violence. And I promise you this: we will not let Redstone be consumed by fear."

The crowd shifted uneasily. Some nodded, their shoulders relaxing slightly, while others remained stiff, their skepticism clear. Helen pressed on.

"Earlier today, one of our own—Sierra Castillo—was injured while standing up for this community, for our connection to this land. That's what's at stake here. This is not just about ley lines or land; it's about who we are. And let me be clear: I will not let this community be torn apart by greed or fear."

Behind her, Chief Martin Vega stepped forward, his uniform as crisp as his tone. "This town was built on trust," he said, his voice even but deliberate. "That trust is being tested, but it's not broken—not yet. We need your vigilance. Your eyes, your voices, your unity. Together, we can hold the line against those who would see this town divided."

For a moment, the crowd quieted. Helen scanned their faces, looking for a sign that her words were landing, but a rustle of dissent rippled through the edges. The murmurs began to grow again, discontent spilling back into the air.

"Words won't stop them, Mayor," a man called out from near the middle of the group. "What are you going to *do*?"

Another voice joined in. "They're already taking what they want. Flyers, threats, their people showing up on our property—it's happening right under your nose!"

The crowd's hum grew louder, sharper. Helen straightened, her jaw tightening. "We are investigating every report, and Chief Vega's team is monitoring the situation closely," she replied. "But we need time, and we need your trust."

Time was not what the crowd wanted. Whispers turned to shouts, and pockets of people broke into urgent discussions, their voices rising above the mayor's steady tone. Vega leaned closer to Helen, his voice low.

"They're slipping, Helen. We're losing them."

Helen exhaled through her nose, her eyes scanning the growing disarray. "We need to be visible. If they see us out here—if they see us working for them—it might hold things together. For now."

As Helen and Vega spoke in hushed tones, the mood of the crowd continued to shift. Near the back, Tom Barker stood with his wife, Marianne, holding one of the glossy flyers that had appeared like unwelcome messengers. *"THE FUTURE IS NOW!"* it read in bold, brazen letters. Below it, an image of a sleek building imposed over a desert backdrop mocked everything Redstone had fought to protect.

"This isn't the future," Tom muttered, crumpling the flyer in his fist. "This is robbery."

Marianne's hand rested lightly on his arm. "What do we do, Tom? If this keeps going…"

Tom glanced toward the fringes of the crowd, where shadowed figures exchanged quiet words, their postures hunched, their faces obscured. His jaw clenched, his voice low. "We stand by Helen for now. But if they think they can take what's ours—they're wrong."

Marianne hesitated, her expression tight with worry. "Don't let this turn into something we can't take back."

Tom didn't answer. His eyes remained fixed on the shadows at the edge of the gathering, his fists tightening at his sides.

Back on the steps, Helen raised her hands, trying to regain control. "This is our town. These are our lives. And together, we will protect them."

But her voice was almost drowned out now by the growing unrest. Groups splintered off, their discussions urgent and clipped. Flyers fluttered across the pavement like taunts in the cooling wind. The sharp glow of streetlights only deepened the sense that the edges of the gathering were fraying, and distrust was seeping into the cracks.

Vega stepped closer to Helen, his expression grim. "We're walking a fine line, Helen. If we don't do something concrete soon, this fear is going to turn into action—and not the kind we want."

Helen's jaw tightened, her gaze hardening as she surveyed the restless crowd. "Then we act," she said. "We can't let this spiral."

In the shifting shadows at the edge of the group, Tom turned toward Marianne. "If they won't stop this, we'll have to," he said, his voice steady but dark. His gaze lingered on the shadowed figures nearby before turning back toward the mayor.

Marianne's eyes filled with unease, but she didn't argue.

Chapter 58

THE BACK ROOM of Redstone's hardware store was shrouded in a dense quiet, broken only by the sound of Marla's restless pacing. Her boots scuffed against the concrete floor as she moved, her hands clenching and unclenching at her sides. Around her, shelves cluttered with dusty tools and cans of paint closed in like silent witnesses.

Veronica sat at the edge of a battered desk, her posture composed, her notebook resting neatly in her lap. Her gaze followed Marla's movements, patient and calculated. When she finally spoke, her voice was crisp, slicing through the room like a blade.

"Ladawn is hesitating," Veronica said. "She's becoming a liability."

Marla stopped mid-step, turning toward Veronica. "She's soft. It's her problem. She doesn't want to risk the bakery, the kids, her entire perfect little world. And that hesitation—" her hand waved in frustration, "—it's slowing everything down."

"And that," Veronica said, leaning forward slightly, "is where we step in. Hesitation is a crack. You press hard enough, and it'll shatter."

Marla hesitated, her fingers drumming against the edge of the desk. "She cares too much about what people think. The bakery, her customers—it's all tied up in her sense of herself. If that cracks..."

She trailed off, her gaze shifting toward the door.

Veronica tilted her head. "What are you thinking?"

Marla pulled her phone from her pocket, scrolling quickly before holding it up. The photo of Ladawn's bakery glowed on the screen—the bright awning, the inviting windows. A place that felt warm and unshakable, the kind of spot people assumed would always be there.

"This," Marla said quietly, her voice harder now. "This is where we press. It's where she feels safest. If we shake it—just enough—she'll come around."

Veronica studied the image for a long moment, her lips curving into a faint smile. "Direct, but effective. Controlled chaos, not destruction. We send a message, one she can't ignore."

Marla nodded, her resolve sharpening as she slid the phone back into her pocket. "I'll do it myself," she said firmly. "It'll be clean, quick. No mistakes. And it'll look like an accident. No one will connect it to us."

Veronica's gaze didn't waver. "And you're sure you can keep it quiet?"

"Quiet isn't the problem," Marla said. "The problem is hesitation. She'll understand the stakes when she sees what's at risk."

Veronica leaned back in her chair, tapping her pen against her notebook. "Good. And while you're busy... creating clarity for Ladawn, I'll make sure the narrative stays where we want it. Sympathy, public support, solidarity. The works."

Marla's jaw tightened, her hand resting on the back of the chair nearest her. "And Hiram?"

Veronica smirked. "Hiram doesn't need to know the details. He wants results, and this is how we deliver. He trusts us to handle the hard calls."

Marla exhaled slowly, nodding. "Then we make sure this gets handled right."

Veronica snapped her notebook shut, her tone final. "It will be.

By the time we're done, Ladawn will fall in line—and Redstone will know exactly who holds the cards."

The two women exchanged a glance, unspoken understanding passing between them. Marla turned toward the door, her steps deliberate as she left the room. The plan had crystallized in her mind, each detail falling into place. The bakery wouldn't burn, but the mark it would bear would be unmistakable.

As the hardware store door clicked shut behind her, Marla's gaze lingered down the street. The faint glow of Ladawn's bakery windows stood out against the darkening sky, a beacon of warmth. But soon, that glow would flicker, its certainty shaken.

And Ladawn would know why.

———

Susan moved through the Redstone Inn's dining area with practiced ease, the coffee pot steady in her hand as she made her rounds. The evening crowd was thinner than usual, the hushed conversations and clinking silverware adding to the subdued atmosphere. Yet one table, tucked into the corner near the wide bay window, seemed to carry a weight that made her steps falter.

Hiram Caldwell and Marla Jenkins sat together, their heads bent low over a spread of blueprints and thick stacks of documents. The table between them was cluttered but deliberate—papers arranged in precise, functional layers. Caldwell leaned back in his chair, his movements measured and contained, while Marla's posture was tense with energy, her hands darting to the pages as if her thoughts moved faster than her words ever could.

Susan approached carefully, pouring coffee for a couple at a nearby table while keeping Caldwell and Marla within her peripheral vision. She couldn't hear their conversation, but their focus on the blueprints was unmistakable. Marla gestured emphatically toward something on the page, her body language brimming with excitement, while Caldwell's gaze followed her hand, his expression sharp and calculating.

Susan adjusted her apron and stepped closer, the coffee pot warm in her hand. She lingered at the edge of their table, pretending to straighten a salt shaker as she observed them more closely. Marla reached out, her fingers brushing Caldwell's arm lightly—a gesture Susan recognized immediately. It wasn't a casual touch. It was something more deliberate, almost eager.

When Caldwell turned his head slightly, Susan caught a glimpse of his face—a faint smile, rare and fleeting, but genuine enough to hold her attention. He nodded at whatever Marla had said, and Susan watched as Marla leaned back in her chair, her expression one of barely contained satisfaction. Whatever they were discussing, it was big.

Susan cleared her throat gently to announce her presence. "More coffee for you, Mr. Caldwell?" she asked, keeping her tone polite but neutral.

Caldwell gave a curt nod, his attention already drifting back to the documents. Marla, however, glanced up briefly, offering Susan a distracted smile before refocusing on the table. Susan poured the coffee, the scent mingling with the lingering spice of their Southwestern meal. As she turned to leave, she felt the weight of the moment pressing at the back of her mind.

Something about the intensity of their interaction stuck with her. The way Marla leaned forward, her eyes darting between Caldwell and the blueprints; the subtle but clear exchange of power in their body language. Susan didn't know what they were planning, but whatever it was, it wasn't small.

Minutes later, Caldwell rose from his seat, smoothing his suit jacket as he prepared to leave. His movements were crisp, decisive, as though the conversation had resolved something significant. "Next week," he said, his voice carrying just enough for Susan to catch. He nodded to Marla and strode out of the dining area without a backward glance.

Marla lingered, her expression softened by something Susan could only describe as triumph. She began gathering the papers, stacking them neatly before sliding them into a leather portfolio. In her rush, one folder slipped from the pile, landing on the floor beside her chair. Marla didn't notice, her focus on packing up and leaving as quickly as Caldwell had.

Susan stepped forward, retrieving the folder before anyone else noticed. She glanced briefly at its cover—a plain but sturdy binder with no markings—and then toward the door as Marla disappeared into the lobby. Something about the folder's weight in her hands, its unassuming exterior, made her pause.

The young server clearing a nearby table caught her eye. "Everything okay?" they asked.

Susan nodded, tucking the folder under her arm. "Looks like they left something behind. I'll take care of it."

She knew someone who might be interested in its contents.

Chapter 59

MARLA JENKINS PERCHED on the edge of the bed, her hands twisting the hem of her skirt. The grooves in the worn wooden floor seemed to pull her gaze, their patterns catching the dim light from the window. Each line felt heavy, like the weight of the choices she couldn't yet put into words. Across the room, Hank Jenkins stood by the window, his broad shoulders outlined against the last faint glow of twilight. The wind rattled the glass, filling the room with its restless hum.

"Marla," Hank said, his voice quiet but steady, "there's something about Caldwell I can't shake. The way he talks... it's like he's already decided this land is his. Like it's just another deal to close, another profit to count. But this isn't just land." He paused, his tone softening. "This is home."

Marla's head snapped up, her eyes narrowing. "Home doesn't pay the bills, Hank," she said, her voice rising, edged with desperation. "It doesn't keep the roof from caving in or the lights on when the power company sends another notice. Caldwell's offering us a future—a real chance. Can't you see that?"

Hank turned from the window, his expression caught somewhere between disbelief and sadness. "A future built on what? On promises he has no intention of keeping? On debts we'll never crawl out from under?" He took a step toward her, his hand half-raised as though reaching for something fragile. "Marla, you know this doesn't feel right."

She stiffened, crossing her arms over her chest as if to shield herself. "You think I'm naive?" she shot back. "You think I don't know what I'm doing?"

"No," Hank said, his voice thick with emotion. "I think you're scared. And I think Caldwell knows it. I think he's using that fear to make you see something that isn't there."

Marla's knuckles whitened as her grip tightened on the edge of her skirt. "You couldn't make it happen, Hank," she said, her words trembling with the force of her frustration. "The loans, the grants, the meetings—none of it worked. You tried, but it wasn't enough. And now Caldwell is offering us something real, and you want to throw it all away because of a...a feeling."

Hank's breath hitched, but he held her gaze. "Is that what you think of me?" he asked quietly. "That I've done nothing but fail you?"

Marla turned sharply, her back to him now, her shoulders rigid. "I think we don't have any other choice."

Silence stretched between them, vast and suffocating. Hank rubbed his temples, his voice dropping to a raw whisper. "Marla... has something happened between you and Caldwell?"

Her shoulders stiffened further, and for a moment she didn't move. When she finally spoke, her voice was low and strained. "What are you asking me, Hank?"

He shook his head, a pained expression softening the lines of his face. "I need to understand why you trust him so completely. Why you look at him like he's the answer to everything."

Marla turned back to him slowly, her face drawn with exhaustion. There was something deeper in her expression now—regret, guilt, or perhaps a weariness that seemed to reach down into her very bones. "Because I have to believe in something," she said, her voice cracking. "If I don't, everything we've fought for—everything we've lost—it's all for nothing."

Hank closed his eyes briefly, nodding as if he'd expected her answer but hoped for something different. "I can't do this, Marla," he said finally, his voice breaking. "Not tonight."

He crossed the room and grabbed his duffel bag from the corner. Marla's voice cracked as she asked, "Where are you going?"

Hank didn't turn around. "Somewhere quiet," he said. "Somewhere I can think."

Sierra's Dream

The desert stretches out before her, endless and trembling, its cracked surface etched with veins of pale light. They pulse like the shallow breath of a sleeping giant, and the earth beneath bare feet hums with something ancient and unyielding. Above, the sky hangs heavy with dusk—clouds bruised and rolling slow, as though time itself is reluctant to move forward.

She stands still, her braid caught in the wind, dark eyes fixed on the horizon. The world feels suspended, fragile, waiting for something to break.
A voice stirs—not a sound, but a vibration, deep and resonant, moving through the ley lines and into her bones.

"Sierra."

She stiffens, her mind sharp as she turns toward the horizon. At the edge of vision, just beyond the shimmer of heat rising from the desert floor, a figure stands. Shoulders heavy with shadows, eyes locked onto hers with a clarity that feels unbearable. The figure looks as if they've already been through the storm.

"They will fall," the voice murmurs through the wind, through the ground, through everything. It is not unkind, but it is inevitable. "They will shatter like glass beneath a hammer. The desert will take them, bury them in dust and silence. But they will rise. Not as they

were, but as something bound to this place—to the light and the silence and the breath between moments."
The air thickens around her, and she doesn't move. Her breath comes shallow as flickering images fill the space behind her eyes. The figure, collapsed on cracked earth. Blood smeared into dust. The faint, weakening glow of ley lines beneath their still form. But then—a pull, a gasp of light, and their chest rises again. Energy surges back into them, raw and unyielding.

She sees herself there, too. Standing beside them at the convergence of ley lines, their hands pressed together, light gathering at their fingertips. Around them, the earth exhales—a slow breath of flowers and green shoots, of water carving paths through lifeless stone. But even here, joy is shadowed by grief. Their faces are etched with sorrow, with loss.

The storm clouds press closer, shadows swallowing the horizon, lightning carving jagged scars across the sky. The air crackles, and the ley lines beneath her feet hum faster, more erratic, until the sound becomes almost unbearable.
"The land will endure," the voice says, final and sharp. "But only if you endure. Only if you hold the line. Only if you listen."

She sinks to her knees, hands pressed flat against the trembling earth. The hum rises through her palms, relentless and desperate, as though the desert itself is pleading with her. Her breath catches in her throat as the moment settles over her, heavy and inescapable.

Chapter 60

LUCAS STOOD IN the doorway of Sierra Castillo's adobe home. The fading sunlight framed his figure against the warm, earthy walls, casting long shadows across the room. Dust swirled in the golden light stretching across the floor, moving slowly as if the air itself held its breath. Inside, Sierra stood beside the dining table, her arms crossed tightly against her chest and her expression unreadable.

"Come in," she said, her voice firm but quiet.

Lucas stepped inside, each footfall soft against the worn floor. He carried the folder in both hands, his grip careful, his posture tense. As he approached the table, he set the folder down. "Susan got this from Sarah," he said. "It's worse than we thought."

Sierra pulled out a chair and sat, touching the folder's edge for a moment before opening it. Maps, schematics, and emails spilled across the table in chaotic order. Her eyes scanned the pages, her brows drawing together as her gaze sharpened. "Caldwell isn't just developing the land," she said. "He's severing the ley lines. He's breaking something fundamental."

Lucas leaned over the table and pointed at several sections of the documents. "Look here. Veronica has been providing him with insider information. Marla's been relaying it to his lawyers. And this—" he slid another page toward Sierra—"Ladawn Greer.

Eviction proceedings have already started."

Sierra's breath faltered, and her fingers pressed hard against the table's surface. "Ladawn? He's targeting the bakery now?" she asked. Her gaze turned to Lucas, a fire igniting in her eyes. "That place isn't just a business. It's where people gather, where we remember who we are. If he takes that, what's left of Redstone?"

Lucas's jaw tightened as he met her gaze. "That's exactly why he's doing it. He isn't just reshaping Redstone—he's erasing it."

Sierra pushed the folder aside, her focus shifting to Lucas. "Then we won't let him. He's taken enough."

Lucas exhaled, rubbing his hands together as he weighed their next steps. "We need more people on our side—Ladawn, Mayor Jones, maybe even Chief Vega if we can get him to stand with us. This won't be easy, Sierra. Caldwell's not just trying to take the town; he's trying to bury us."

Her voice turned colder, more resolute. "Then we push back harder. We've given him too much room already."

They worked into the night, their focus unbroken as plans began to take shape. Notes covered the maps sprawled across the table, forming connections between names and places, marking the cracks they would expose in Caldwell's ambitions. The quiet murmurs of their conversation carried an urgency that filled the room, a reminder of how much was at stake.

When Lucas stood to leave, he gathered the remaining papers. Sierra's hand reached out, her grip steady as she stopped him for a moment. "Thank you for being here, Lucas," she said. "I needed this."

Lucas nodded, meeting her gaze. "We're in this together, Sierra. We won't let him win."

Outside, the stars spread across the desert sky, their cold light stretching over the quiet landscape. The air carried a stillness that felt fragile, ready to shift with the decisions made inside the adobe walls. Lucas walked to his truck, his thoughts focused on the fight ahead.

Inside, Sierra returned to the table. Her gaze moved over the maps and notes, taking in the plans they had built. Each name and mark represented resistance, a refusal to surrender what made Redstone whole. Whatever Caldwell thought he could take, Sierra would ensure he faced something far stronger than he had anticipated.

Chapter 61

As Caldwell's sleek black car glided into the driveway, Ladawn watched from the window, her pulse quickening with every inch it crept closer. The setting sun stretched long shadows across the cracked pavement, its fading light catching the edges of the bakery's weathered sign in the distance. Inside, the faint laughter of her children drifted from the kitchen, their carefree joy a sharp contrast to the storm she could feel gathering.

She stepped into the hallway, her voice steady but firm. "Upstairs, kids. Time to get ready for bed."

There was a brief pause, followed by the sound of small feet pattering up the staircase. Their voices rose in a playful argument over whose turn it was to brush their teeth first, and Ladawn allowed herself a fleeting moment of comfort. They trusted her implicitly. She needed to be strong enough to protect that trust.

With a steadying breath, Ladawn opened the front door.

Hiram Caldwell stood on the porch, his tailored suit immaculate even in the fading light. The faint scent of his cologne mixed with the evening breeze. His shark's smile stretched across his face, his sharp eyes scanning her with an unnerving precision—reading her posture, her exhaustion, the tremor she tried to conceal in her fingers.

"Good evening, Ladawn," he said smoothly, taking a single step closer to the threshold.

Ladawn planted herself firmly in the doorway, her hand gripping the frame. "What do you want, Hiram?" she asked, her tone sharp but controlled.

Caldwell's smile didn't falter, but his gaze sharpened, betraying the edge beneath his polished demeanor. "Straight to business. I like that." He gestured lazily toward the bakery sign in the distance, its faded paint barely visible through the encroaching dusk. "I'm here to make you an offer—one I think you'll find... compelling."

"I'm not interested," Ladawn said, her voice clipped.

"Don't be so quick to decide." Caldwell reached into his coat pocket and produced a crisp envelope, its pristine edges catching the last light of the day. He held it out to her, tilting it slightly as if to make the contents within seem heavier. "One hundred and fifty percent of your bakery's appraised value. Cash. A life-changing sum."

Ladawn's eyes flicked to the envelope, the pristine white standing out against Caldwell's dark suit. For a moment, uncertainty rippled across her face, but she steadied herself, her fingers gripping the doorframe harder.

"This bakery isn't just numbers on a ledger, Hiram. It's my family's history. It's where this community gathers. You can't buy that."

Caldwell tilted his head, the smile thinning into something harder. "Ladawn, be practical. Think about your children. This is college funds, opportunities, security—all handed to you with no strings attached. Isn't that worth more than sentimentality?"

Ladawn straightened her back. "Security isn't just a bank account balance. It's showing my children what matters—what has real value. This bakery is part of that. It's heritage, Hiram. It's purpose."

Caldwell's jaw tightened, his polished mask slipping just enough to reveal irritation beneath. "You're letting nostalgia cloud your judgment. Sentimentality won't save you when things start falling apart. You don't want to put yourself in a position where you regret this."

The air between them seemed to hum with the tension, the streetlights buzzing faintly in the background. Ladawn's breath slowed, her eyes narrowing. "Is that a threat?"

Caldwell's tone remained measured, but his words carried a deliberate weight. "It's reality. This isn't just about you, Ladawn. This is about what happens when people refuse to adapt. When the dust settles, I hope you'll remember that I gave you a choice."

He stepped back from the doorway, his shoes clicking against the wooden porch with precision. "I offered you an out," he said, his voice almost regretful. "Remember that."

He glanced at her once more, his shadow stretching long and angular under the porch light, before turning and walking to his car. The engine roared to life, breaking the silence of the evening as he pulled away, the taillights glowing like embers in the encroaching dark.

Ladawn shut the door, leaning against it as her breath escaped in slow, measured increments. Her gaze drifted to the mantel, where a framed photo of her children stood in the soft glow of the living room lamp. Their faces beamed with joy, their small hands clutching cookies they had helped her bake.

Chapter 62

HIRAM SAT on the edge of the ridge, his coat snapping against him in the relentless wind. Below, Redstone sprawled out in scattered lights, its stillness deceptive. From here, it looked whole, untouched by the fractures running beneath its surface. The horizon stretched endlessly, the bruised sky above streaked with deep purples and the last molten traces of sunlight retreating behind distant mesas. The day was dying, and so, it felt, was the clarity Hiram had once relied on.

The briefcase sat beside him, its polished leather catching the dim light. Inside were the artifacts of his ambition—contracts, schematics, spreadsheets—all meticulously arranged to reflect control and purpose. But their precision mocked him now, reminders of how far the project had spun beyond his grasp. Every line was a promise, every signature a weight pressing against his chest.

Behind him, Mika's quiet footsteps approached, steady against the gravel path. There was a presence about the elder that seemed to absorb the chaos around him, an unshakable calm that contrasted sharply with the storm unraveling inside Hiram. Mika stopped a few paces away, his outline framed by the darkening sky.

"You've felt it, haven't you?" Mika's voice carried, low and deliberate, just loud enough to reach Hiram over the wind. "The land doesn't let go easily. You can't ignore it, no matter how hard you try."

Hiram didn't turn. He stared down at the lights of Redstone, his jaw tight, his breath uneven. "I know I've pushed too far," he said finally, his words clipped. "Every day, I tell myself to move forward, to stick to the plan. But it's different now. I stood in that valley, Mika. I felt something there. And now... I can't unfeel it."

Mika stepped closer, his voice gaining a sharper edge. "What you felt wasn't a warning, Hiram. It was an invitation. But that invitation comes with responsibility. The ley lines, the energy, the stories—they aren't yours to reshape. If you keep pushing forward without listening, without understanding, do you know what will happen?"

Hiram turned to face him, his eyes raw with exhaustion and something closer to fear. "You think I don't already feel the cracks? I can't stop this, Mika. If I walk away, everything falls apart. My investors, my board—they'll destroy me. They'll bury me."

"And if you keep going?" Mika's tone softened, but the weight of his words didn't. "What will you be left with? Broken land, broken people, broken promises. What good is success if it leaves nothing worth having?"

The wind shifted, scattering dust across the ridge. Hiram dragged a hand over his face, his fingers trembling as he pressed them against his forehead. "I don't know how to fix this," he admitted, his voice fraying. "This was supposed to be simple. Just a project. Just another deal."

"It was never just a project," Mika said. "Not to the people here. Not to the land itself."

Hiram sank onto the rocky ground, his knees drawn up as he stared out at the expanse below. The quiet that followed wasn't peaceful; it was the stillness before a collapse. "If I stop now, it's over. All of it."

"Maybe," Mika said, stepping closer. "But stopping is the only way to begin something new. This isn't about undoing the damage you've done—it's about choosing not to do more. You have to stop thinking like a businessman, Hiram, and start thinking like a guardian."

Hiram let the words hang in the air, their weight undeniable. He closed his eyes, the memory of the valley flooding back—the stillness, the hum beneath the earth, the sense of something ancient and alive pressing against his chest. He had dismissed it at first, chalked it up to nerves, to fatigue. But now, it felt undeniable.

"Do you really believe I can fix this?" he asked, his voice barely audible.

Mika crouched beside him, his hand resting firmly on Hiram's shoulder. "You can try. But it starts with listening. The land isn't silent, Hiram. It's telling you what it needs. You just have to be willing to hear it."

Hiram opened his eyes, the ridge and the lights below coming back into focus. The scattered glow of Redstone seemed different now—not just a town but a fragile thread connecting everything he had worked for and everything he had broken. The wind picked up again, scattering loose papers from the briefcase, their pristine lines crumpling as they tumbled across the ground.

"It's not too late," Mika said. "But you have to act now."

Hiram nodded faintly, though his gaze remained fixed on the horizon. The decision loomed like a shadow, and the man who had once thrived in the certainty of risk now found himself unmoored.

Neither man spoke as the stars began to pierce the deepening sky, their quiet emergence a silent reminder that the world was watching, waiting for him to choose.

Chapter 63

THE GRAVEL LOT behind Ladawn's bakery was a void of shadows, the faint hum of streetlights doing little to push back the dark. Ladawn killed the engine of her car, the dashboard clock glaring *4:30 AM* like a warning. Her hands lingered on the wheel, the ache of exhaustion settling in her chest. With Tara unavailable, the day loomed before her, every chore stretching endlessly. The silence felt heavier than usual, as though the world itself was holding its breath.

Stepping out of the car, the chill of the desert air bit at her skin. The wind carried an eerie stillness, stirring dust and making the bakery's faint silhouette flicker in the pale glow of the backdoor light. That bulb, perpetually flickering, now seemed to sputter with purpose, as though it too felt the tension in the air.

She approached the door, her keys jangling louder than they should have in the silence. But the lock didn't resist. The door stood slightly ajar, a thin sliver of yellow light spilling out onto the concrete. Ladawn froze, unease prickling at the edges of her thoughts.

"Maybe I forgot to lock it," she whispered to herself, but the words carried no conviction. She pushed the door open, her steps hesitant as the hinges creaked in protest.

"Hello?" she called, her voice thin against the quiet. No answer came. She stepped inside, the faint scent of smoke prickling her nose. The door swung shut behind her, the sound sharp and final.

"Is anyone there?" she called again, louder this time, her voice trembling.

Her footsteps echoed as she made her way toward the front of the store. Her gaze darted to the walls, the shadows twisting and contorting with each step. At the threshold to the front room, she froze. The acrid smell of smoke thickened, and the crunch of glass beneath her foot shattered the stillness. She reached for the light switch, her fingers fumbling against the wall.

The scene illuminated in the fluorescent glow stole her breath. The bakery was in ruins. Display cases lay shattered, their glass shards catching the light like jagged stars. Tables were overturned, chairs broken and strewn about as though a storm had torn through. The ley line map that had hung above the counter—a centerpiece of history and pride—was torn from its frame, crumpled and discarded among the wreckage.

"No," Ladawn whispered, her hands trembling. She took a shaky step forward, glass crunching beneath her shoes. "Who... who would do this?"

A sharp shove from behind sent her sprawling forward, her hip slamming against the counter. The impact shot pain through her side, leaving her gasping. She tried to turn, but another blow landed hard against her back, driving her to the ground.

"You should've stayed out of it," a woman's voice hissed behind her.

The world tilted as Ladawn tried to push herself up, her hand slipping on shards of glass. "Why?" she gasped, her voice cracking. "Why would you...?"

A final strike sent her head crashing against the corner of a heavy mixer. The impact rippled through her skull, pain blooming and then fading as darkness crept in. Her body slumped to the floor, her vision narrowing to a hazy view of the shattered bakery around her.

Before unconsciousness claimed her, she saw the broken map, its torn edges fluttering in the breeze from the open door. She thought of her children, their laughter only hours ago. "I just wanted to..." she tried to say, but the words dissolved into the void.

———

By the time the sun began to rise, the bakery had drawn a crowd. Police tape fluttered in the early morning wind, cordoning off what was now a crime scene. Smoke lingered faintly in the air, carrying the sharp reminder of something broken beyond repair. The usual scent of bread and cinnamon was gone, replaced with burnt remnants and cold ash.

Veronica Miller stepped out of her car, the sharp click of her heels cutting through the murmurs of the crowd. Her coat billowed in the breeze as she approached the police barricade, her eyes scanning the destruction inside. Broken glass and splintered wood littered the floor. The space that had once buzzed with warmth now exuded only tension.

She ducked under the tape, ignoring the murmurs of protest from an officer. Chief Vega stood near the entrance, his face lined with exhaustion as he spoke to one of his team. Veronica moved closer, her phone buzzing in her hand.

"What's the status?" she demanded, her voice low and clipped.

Vega glanced at her, his jaw tightening. "Ladawn's in the hospital. Critical condition. We don't know if she'll make it."

Veronica didn't flinch, but her grip on her phone tightened. She stepped away, answering the buzzing call with a terse, "This has gone too far. We need to contain it—immediately." She ended the call without waiting for a reply.

Outside, Mayor Helen Jones arrived, her presence commanding

as she threaded through the gathered crowd. She raised her hands to quiet the whispers.

"This is not random vandalism," Helen said, her voice cutting through the air. "This is a message. Caldwell's plans have pushed us to a breaking point, but we will not break. Redstone will not be silenced, and we will not back down."

The crowd murmured, anger simmering just beneath the surface. "What about justice?" a voice called out. "When will we see action?"

Chief Vega stepped forward, his voice gravelly and firm. "We're working on it. But standing here shouting won't help Ladawn or this town. Go home. Let us do our job."

The tension didn't dissipate, but the crowd began to thin, their frustration turning inward. Veronica lingered near the scene, her gaze fixed on the shattered bakery window. The damage was done—irreversible.

———

At the Redstone Inn, Sierra sat across from Elana, their breakfast forgotten. Sierra's voice shook as she recounted the scene. "The bakery's gone, Elana. Ladawn's barely hanging on. We've been so caught up in our own battles that we let this happen."

Elana's jaw tightened, her voice steady. "No more excuses, Sierra. No more divisions. Caldwell's tearing this town apart, and we've been too blind to stop it."

Sierra nodded, her throat tightening with emotion. "It's time. We fight together. No more hesitation."

Elana leaned forward. "Then let's make sure this fight counts."

Chapter 64

THE EVENING AIR HUMMED with the tension of unspoken thoughts as Redstone's Solstice Festival unfolded under the glow of lanterns strung between weathered poles. The laughter of children and the sound of a distant guitar created a fragile backdrop to the fractured mood. Beneath the surface of celebration, something darker lingered, a pulse of unease that Sierra felt in the cool wind brushing her face.

She stood at the edge of the festival grounds with Lucas, Tara, Elana, and a small knot of others. The quiet murmurs of their conversation set them apart from the crowd. Beyond the festival lights, the cliffs rose crimson and stark against a bruised sky, their jagged edges sharp as the choices before them.

Lucas adjusted his glasses, his fingers gripping the edges of his notebook. The detachment he once carried, the calm of a man tethered to science, had vanished. "Caldwell's ambitions have taken root, and this town is suffering for it," he said, his voice low but urgent. "This isn't just about greed. It's about erasing everything that gives Redstone its meaning."

Sierra crossed her arms, her gaze fixed on the distant lights of the festival. "He's not just taking the land," she said, her voice taut with anger. "He's severing the ley lines—cutting through our stories, our history, everything that binds us here. If we let him, he'll hollow this place until there's nothing left."

Elana leaned against a nearby post, her face unreadable but her presence weighted with purpose. "We've been talking about action for weeks," she said. "But Ladawn's bakery—what happened there—shows that Caldwell isn't waiting anymore. Why should we?"

Tara's jaw tightened. "We can't waste time debating what to do next. Caldwell and his people are already two steps ahead, and we're still picking up the pieces."

Lucas nodded. "Then we stop picking up pieces. We build something they can't break." He turned to Sierra, his voice steady. "We have to go public, loud and visible. Caldwell thrives on control, on keeping people in the dark. We drag his plans into the light and make sure everyone sees what he's doing—to the ley lines, to Redstone, to Ladawn."

Sierra looked at him, the fire in her chest barely contained. "It's time to fight back," she said. "Not just with words, but with action that can't be ignored."

A small group of festival-goers had edged closer, their curiosity piqued. One man, younger than Sierra but with lines of exhaustion etched into his face, stepped forward. "What are you asking us to do?" he asked, his voice uncertain.

Sierra stepped forward, her voice clear and sharp as glass. "I'm asking you to stand up. To organize, to share your stories, to make sure no one can look away. We need to tell the world what Caldwell is doing—through social media, through the press, through every conversation we have. This isn't just a protest. This is a fight for the soul of Redstone."

Lucas's calm voice followed hers, grounding the moment. "We'll need coordination. Volunteers who can manage logistics, craft messaging, and ensure our efforts stay unified. This isn't just about one approach. It's about a movement."

The group exchanged glances, the weight of the moment settling in. Tara stepped forward, her tone resolute. "We'll also need people watching Caldwell's team. If they make a move, we need to know about it—before it's too late."

Elana added, her voice steady but intense, "This has to be relentless. Every day, every hour, we make noise. Caldwell needs to feel the pressure until he has no choice but to stop."

From the growing circle, a woman with gray streaks in her hair stepped closer. Her voice cut through the gathering. "And if he doesn't stop? What then?"

Sierra turned to her, her gaze unwavering. "Then we don't stop either. If they push, we push harder. If they dig, we block their path. This is our home. We defend it with everything we have."

The group's murmurs grew louder, their resolve hardening as they began to exchange ideas. Names and numbers were shared, plans taking shape in a flurry of whispered determination. Someone suggested creating banners; another volunteered to lead a social media campaign. Sierra moved through the gathering, offering quiet encouragement, her hands brushing shoulders, her voice steady as she reminded them of what they stood to protect.

Nearby, Lucas jotted notes into his notebook, his focus razor-sharp as he captured the momentum. Elana pulled Tara aside, speaking in urgent tones about who they could reach out to for support. The air around them buzzed with a sense of inevitability, a rising tide that couldn't be turned back.

Sierra paused for a moment, her gaze lifting to the cliffs beyond the festival. The distant music from the main square still lingered, faint and dissonant against the energy crackling around her. The Solstice Festival had always been about celebration, about renewal and light. But tonight, its warmth felt like a fragile shell over the urgency of their cause.

"We start now," Sierra said aloud, her voice carrying over the murmurs. "Not tomorrow. Not next week. Right now."

Lucas stepped to her side, his tone firm. "We make our voices impossible to ignore. Together."

The group dispersed into action, their energy palpable. Sierra watched them go, the fire inside her burning brighter with each passing second. She turned to Lucas, her words quiet but unshakable. "No matter what happens next, we don't back down."

Lucas met her gaze, his expression resolute. "No turning back."

As the festival lights flickered in the distance, the cliffs loomed above them, their silent presence a reminder of all they were fighting for. The ley lines hummed faintly beneath their feet, steady and unbroken, as though waiting for the battle to come.

Chapter 65

THE WAREHOUSE WAS DIM, the pale moonlight threading through cracked windows and casting jagged patterns across the concrete floor. Dust swirled in the air, catching the faint glow. Around a scarred wooden table, Tara, Tom, Ashley, Sarah, and Derek gathered, the silence between them taut. Maps and sketches lay scattered across the surface, but all eyes kept flicking to the small wooden hawk at the center. Its carved wings, outstretched as if bracing for flight, seemed to hold the room's unspoken tension.

Tara paced, her boots scuffing against the floor. She gripped the back of a chair, her knuckles pale against the worn wood. "Ladawn's bakery wasn't just vandalized," she said, her voice tight. "It was a warning. Caldwell and his people are telling us to back off, but we can't. If we let them keep tearing up this land, there won't be anything left to save."

Tom stood with one hand resting on the edge of the table, his gaze fixed on the hawk. "We've tried everything—meetings, protests. They don't care. Caldwell's already sent in more machines, more guards. They're daring us to do something."

Ashley shifted in her chair, her tone calm but sharp. "So, we do something. If those machines stop working, Caldwell loses money. That's the only language he speaks."

Sarah leaned against the wall near the window, her face half-lit by moonlight. "Back home, they tore up sacred land while we begged them to stop. The only thing that worked was making sure their equipment couldn't run. They couldn't finish what they started."

Derek sat on an overturned crate, his arms resting on his knees. "If we sabotage the machines, we do it clean. No one gets hurt—not us, not the workers. We send a message, not an invitation for retaliation."

Tara stopped pacing and faced Tom. "You've lived here longer than any of us. Is this the right move?"

Tom ran a thumb over the edge of the hawk's wing, his face lined with thought. "Caldwell doesn't care about our voices, Tara. He cares about profits and deadlines. If we hit him where it hurts, he'll feel it. But if we do this, there's no going back."

The group exchanged glances, their shared hesitation giving way to resolve. Ashley stood, her boots crunching on the floor. "We do it smart. We disable the machines, slow them down, make them rethink their timeline. No casualties, no destruction. Just disruption."

Sarah's voice cut through the gathering tension. "This only works if we're together. If one of us hesitates, it all falls apart. Are we in this?"

Tara's fingers closed around the wooden hawk. She traced its carved feathers, the familiar grooves steadying her. "We do this. No reckless moves. No one gets hurt. But Caldwell has to know we're not standing aside anymore."

Derek nodded, his voice measured. "We'll need schedules, blueprints, and someone watching their movements. We can't afford mistakes."

Tom placed a firm hand on Tara's shoulder. "We're with you. We'll make it count."

The group leaned over the table, their shadows merging under the flickering moonlight. They spoke in low, urgent tones, marking maps and drafting plans. Outside, the wind pressed against the warehouse, carrying the promise of a storm. The wooden hawk remained at the center, its wings spread, its carved eyes unblinking, as if watching the leap they were about to take.

Chapter 66

LUCAS STOOD on the outskirts of the town square, arms crossed over his chest, watching the gathering unfold. The night air was thick with anticipation, the distant hum of drums and flutes rising into something more—a pulse, a current that seemed to ripple through the earth beneath his boots.

At the center of the square, Sierra stepped forward. Her silhouette was etched sharply against the glow of lantern light, her movements fluid and purposeful. She raised her arms, her fingers tracing invisible patterns in the air, her body swaying in slow, deliberate circles. The music responded to her, deepening, resonating, as if drawn to her presence.

The townspeople edged closer, hesitant at first. Mothers guided wide-eyed children forward, elderly couples clasped hands tightly, and younger townsfolk lingered at the fringes. One by one, they stepped into the circle, feet tapping cautiously against the dusty ground. But the rhythm took hold. Caution gave way to confidence, and soon they were moving with joy, their motions synchronized with the music's steady rise.

Lucas felt it too—a faint vibration at the edge of his consciousness, a hum that didn't come from his instruments but from somewhere deeper, somewhere beyond measurement or logic. It unsettled him. His instinct was to retreat, to reduce this feeling to data points and analysis. But he stayed rooted to the spot.

His eyes found Sierra's across the crowd. Her gaze was steady, calm yet intense, pulling him forward without a word. Around her, the ley lines seemed to hum in harmony with the rising energy of the people.

"Lucas," a voice said beside him. It was Elana. She stood nearby, her face illuminated by flickering lantern light, her eyes reflecting a quiet understanding. "You feel it, don't you?"

He swallowed hard, his throat dry. "I don't know what I feel, Elana. But it's... it's real."

She smiled faintly, her voice gentle. "Then don't fight it. Go to her."

Lucas hesitated for a moment longer, then took a breath and stepped forward. His feet felt heavy, his movements stiff and awkward as he crossed into the circle. But the music pulled him onward, and Sierra's smile—soft, patient—anchored him.

When he reached her, she extended a hand. The world seemed to still. The music softened, the crowd faded, and even the faint hum of the ley lines quieted. Lucas hesitated, then took her hand.

They began to move together, first tentatively, then with growing confidence. Each step seemed to unravel a knot inside him, loosening the tight threads of doubt and skepticism. He wasn't thinking about measurements or charts, wasn't dissecting the ley lines' energy. He was simply... there. Present. Grounded in the moment.

Elana joined them moments later, her hand brushing briefly against Lucas's before she was swept into the dance by an older woman with silver hair and bright eyes. The three of them—Sierra, Lucas, and Elana—moved together, carried by the pulse of the music and the shared rhythm of the crowd.

For Lucas, it was unlike anything he had ever experienced. The threads of science, belief, and humanity wove together into something transcendent, something whole. In that fleeting moment, Lucas understood—not with data or theories, but with his heart— what Sierra had been trying to show him all along.

The ley lines weren't just magnetic anomalies or energy pathways plotted on a map. They were connection. And tonight, Lucas felt tethered—not just to Sierra, not just to Elana, but to the very soul of Redstone.

When the dance finally slowed and the music faded into the stillness of the night, Lucas turned to Sierra. She was watching him, her eyes filled with quiet knowing.

"And with that," she said, "you have taken your [next, final, irreversible?] step.

He let out a breath he hadn't realized he'd been holding. "Thank you," he said.

Chapter 67

THE WALLS of the Jenkins ranch house held the day's heat, the air inside thick despite the steady hum of an old ceiling fan. Caldwell stood near the table, his phone pressed tightly to his ear. Outside, the desert stretched out in endless, golden stillness, interrupted only by faint gusts of wind kicking up loose dust.

"Double the security," he said, his tone sharp and clipped. "Every entrance and exit. Drones in the air by tonight. No gaps. No excuses." He ended the call abruptly, lowering the phone as his attention returned to the digital map on the table. The glowing lines of security perimeters and access routes seemed to mock him with their neatness. He stared at them for a moment longer before speaking.

"They're planning protests," he said, his voice quieter now but edged with frustration. "Chanting, prayers, stacking rocks—like any of it will stop bulldozers." He rubbed his temples, his fingers pressing hard against the skin as if trying to banish the creeping pressure in his head. "Construction starts next week. We can't afford delays."

The legal team exchanged uneasy glances. Lisa Chen flipped through her notebook, the scratch of her pen breaking the silence. "We've prepared counters for any injunctions," she said, her words precise and quick. "Economic benefits, job creation, infrastructure improvements—it's all solid."

Caldwell nodded once, though his focus remained fixed on the map. His fingers traced one of the marked perimeters, moving slowly as though trying to steady himself. "Good. We'll issue a press release. Make it about cultural preservation or a scholarship program. We need to show we're invested."

Tomás Herrera leaned back in his chair, his arms crossed. His hesitation showed in the tightness of his posture. "Hiram, we're already pushing the locals. If we ramp up security—"

"We're not escalating," Caldwell interrupted. His voice cut through the room, sharp but controlled. "We're maintaining order. That's the point."

Near the window, Marla Jenkins stood apart from the others. She shifted slightly, her gaze fixed on the horizon beyond the glass. Her arms folded tightly across her chest, holding in an unease she couldn't shake. "What if they don't stop?" she asked, her voice measured but softer than the others'. "What if this turns violent?"

Caldwell turned toward her. His eyes met hers for a moment, and the weight of the question hung between them. "Then we deal with it," he said after a pause, though his voice lacked its usual conviction. "But we're not there yet. We can still manage this."

Lisa tapped her pen lightly against her notepad, the faint rhythm underscoring the tension. Tomás stayed silent, his attention fixed on the table. Marla shifted her focus back to the window, her reflection faint in the glass.

"I'll keep watching the locals," she said, her tone steady but detached. "If anything changes, I'll let you know."

"Good," Caldwell replied, though the word carried no satisfaction. He held her gaze for a moment longer before she turned away.

Marla's movements toward the door were deliberate. Her hand brushed the edge of the window frame, but she didn't linger. Her thoughts churned as she walked, the memory of the bakery haunting her with every step. She could still see the shattered glass, still feel the mixer's cold metal edge under Ladawn's hand before she fell. Veronica had called it necessary—decisive—but now Marla wasn't so sure. She didn't know what Caldwell would do if he found out, and the thought twisted in her chest.

Behind her, Caldwell remained by the table, his hands gripping its edge. The glow of the map filled the room, but it no longer offered clarity. The boundaries and routes looked fragile now, like barriers that could crumble at the first push.

Lisa gathered her notes quickly, her hands moving with precision but not confidence. Tomás rose slowly, his hesitation clear as he lingered near the door before stepping into the hallway. Marla didn't look back at either of them, her pace measured as she exited the room.

Caldwell stayed where he was, staring down at the map. His hands pressed harder into the table, his knuckles pale under the strain. The lines on the map blurred slightly, but he didn't blink, didn't move. The silence of the room pressed in around him.

The faint sound of the door clicking shut behind Marla pulled his focus briefly. Her presence lingered in his mind, not as a comfort but as a question. Something about her hesitation unsettled him, though he couldn't pinpoint why.

Outside, the desert air cooled as the sun dipped lower, staining the horizon in deep orange and muted purple. The faint outline of the town below flickered with scattered lights, a fragile mirror of the order Caldwell was trying to maintain. He stood motionless as the edges of his vision darkened with fatigue, and the sense that something irreparable had already begun to slip from his grasp.

Chapter 68

THE MORNING SUN FILTERED through the cracked walls of the abandoned shed, painting streaks of gold across the concrete floor. Dust hung in the air, catching the light like suspended time. Five figures stood in a loose circle, their faces lined with exhaustion. The air inside the shed felt heavy, the faint hum of distant construction equipment vibrating through the ground.

Derek entered last, pulling the door shut behind him with a sharp scrape. He guided a woman forward, her stiff posture betraying unease. "This is Jenna," he said, his tone brisk. "She works for Vega."

The group exchanged wary glances. Tara, standing near the door, tightened her arms across her chest. Ashley paused mid-motion, her fingers hovering over the straps of her heavy backpack. Jenna offered a faint nod, clutching a crumpled paper that was smudged with ink and sweat.

"She's got the details," Derek added. His words hung in the air, unanswered.

Tom Young adjusted his faded cap, the brim shadowing his face. "Let's hear them," he said, his voice gruff but steady.

Jenna unfolded the paper with trembling hands, her voice barely rising above the tension in the room. "The equipment's leaving the depot in under an hour. If we intercept it on the access road, we can stall them before they reach the site. It's a narrow window, but it's possible."

Ashley straightened, her hands steadying as she pulled the straps of her backpack tight. "We'll need the march to keep their attention on town," she said, her words measured. "But after that, we move. This isn't about slogans anymore. This is about stopping those machines."

Derek paced near the door, the soles of his boots scuffing the concrete. "Stopping them isn't enough," he said, his tone sharp. "They'll regroup and start again tomorrow. Those machines need to be… out of play."

Tom's head lifted abruptly, his jaw tightening. "You're talking about sabotage."

Derek stopped pacing and turned to him. "I'm talking about making a statement. If we don't act, this keeps happening."

Tom exhaled, his eyes flicking toward the faint light breaking through the walls. "That's jail time, Derek. Serious jail time."

Tara shifted uncomfortably, her voice low and unsteady. "But if we back out now, everything we've done—everything we've risked—was for nothing."

Ashley's gaze swept the group, her shoulders squared. "If it feels wrong, we stop. No arguments. No reckless moves."

The group fell silent, the tension thickening. Outside, the hum of Caldwell's machinery grew louder, each vibration a reminder of what they faced. Jenna's voice broke the quiet, trembling but determined. "I can't stand by and let them tear this place apart. I'm in."

Tom adjusted his cap again, his hand lingering on the brim. "This isn't about making headlines. It's about buying time. Enough time for people to see what's happening."

Tara inhaled sharply, her words faltering. "Alright. But let's be careful."

Ashley slung her backpack over her shoulders, her fingers curling into fists. "We stay focused. We stay calm. And we stay together."

The morning sun grew brighter, slicing through the cracks in the shed walls and illuminating the group's faces. Their expressions carried the weight of their decision—fear, resolve, and the quiet understanding that nothing would be the same after today.

No one spoke as they filed out of the shed, their steps muffled by the sandy ground. The sound of the distant machinery droned on, relentless and unmoved, as if daring them to act.

Chapter 69

THE FIRST RAYS OF DAWN painted the horizon in streaks of amber and red, casting long shadows across the square where the people of Redstone gathered. The sharp scent of sagebrush mingled with the earthy warmth of sunlit rock, and the rustle of banners filled the air. Sierra tightened her grip on the wooden pole of a hand-painted sign. Around her, the low hum of voices built steadily, fueled by quiet determination.

Elana moved through the crowd, her movements purposeful. She pressed a sign into Sierra's hands without a word, their shared resolve unspoken but undeniable. "Glad you're here," Sierra said, her voice steady despite the tension building inside her.

Elana's jaw tightened, her knuckles white against her own sign. "There's no other place I could be. Today, Caldwell learns what Redstone stands for."

Lucas stood nearby, shifting a banner into place. His hands stilled as he turned to Sierra. "Will this be enough?" he asked, his words deliberate, as though weighing each one.

"It has to be," Sierra replied. Her focus moved over the gathering crowd, taking in every detail—the ranchers in weathered boots, shopkeepers in flour-dusted aprons, the wide-eyed children darting between clusters of marchers. "Caldwell needs to see this land isn't just dirt to dig up. It's alive, and it's ours to protect."

The crowd thickened, voices rising as more people joined. Tourists with cameras slung over their shoulders lingered at the edges, drawn by the spectacle. Chief Martin Vega arrived, his uniform crisp against the desert backdrop. He approached Sierra and Lucas, offering a nod that carried more than formality. It was an acknowledgment of shared purpose.

Sierra turned toward him. "We're glad you're here."

"I should've been here sooner," Vega said. His voice carried a quiet gravity that seemed to ripple through the nearby marchers.

The makeshift stage at the center of the square waited, a simple platform framed by banners snapping in the wind. Sierra climbed onto it with measured steps. The murmurs faded into silence as she faced the crowd. Her voice carried over the assembly, clear and unwavering. "We stand here today not for ourselves, but for every generation that came before us and every one that will follow."

She paused, scanning the crowd. She didn't see strangers or skeptics—she saw neighbors, friends, and the shared history that tied them all to this place. "The ley lines beneath our feet are not just myths or stories. They are the memory of this land, a connection to our ancestors, and a promise to those who come after us. To destroy them is to destroy the very spirit of Redstone."

Lucas stepped up beside her, the crowd shifting as they turned their attention to him. His movements were precise, but his voice held a new intensity. "This isn't just about preserving the past. The ley lines are tangible. They are energy, connecting the physical and the spiritual. If we let them be destroyed, we lose something we will never recover."

A voice called out from the crowd, sharp and questioning. "What if Caldwell ignores us? What if this doesn't work?"

Lucas met the question head-on. "Then we stay louder. We make it impossible for him to dismiss us. The strength of this town is in its people, in the stories we carry and the actions we take."

Vega stepped forward, his presence grounding. "As your chief, my oath is to protect this town and its people. But this fight is personal. This land is in my blood, just as it's in yours. My abuelo taught me that protection isn't just about laws—it's about heart. And I promise you, I'll give everything I have to defend what matters."

The crowd erupted into applause, a wave of sound that carried through the square. Sierra descended from the platform, Lucas and Elana following close behind. They wove through the marchers, stopping to listen to quiet concerns and share words of reassurance.

Elana leaned toward Sierra, her voice barely audible over the swell of voices. "We need to be ready for Caldwell's response. He won't let this go unanswered."

Sierra's response was calm but firm. "Then we'll face it head-on. Together."

The morning sun climbed higher, casting sharp shadows across the square. The marchers moved with a shared rhythm, their banners rising and falling in unison. Sierra paused for a moment, looking out over the crowd. This wasn't just resistance—it was a declaration, a living reminder that Redstone would not be silenced.

Chapter 70

NOT FAR FROM THE SQUARE, Derek's team moved in near silence, slipping through backstreets and shadowed alleys. The chants and music provided a cover, masking their purposeful steps. The distant hum of tambourines and guitars faded as they neared the construction site. When they reached the chain-link fence, the towering machinery loomed before them, inert but menacing. Excavators and bulldozers stood still under the harsh glow of floodlights, a stark reminder of what they fought to stop.

In the square, the crowd had begun to march. Banners fluttered above the procession, their slogans bold against the fading light. The parade wound its way through Redstone, past old markets and shuttered shops. Vendors paused their work, shouting encouragement as the marchers passed. Children darted along the edges of the procession, their laughter a sharp counterpoint to the determined chants.

At the edge of the construction site, Sierra knelt, her fingers sifting through the dry earth. The younger marchers gathered near her, their faces lit with curiosity and reverence. She let the soil fall from her hand, scattering back to the ground. "This isn't just dirt," she said, her voice carrying over the faint hum of distant chants. "It holds our stories. Every step we take leaves something behind—memories, intentions, a mark of who we are. That's what we're here to protect."

Lucas stood nearby, watching her with a mixture of respect and uncertainty. The gesture was simple, almost ordinary, yet it carried a quiet power that reached past his instinct for logic and reason. As she spoke, the tension in his shoulders eased, replaced by a sensation he couldn't name—a connection he couldn't measure. He stepped closer, feeling the ground beneath his boots, as if the energy Sierra described might make itself known if he just stood still long enough.

The marchers approached the construction site, their voices lifting into songs that blended old verses with new refrains. The melodies threaded through the air, weaving a connection between past and present. Security guards in dark uniforms lined the perimeter, their stances rigid, their eyes scanning the crowd. Among them, one guard stepped forward, his hand brushing the baton at his side.

The crowd faltered, their steps slowing as the tension crackled. Lucas's pulse quickened, the potential for conflict a sharp undercurrent in the moment. Before anyone else could act, Elana moved forward, her expression calm but resolute.

"We're here to be heard," she said, her voice clear but not confrontational. "Nothing more." Her words hung in the charged silence, steady and unyielding. The guard hesitated, his hand lingering at his belt before he stepped back into line. The air between the crowd and the guards softened, the tension easing like a released breath.

Sierra joined the marchers again, her voice rising into the chorus of a song that flowed through the assembly. The music carried the weight of their heritage, its rhythm pulling the crowd into step. Lucas listened intently, the cadence of their voices a revelation. These weren't just songs; they were living artifacts, threads binding the people to their land and to each other.

As the singing swelled, Derek's team reached the far side of the construction site. They crouched low, working with quiet efficiency, their focus unwavering. The hum of distant chants and the vibrations of drums reached even here, an echo of the defiance surging through the town.

At the site's edge, Lucas glanced toward Sierra. She stood at the center of the crowd, her presence a still point in the movement around her. He couldn't explain it—didn't need to—but in that moment, he understood why she was the one leading this fight.

The songs rose higher, carrying into the night, their power undiminished. Around them, the protest pressed forward, and the line between resistance and transformation blurred.

Chapter 71

THE SUN BLAZED OVERHEAD as Tara moved through the swelling crowd of protesters, their chants rising and falling like waves against the dry desert air. The cracked asphalt shimmered, and the fenced outline of the construction site loomed ahead, framed by chain-link fences and watchful guards. Derek followed Tara, Sarah at his side, while Tom, Jenna, and Ashley wove through the crowd, their faces taut with focus.

The plan unspooled in Tara's mind—they were counting on timing, precision, and trust. Ashley leaned in close, her voice low but firm. "We're almost there. You ready?"

Tara nodded sharply, her eyes fixed on the guards near the fence line. "Stay close to me. Please."

The crowd swelled and surged, the noise peaking and ebbing like an unstable tide. Derek's voice cut through the chants, tight with purpose. "Alright, let's split!"

The six of them broke away, slipping into the narrow shadows of a maintenance road. The noise of the crowd fell away, replaced by the crunch of gravel beneath their boots and the distant, mechanical hum of construction equipment. The air was sharper here, charged with risk and purpose, Tara's every breath tight.

Derek and Sarah darted along the perimeter fence, their footsteps unable to muffle by the crunch of gravel. Derek gripped a crowbar in one hand, knuckles white, while Sarah carried a satchel of industrial glue and bolts close to her chest.

"They're staging everything here—forklifts, heavy loaders, fuel reserves," Derek, scanning the sprawl of equipment. "We hit the ignition points, they'll be dead in the water."

Sarah dropped to her knees beside a forklift, hands flying as she jammed glue into ignition keyholes and fuel latches. Her movements were sharp, efficient, but her breath came fast and shallow.

"Hurry, Sarah," Derek urged, glancing over his shoulder as a distant voice barked an order.

Sarah slapped the satchel shut. "Done."

Derek swung the crowbar, splitting a hydraulic line with a brutal crack. A geyser of fluid sprayed across the gravel, the sharp scent burning their noses.

From somewhere close, a radio squawked. Sarah froze.

"Move!" Derek barked, grabbing her arm and pulling her into the tangled shadows of stacked pallets.

They melted back into the maze of machinery, heartbeats hammering against the fragile silence around them.

Tom and Jenna sprinted toward a storage shelter, their breath sharp in the scorching noon air. Inside, wooden pallets leaned haphazardly, tarps hung limp like dead skin, and old blueprints lay scattered in the dust. Sunlight slashed through the corrugated walls, turning the shelter into a fragile house of cards.

"Dry as bone," Tom hissed, yanking back a tarp. "This'll burn fast and bright."

Jenna's hand trembled as she unscrewed the lighter fluid canister. "Tom, if we mess this up—"

Tom's voice cut her off, low and firm. "We do this clean, Jenna. No one gets hurt. Just enough fire to make them stop and look."

Jenna swallowed hard, then nodded. She crouched and poured lighter fluid across the pallets, the sharp chemical scent filling the tight space. Tom's hand fumbled in his pocket until he pulled out a matchbook. He struck one, the flame a flickering speck in the gloom.

"Ready?" he whispered.

She gave a sharp nod.

Tom dropped the match.

The fire erupted, leaping hungrily across the pallets. In seconds, the flames roared, devouring wood and blueprint paper with crackling fury. Smoke billowed, thick and choking.

"Go!" Tom barked, grabbing Jenna by the wrist. They bolted out of the shelter just as a guard's voice shouted nearby.

"Hey! Over there!"

Jenna's breath hitched as they ducked behind a pile of scrap metal. Alarms blared, and the sky above the shelter darkened with curling smoke.

Tom's voice was sharp. "Keep moving. Don't stop."

They plunged into the chaos, the crackle of fire and distant shouts echoing behind them.

Ashley yanked Tara through a narrow maintenance door into a stifling electrical control room. Shafts of noon sunlight stabbed through a cracked skylight, carving jagged lines across the walls tangled with conduits and blinking control panels. The smell of metal and ozone clung to the stale air.

"This is it," Ashley said, her voice tight, pointing to the thick conduit snaking along the far wall. "Cut this, and the whole site goes dark. They'll need hours to recover."

Tara's breath was sharp, her chest rising and falling as adrenaline clawed at her ribs. Ashley dropped to her knees, fingers moving fast, stripping wires with surgical precision.

A distant shout outside. Footsteps. The metallic clang of

something heavy hitting the ground.

"Hurry," Tara hissed.

Ashley's hands shook as she severed the final cable. Sparks spat, the lights flickered—and then everything plunged into a suffocating silence, broken only by the faint hum of the emergency bulb casting a crimson glow over them.

Ashley exhaled sharply. "We did it. Tara, we actu—"

But Tara was already moving. The space between them evaporated as she shoved Ashley against the cold metal wall, their breaths colliding in the tight gap. Tara's lips found Ashley's in a bruising, desperate kiss, raw and electrified.

Ashley gasped into her mouth, her back arching against the unyielding wall as Tara's hand slid up her side, fingers trembling as they brushed over the curve of her breast. The thin fabric of Ashley's shirt did little to dull the sharp jolt of sensation.

A faint voice crackled over a nearby radio. Footsteps echoed somewhere close.

Ashley pulled back, her breath ragged, eyes wide and searching Tara's face. "Tara… we—"

Tara pressed her forehead against Ashley's, her voice low, hoarse. "Not now. Move."

They broke apart, their bodies still humming with unspent energy, and slipped back out into the blinding desert light. Behind them, the electrical room sat dark and still, a heartbeat away from discovery.

One by one they rejoined the others at the main gate of the construction site, where the march had stopped. Derek clapped Tom on the shoulder, Sarah gave a brief nod, and Ashley lingered closely behind Tara, her expression unreadable.

In the distance, smoke billowed skyward, faint alarms howled, and distant shouts carried on the wind. Their work was far from invisible—but it was enough.

Tara scanned the group, her chest heaving from exertion and adrenaline. "We did what we came here to do. Now let's disappear before they realize just how deep we've cut."

One by one, they slipped back into the crowd, leaving chaos—and a fragile ember of hope—in their wake.

Chapter 72

THE CROWD'S SIGNS BOBBED in rhythm with their chants, voices rising and falling with defiant energy. Lucas stood at the edge of the gathering, Sierra beside him, her words clear and firm as she addressed the protesters. "This isn't a battle to destroy—it's one to protect. We're here to honor what's sacred."

Lucas shifted his attention to the crowd, the faces around him reflecting hope, determination, and the faint unease that came with facing the unknown. The protest had settled into a steady rhythm when distant shouts broke through the harmony. A plume of black smoke rose beyond the crowd, stark against the pale desert sky. Lucas tensed, his pulse quickening. "What's going on?" he asked.

Sierra's expression hardened. "Something's wrong." She moved quickly, weaving through the protesters with Lucas close behind. The growing tension in the crowd pressed against them, the chants faltering as confusion rippled outward.

When they reached the front, the scene struck Lucas like a physical blow. A bulldozer burned fiercely, flames consuming its metal frame, warping it into jagged shapes. Smoke poured from a storage building nearby, the acrid stench of scorched fuel and rubber filling the air. The once-quiet machinery now seemed alive with chaos.

"This isn't us," Sierra said. Her fists clenched at her sides as she surveyed the destruction.

A black SUV screeched to a halt at the edge of the site, its tires kicking up clouds of dust. Caldwell stepped out, his movements deliberate, his face etched with fury. He strode forward, his voice cutting through the murmurs of the crowd. "This is what your so-called 'peaceful protest' looks like!" he bellowed. "Violence. Destruction. Is this your message?"

Lucas stepped forward. "We had nothing to do with this, Caldwell. We're here to protect, not destroy."

Caldwell's sharp expression darkened further. "Convenient, isn't it, Mr. Grant? My equipment is in flames, and you claim innocence?"

Sierra took a step forward. "Look around, Caldwell. These are families, neighbors, people standing together for their home. This isn't their doing."

Caldwell turned to survey the crowd. His eyes narrowed, his silence louder than the accusations that had come before.

A new voice cut through the rising tension. "That's enough." Said Chief Martin Vega appeared His tone carried the authority that quieted the crowd, though it did little to soften Caldwell's glare. "We'll get to the truth," Vega said. "But right now, speculation helps no one."

Caldwell turned to him "Your 'truth' doesn't matter, Chief. I'll handle this my way."

"You'll handle it my way," Vega replied. "This is Redstone, Caldwell. Not one of your boardrooms."

Lucas caught Sierra's eye. The look on her face mirrored his own worry. They had worked so hard to frame their movement as peaceful Now the flames in front of them threatened to unravel everything.

Caldwell stepped closer to Lucas, lowering his voice so only a few could hear. "If I find out you or your people are behind this, there won't be enough left of your little movement to rebuild."

He turned on his heel and strode back to the SUV. The engine roared, and the vehicle sped away, leaving a haze of dust and anger in its wake.

The crowd began to break into smaller groups, their voices low as they speculated about what had happened. Sierra remained beside Lucas, her shoulders stiff. Her focus fixed was on the smoldering bulldozer.

"This changes everything," she said quietly.

"It does," Lucas agreed.

Lucas and Sierra stood at the thin line between the protestors and Caldwell's security team. The guards' stances were rigid, their hands hovering near radios and batons, eyes darting between the advancing crowd and the leaders standing in front. Behind Lucas and Sierra, the chants from the protesters faltered, replaced by a hum of nervous energy.

"Stay back!" Sierra shouted, turning to face the crowd. Her voice cut through the rising murmur. "Do not push forward! Hold your ground!"

On the other side, the guards tensed visibly. One reached for his belt, his fingers brushing the handle of a baton. Chief Vega stepped forward, his voice sharp and steady. "Stand down!" he said, directing the order toward the guard. "No one moves."

Lucas stepped to Sierra's side, raising both hands in a gesture of calm. His throat tightened as he noticed one of the guards speaking into a radio, his voice low but urgent. "Sierra, this is about to spiral."

A commotion broke out deeper in the crowd. Someone pushed forward, shouting angrily, and Sierra's eyes locked onto the movement. She darted toward the source, shoving her way past shoulders and waving signs. "Get back!" she yelled at the protestor.

"You're going to ruin this for all of us!".

The guard with the baton moved forward a half-step. Sierra turned to him, her voice cutting like a blade. "Don't even think about it. You swing that thing, and this explodes. No one wants that. Not you. Not us."

Vega placed himself directly in front of the guard, his expression unreadable but firm. "You heard her. Stand down."

Lucas barely heard. His attention was fixed on the guards. One of them had stepped forward, with his hand now gripping a stun gun. Before the guard could move, Lucas blocked the man's advance, stepping between him and the crowd. "Put that away."

———

Near the front of the crowd, a young man stood rigid, his fists shaking at his sides. His face twisted with frustration and despair, and he bent sharply, snatching a jagged rock from the ground. Before anyone could react, he hurled it. The rock spun through the air, landing just short of the security line with a dull thud in the dust.

The silence that followed was deafening. Protesters froze, guards stiffened, and for a single breath, the world seemed to teeter. The rock hadn't harmed anyone, but its meaning was unmistakable—a spark in dry tinder.

The security team reacted first. Batons came free from their holsters, the guards stepping forward with cold precision. Their line tightened, boots scraping against the gravel as they began to advance.

"No!" Sierra's voice tore through the air, sharp and desperate. She surged forward, her arms raised, the protestors parting just enough to let her through. "Stand down! This is peaceful!"

Lucas was beside her, his sign dropped in the dirt as he mirrored her motions, his voice rising to match hers. "Stop! Don't move forward!" The crowd behind them churned, caught between fear and defiance, their energy unsteady and growing dangerously chaotic.

Chief Vega pushed his way into the fray, his commanding presence cutting through the rising noise. "Hold your positions!" he barked at the guards, his hand shooting up like a signal flare. "This is a peaceful assembly. You do *not* engage."

But the crowd was already breaking. People at the edges began to scatter, their retreat creating more confusion as others surged forward in defiance. A scuffle broke out on the left flank where a protestor pushed back against an advancing guard. Sierra turned toward the disturbance, her breath catching when she saw a baton swing down toward an older man who had stumbled.

"Lucas!" she shouted, but she was already moving.

Her body collided with the man's just as the baton came down. The blow glanced off her raised arm, sending a jolt of pain through her shoulder, but she stayed upright. The older man scrambled back, his face pale, muttering apologies as Sierra placed herself firmly between him and the guard.

"Back off!" she yelled, her voice raw with urgency. The guard hesitated, his baton raised, his indecision flickering in the tightness of his grip. Around them, the crowd surged, pushing and pulling like a living tide.

"Sierra!" Lucas's voice drew her attention. She turned to see him trying to hold back a small group of protestors shoving against the security line. Behind them, Elana Rossi had climbed onto a concrete barrier, her phone raised high as she filmed the unfolding chaos. Her face was pale but focused, her free hand gripping the edge of the barrier for balance.

"Everyone, stop!" Sierra shouted, her voice cutting through the clamor. She pushed forward again, her injured arm hanging awkwardly as she raised her other hand. "Pull back now! Don't give them a reason to escalate!"

The young man who had thrown the rock was still near the front, his face pale as he realized what he'd done. Sierra reached him, her voice low but firm. "Leave. Now. Before this gets worse."

He nodded stiffly and backed away, disappearing into the crowd just as another protestor began shouting at the guards. The energy was slipping out of control, and Sierra felt it pressing down on her—every choice, every movement threatening to tip the fragile balance into outright chaos.

"Lucas!" she called, forcing her way back to his side. "We need to pull them out. Get them to retreat."

"I'm trying," Lucas replied, his voice tight with frustration. "They're not listening."

———

Caldwell stepped forward, his face a mask of cold fury as he pointed directly at Lucas. "Get those people to stand down," he ordered, his voice sharp and cutting through the cacophony.

The crowd roared back, their voices cresting like a wave, defiant and unrelenting. Sierra scanned the crowd, sensing the shift—a volatile energy coiling tighter with every passing second. What had been a demonstration on the edge of control was now teetering dangerously toward a breaking point.

The protesters surged forward, their chants swelling into a single, powerful roar. The thin line of security guards wavered, their formation breaking as some stepped back. Sierra's chest tightened when her eyes landed on one of the younger guards, his pale face betraying his inexperience. His hand hovered near his holster, fingers twitching with hesitation.

"Sierra stepped forward, her arms raised high, palms out. "Stay peaceful!" she shouted, her voice cutting through the crowd. "Do not push forward!" She turned toward the guards, her focus locking onto the trembling young man. "We don't want violence!"

The guard's chest heaved as his panicked gaze darted from Sierra to the sea of angry faces behind her. Sweat trickled down his temple, and his lips moved wordlessly, as if he were trying to convince himself of something.

Sierra's heart sank as she realized the danger.

"Stay calm!" Sierra shouted, her voice edged with desperation. She stepped closer to the guard, her open hands trembling slightly. "Don't draw it. You're safe. Just hold your position."

The guard's breath quickened. He flinched as a bottle shattered against the ground nearby, the sharp sound slicing through the noise like a warning shot. His hand jerked toward his holster, and before Sierra could close the gap between them, his fingers found the grip.

"No!" Sierra screamed, lunging forward, but the guard's panic erupted into action. His hand moved reflexively, pulling the firearm free.

The crack of the gunshot shattered the chaos into silence.

Lucas staggered, his breath catching audibly. His wide eyes locked onto Sierra's as the crimson bloom spread across his shirt, staining the fabric in jagged patterns. He stumbled, his legs giving out beneath him, and collapsed to the ground.

Sierra's body moved before her mind could catch up, her knees hitting the ground as she reached for him. "Lucas!" Her voice broke as she pressed her hands against the wound, warm blood seeping through her fingers. The metallic scent of it mixed with the acrid air, turning her stomach.

The guard froze, his arm slack, the firearm slipping from his grip and clattering to the ground. His pale face twisted with horror as he stared at Lucas. "I—I didn't mean—"

Caldwell froze as the scene unraveled before him. The crowd, once a manageable force of defiance, had transformed into chaos. Shouts collided with screams, and the raw panic in the air clawed at him. His sharp commands faltered, swallowed by the tumult.

"Stand down! Everyone, stop!" he yelled, but his voice barely registered in the maelstrom.

Then he saw Lucas on the ground, Sierra hunched over him, her hands pressing against the crimson bloom spreading across his shirt. The metallic scent of blood hit Caldwell like a blow. His polished exterior cracked.

He shoved his way forward, his movements uncharacteristically urgent. "Move! Let me through!" he barked at the crowd.

Reaching Lucas, Caldwell knelt, his carefully curated arrogance giving way to something raw and unguarded. "I didn't want this," he said, his tone low, almost pleading. "I'll get help. We'll fix this."

Sierra's head snapped up. Her hands stayed firm against Lucas's wound, her fingers slick with his blood. "Fix this?" she hissed. Her eyes burned, her voice cutting through the chaos with cold fury. "This is what your greed has done. His blood is on you. On *your* plans."

Caldwell didn't respond. Her words struck deeper than he wanted to admit. He stayed there, kneeling on the dusty ground, watching Lucas struggle to draw a breath. The noise around him seemed to fade, replaced by the crushing reality of what he had unleashed.

Chapter 73

CHIEF VEGA KNELT beside Lucas, his uniform smeared with dirt and blood as his steady hands hovered over the wound. The chaos surrounding them—blaring sirens, shouts, and the hum of frantic motion—faded as his focus locked on Lucas's shallow breaths. The acrid scent of smoke and metallic tang of blood hung thick in the air, a grim reminder of the escalation no one had been able to stop.

A paramedic slid in beside Vega, her voice sharp and precise. "Pressure on the wound! Tight and steady. Where's the stretcher?" She didn't wait for answers, her gloved hands already assessing the damage. Her face betrayed no hesitation, her motions practiced and swift.

"Here!" another paramedic called, rushing forward with a collapsible stretcher. They worked in tandem, their efficiency honed by countless emergencies.

Vega rose to his feet, his knees stiff, and turned his attention to the source of his simmering rage—Caldwell. The man stood a few yards away, flanked by officers, his wrists bound in cuffs. His face, calm but unreadable, only deepened Vega's anger.

"Get him out of here," Vega barked, his voice low but dangerous. Caldwell was led away, and Vega turned back to the scene that mattered most.

Sierra knelt on the other side of Lucas, her hands stained red as she pressed down on his wound. Her breathing was shallow, but her grip was steady. "Lucas," she whispered, leaning close. "We're not losing you. Do you hear me? Stay with us."

The paramedics moved to lift Lucas onto the stretcher. "Keep him stabilized," the lead paramedic ordered. "Oxygen mask now."

Sierra refused to let go of Lucas's hand as they secured him to the stretcher, her grip desperate and unrelenting. "You're stronger than this," she said, her voice trembling but firm. "We've got you. Just hold on."

The stretcher was wheeled toward the ambulance, the crowd parting in stunned silence. Sierra stayed close, walking in lockstep with the paramedics. She barely registered the flashing lights or the murmurs rippling through the bystanders. Her entire world had narrowed to Lucas—the rise and fall of his chest, the faint warmth of his hand in hers.

When they reached the ambulance, the lead paramedic hesitated. "Ma'am, we need to go now."

Sierra's hand lingered on Lucas's for one last moment. "You fight, Lucas. Do you hear me?" Her voice cracked, and she stepped back as the doors swung shut. The ambulance roared to life, its sirens cutting through the tension like a blade as it sped off into the night.

Sierra stood frozen, the warmth of Lucas's blood still clinging to her hands. Her breaths came in shallow gasps as the weight of the moment pressed down on her. She turned, scanning the crowd, and caught sight of Elana weaving toward her.

Elana reached her, and without a word, they embraced. Sierra's shoulders trembled, but she didn't cry. Not yet.

"He's strong," Elana murmured, her voice steady despite the quaver in her eyes. "He'll make it."

Sierra pulled back, her breath shaky but her resolve hardening. "He has to." Her voice was raw, but her determination was unwavering. "And so will we."

———

Caldwell watched the ambulance vanish into the distance, its sirens wailing like a judgment passed down. The faint red-and-blue flashes still danced on the edges of his vision as he stood in the churned dirt of the construction site, his jaw locked so tightly it ached. The scattered crowd lingered, their murmurs rising and falling in an uneven rhythm that felt like the thrum of his own pulse.

He turned sharply to his head of security, a broad man with a perpetual scowl etched across his face. "What in hell just happened?" Caldwell barked, his voice cutting through the murmurs like a whip.

The security officer, already pale, stiffened under Caldwell's glare. "One of the rookies panicked," he stammered. "We—uh—we didn't mean—"

"You didn't *mean*?" Caldwell's voice rose dangerously. He stepped closer, forcing the man to look him in the eye.

The officer glanced toward the remaining guards, who were shuffling awkwardly near the protestors still lingering by the fence. "It's under control," he offered weakly.

"Does this look under control to you?" Caldwell growled, gesturing toward the bloodstained dirt and scattered protest signs. "Get your men off this site. Now. Before someone does something even more idiotic."

The guard hesitated, then nodded curtly, retreating to bark orders at the team. Caldwell rubbed his temples as he turned away.

Veronica Miller appeared at his side, her heels crunching against the gravel. "This is salvageable," she said. "We spin it. The protest turned violent. Your security acted in defense."

Caldwell shot her a sneer. "Spin it?" He stepped closer, lowering his voice. "A man just got shot, Veronica. On my watch. On this *site*.

And you want to talk about spinning?"

"Because that's what we *have* to do," Veronica snapped. "If you don't control the narrative, someone else will. They won't be kind."

———

Caldwell stood at the edge of the chaos, his eyes fixed on the bloodstain smeared across the dirt. The burned bulldozer, the twisted equipment—it all seemed to close in around him, pressing tighter with every breath.

"Hiram." Veronica's voice pierced the noise, urgent and sharp. "We need a plan. The lawyers—"

He didn't respond. His hands fell loosely to his sides as though drained of purpose. He took a step forward, his movements halting, his focus drifting to the crowd scattered along the edge of the site. A murmur of voices surrounded him, but none of it registered.

"And the press?" Veronica pressed, her tone more insistent now. "We have to control this. Hiram!"

"Stop," he said, his voice low, almost swallowed by the distant sound of sirens. He didn't turn to look at her. "Just... stop."

Veronica hesitated, confusion tightening her posture. "What are you—?"

"I said stop!" Caldwell's voice cracked, louder this time, raw and trembling. He finally turned toward her, and his face, usually etched with authority, sagged under the weight of something different. "Can't you see what's happened? What I've done?"

Veronica lowered her phone, her fingers tightening around it. "Hiram, this isn't the moment for—"

"It's exactly the moment," he interrupted, the words tumbling out. His hand lifted briefly, gesturing toward the destruction, then fell again. "This. All of this—it's my doing. I built this. I made it happen."

He stumbled a step closer to the bloodstain, his chest rising and falling with uneven breaths. The dirt clung to his shoes, unnoticed. His eyes darted across the site, taking in every shattered piece of machinery, every hushed face.

"I thought I was building something," he murmured, more to himself than to her. "Something that would last. But I've been blind. I've been tearing it apart—tearing *everything* apart."

The words hung in the air, fragile and heavy. Veronica's grip on her phone loosened, and for the first time, her composure cracked. "Hiram, you can't—"

"Can't what?" He rounded on her, his tone filled with exhaustion instead of anger. "Admit it? That I've done this? That I've failed?"

The crowd in the distance shifted, whispers spreading like ripples. Caldwell's shoulders sagged as he knelt, lowering himself onto the dirt. His fingers brushed against the earth, dry and cold against his skin. He stayed there, unmoving, the hum of activity around him fading into the background.

"This isn't progress," he said softly, his voice barely audible. "It's destruction. And it's all mine."

Veronica crouched beside him, her words faltering. "Hiram, we can still fix—"

"No." His hand pressed into the dirt. "Not this time. This can't be fixed."

Chapter 74

THE HOSPITAL ROOM was steeped in sterile stillness, punctuated only by the monotonous beeping of machines. Lucas lay motionless on the bed, his breathing shallow. His face was pale and drawn. Sierra stood beside him, her hand resting lightly on the edge of the mattress. Her posture was calm, but her eyes held a quiet intensity.

Behind her, Elana paced. "Sierra," she said, urgency cutting through her voice. "You have to do something. Do you hear me?"

Sierra didn't respond. She closed her eyes and breathed slowly as she focused inward. The antiseptic smell of the hospital receded, and her mind reached out to something deeper. The faint presence of he ancestors stirred within her, subtle but undeniable. She let it ground her, threading her thoughts with the memory of Redstone—the warmth of its sun, the strength of its cliffs, the whispers of its ancient stories.

When she opened her eyes, she placed her hands gently on Lucas's face. "Tawa," she said softly, "Pahana, I call upon you. Mend what is broken. Restore what must endure."

Elana stopped pacing. The room felt still in a way that was hard to name, as though something just beyond sight was holding its breath.

Sierra's voice deepened, steady and resolute. "Earth and air, creation's breath, bind the threads of life once more. Let his spirit rise whole, renewed by the power that sustains us all."

Her hands moved to hover just above Lucas's heart. She focused on the connection she had created with something far greater than herself.

"Where shadows linger, let light prevail," she continued. "Restore balance, as it was and as it will be."

The stillness lingered, stretching out until it felt nearly tangible. Sierra stepped back, her chest rising and falling with controlled breaths. Her hands dropped to her sides. She didn't look at the machines or the monitors. Instead, she kept her eyes on Lucas, willing him to move, to breathe more deeply, to return.

Elana approached hesitantly, her movements careful, as though the stillness of the room might shatter under the weight of her voice. "Sierra, did it... work?"

Sierra didn't answer immediately. Her eyes lingered on Lucas's face, his features slack in the pale light. "We've done all we can," she said at last. Her voice carried no hint of certainty, only the quiet endurance of someone who had given everything and knew it might not be enough. "The rest isn't ours to control."

The room breathed in a rhythm of its own, the monitors marking time in a language neither of them wanted to understand. Sierra leaned back slightly, exhaustion dulling the edges of her movements. Despite the artificial sterility of the hospital, she felt a pulse threading through her awareness like a heartbeat she could only half-hear.

"Do you think he knows we're here?" Elana asked. She was quieter now, as though speaking louder might break the fragile moment.

Sierra turned. "I believe he does. The threads that hold us to this world aren't so easily severed. Even in silence, we're bound to one another." She rested her hand lightly on Lucas's arm. "What's here in this world, in these connections, is more than memory. It's something alive. Something that endures."

"That is what I have always wanted Lucas to understand," Elana said.

Sierra replied. "Belief isn't a matter of certainty. It's the choice to stand in the absence of answers and still move forward. It's the willingness to trust that the unseen matters as much as what we can measure."

She looked down at Lucas again, her fingers brushing the edge of the blanket. "When I was young, I didn't know what the ley lines were. I only knew how they felt—how they tied me to the earth, to everything that had been and everything that would be. That connection didn't promise safety or certainty, but it did teach me that we're never truly alone."

Elana crossed her arms tightly over her chest. "And if it's not enough? If he doesn't come back?"

Sierra's shoulders lifted slightly. "Then we grieve. And we fight for what remains. But we never forget that what we do here, the lives we live, echo far beyond us. That's all we can ever hold onto."

The room turned to stillness except for the steady rhythm of Lucas's breathing and the mechanical pulse of the machines. Sierra's thoughts wandered to the chaos that had brought them here—the violence, the fear, the fractures Caldwell had forced into their lives. She thought of the land, scarred but still alive.

She leaned closer to Lucas, her voice soft. "Whatever happens, we carry the stories forward. That's all that is asked of us. To remember. To protect. To give what we can, knowing it's part of something larger than ourselves."

Chapter 75

A FAINT SOUND BROKE the stillness—a groan, low and unsteady. Sierra froze as her eyes fixed on Lucas's hand. His fingers shifted, almost imperceptibly. Beside her, Elana inhaled sharply, her hands flying to her mouth, her eyes shimmering with tears.

Sierra leaned closer, her voice trembling but steady. "Lucas," she whispered, her lips close to his ear. We're here. Come back to us."

A second passed. Then another. Slowly, his fingers curled around hers. Elana let out a sound somewhere between a sob and a laugh, her disbelief melting into relief.

Lucas's eyelids fluttered. The confusion in his expression softened as his eyes adjusted to the pale light of the room. Soon, recognition came like the first blush of dawn. "Sierra... Elana..." His voice was barely audible. "What... happened?"

Sierra's tears traced silent paths down her cheeks. "You're back," she said.

Lucas swallowed. "I... felt something. Like... I was being pulled... held."

Sierra nodded, her hand tightening on his. "They called you back. We called you back."

Lucas closed his eyes briefly. "It wasn't just me," he murmured. "It felt... bigger. Like the earth itself wouldn't let go."

Elana, her hand still resting on Lucas's forearm, finally spoke. "You were meant to stay, Lucas. Whatever's happening here—this life—it isn't done."

Lucas's tired eyes met Sierra's. "You didn't give up."

"Never," she replied. "None of us did."

The first light of dawn crept through the window, soft and golden. It carried the promise of something new and something whole. Sierra sat back, the tension in her shoulders easing for the first time in hours.

"We've got more to figure out," Elana said. She leaned over and kissed his forehead. "But for now, you need to rest. The rest can wait."

Sierra looked at both of them. The spirits had held him. And they held all of them—bound together by something ancient and undeniable, woven into their lives with a strength that defied explanation.

Chapter 76

CHIEF VEGA SAT across from Caldwell in the interrogation room of the Redstone Police Station. Caldwell, usually polished and composed, appeared frayed at the edges. "Hiram, we're done with excuses," Vega said. "The violence, the sabotage—who's behind it? I need names, and I need the truth."

Caldwell shifted in his chair. His shoulders slumped. "I didn't order the attack on Ladawn's Bakery," he said. "That wasn't my plan."

Vega leaned forward. "But it happened because of the chaos you brought to this town. You set this in motion. If you want to fix it, start talking."

Caldwell's jaw tightened. Vega's expression didn't waver. "Veronica Miller? Where does she fit?"

Caldwell's shoulders. "Veronica was only helping herself. She fed me information, looking for a prize. She believed she could shape this into her winning lottery ticket. I let her think that. I didn't stop her."

Vega took a long breath, assessing Caldwell's words.

Caldwell straightened slightly, his hands still resting on the table. "I'll cooperate," he said. "Whatever you need, I'll do it. I want to fix this."

Vega reached for his radio, his movements deliberate. "Bring

Veronica in," he said.

The door opened moments later, and Veronica Miller stepped inside. Her expression was tight. Her posture was rigid. Caldwell glanced at her, and for a moment, his face flushed with shame.

"You've both made a mess of this town," Vega said. "Veronica, have you been working alongside Caldwell?" Vega asked.

Veronica met him with defiance and resignation in equal measure. She couldn't shake Caldwell's words from her mind: *This project will bring progress and prosperity to Redstone, Veronica. You can either embrace it or get left behind.* Taking a deep breath, she struggled to balance her loyalty to the town she loved with the tempting promises Caldwell had made her.

"Chief, you should know that things aren't always black and white," she said.

As Vega processed her words, Veronica reached into her jacket and placed a stack of photographs on the table. In them, Marla Jenkins could be seen in the chaos at the bakery, bent over an injured Ladawn.

Caldwell didn't hesitate. "She acted on her own. She went too far. She thought she was protecting my vision, but I didn't ask for this."

The chief took a moment to collect his thoughts before keying the radio, "Please bring in Marla Jenkins for questioning."

———

The door swung open once again, and Marla Jenkins entered with a worried expression etched on her face. She avoided looking at Caldwell, instead focusing on Vega who stood with a determined expression. Sensing the gravity of the situation, she took a seat across from him.

"Marla, please sit down," Vega said gently, motioning to the empty chair. "We need to discuss your involvement in the incident at Ladawn's Bakery."

Marla's perched on the edge of her chair, alert and defensive. "I swear Chief, I had nothing to do with that attack," she stated firmly, although a hint of fear lingered in her voice.

Vega interjected, sliding some photographs across the table towards Marla. "Then can you explain these?" he asked.

Marla's composure faltered for a moment as she looked at the images before regaining her resolve. "Those prove nothing," she snapped defensively. "Ladawn was injured. I was trying to help."

Caldwell remained silent, no longer smirking or reveling in the tension. He could sense the seriousness of the situation and didn't want to exacerbate it further.

Vega never wavered as he continued questioning Marla. "Why were you at the bakery? And why did you not report seeing Ladawn in that state?"

Marla hesitated, her fingers gripping the edge of the table tightly. "I. panicked," she finally said "I knew how it would look if I was caught there. But I swear, I had nothing to do with hurting her." Vega leaned in closer, pressing for the truth.

"Did you panic, or are you hiding something more?" he prodded. "Your presence at the scene and these photos don't paint a favorable picture."

Silence filled the room. After a moment, Marla spoke, "I just wanted to give Ladawn a warning. I wanted to persuade her to see reason. She was turning against us. But then she came in sneaking up on me."

———

Veronica paced anxiously outside of Chief Vega's office, her mind racing with guilt and fear. She took a deep breath and steeled herself before entering. As she walked in, she immediately noticed the stress and wariness etched on Vega's face.

"Veronica," he said. "What do you want?"

She closed the door behind her and stood before his desk, struggling to find the right words. "Chief, I... I need to talk to you about everything."

Vega's words were harsh. "Everything? You mean your betrayal?"

Her heart sank at the accusation. "I know how it looks, Chief, but please hear me out."

He leaned back in his chair, his arms folded across his chest. "I'm listening."

Veronica steadied herself. "I did leak information to Caldwell. At the time, I thought I was doing the right thing—trying to navigate the politics of this town and get ahead. But now I see that I was wrong. Infatuation got the best of me. And he took advantage of that."

Vega's eyes never left hers. "Why tell me this now?"

"Because I can't stand what I've become," she admitted. Her voice broke as she spoke. "I can't even look at myself in the mirror knowing that I betrayed everything I stand for. And I know...I know I put this town, and you, in a terrible position."

"Seeing how far Caldwell pulled Marla into all of this," Veronica said. "She didn't deserve to be a pawn in his twisted game. None of us did."

The chief studied her for a long moment. "what makes you think I could trust you again?"

"You can't," she replied. "Not yet. But I want to earn your trust back, Chief. I want to help you. For the sake of Redstone."

Vega remained silent, only one thing wasn't clear.

"I just have one question, Veronica," Chief Vega finally said. "Why were you at the bakery with Marla in the middle of the night?"

299

Epilogue

SIERRA STOOD at the center of the clearing. Her turquoise-trimmed skirt rippled in the desert breeze. The children gathered around her, their eyes wide with curiosity. The sunlight played through her braided hair, casting golden threads amidst the shadows. She held their attention with the quiet strength of someone deeply rooted in the land.

"We are not just here to paint," Sierra began, her voice steady and warm, carrying the resonance of the wind through the canyons. "We are here to remember—stories that live in the earth, whispers of those who came before us, and the ties that bind us to this place."

She extended her hands, revealing a collection of river-worn stones she had gathered under the desert sun. "These stones are not just fragments of the earth," she said, her voice softer now. "They are pieces of its memory. Today, they are our canvas, but they are also our storytellers."

The children, ranging in age from six to twelve, listened eagerly as Sierra wove tales of ley lines—described not simply as channels of energy but as veins of the earth itself, pulsating with life and history. She spoke of how these lines connected the community to one another and to those who had walked these lands before them.

"Today, you will create something that represents your connection to Redstone and the ley lines," Sierra announced, unveiling an array of art supplies. "Use these paints and brushes to bring your vision of the ley lines to life."

While the children immersed themselves in their artwork, Sierra moved among them, offering gentle guidance and encouragement. With a soft touch here and a guiding hand there, she helped transform their abstract thoughts into vivid colors and shapes on canvas.

Midway through the session, an older boy—about ten years old—looked up from his painting with a frown creasing his brow. "Sierra, why is it important to protect these ley lines?" he asked, voicing common skepticism influenced perhaps by ongoing debates about development in Redstone.

Sierra knelt beside him and pointed towards the horizon where the desert met the sky in a perfect line. "Imagine if one day we could no longer see where the sky meets the land, or if we forgot the stories of who we are and where we come from. Protecting the ley lines," she explained, "is like preserving the sacred tales of our ancestors, the whispers of the wind, and the silence of the stars. It's our duty to keep the earth's storybook open for all to read, learn, and remember."

The boy nodded, turning back to his painting with newfound determination in his strokes.

The workshop finally ended, and parents arrived to collect their children. Sierra invited everyone to view the "gallery" of artworks spread out on the grass. Each piece was evidence of the deep connections the children had forged with their heritage during their few hours under Sierra's guidance.

Lucas approached with a smile. "You're not just guarding the ley lines, Sierra. You're ensuring that the next generation understands their value."

Sierra watched the children excitedly show their artwork to their parents. Pride and sadness mingled in her heart, knowing that her dedication to Redstone's heritage often kept her at a distance from moments of personal joy. Yet seeing the children's enthusiasm reaffirmed her resolve to protect what truly mattered.

"It's a start," she said hopefully. "One day, they might be guardians too. Until then, we continue teaching and protecting."

The crowd began to disperse. Whispering Rock stood silently, bearing witness to the seeds of guardianship Sierra had planted that day—a blend of art, story, and an unbreakable bond with the land poised to grow with each passing generation.

———

Elana drove back to Flag staff alone. Redstone, with its mystical allure and secrets hidden beneath the earth, receded in her rearview mirror as she continued on her journey. She wound through the living canvas of the desert—vibrant greens, rich browns, and swaying wildflowers—each mile bringing her closer to a decision that would change her life forever.

Thoughts of Lucas consumed her, despite the beauty surrounding her. His words echoed in her mind. "It's about choosing." His voice had been so sure and so filled with conviction. She had waited for that for years.

As she pulled off the road near a scenic lookout point, her thoughts were drawn back to reality. The vista before her was breathtaking—a sweeping view of the valley below, cradled by towering mountains. Stepping out of the car, she took a deep breath and let herself take in the vastness of the landscape before her. It was only one decision—could she leave everything behind? Simple, right? Was she ready to exchange it all—her family, her career, the life she had meticulously built in Seattle—for a new and uncertain future here?

At the edge of the lookout, her hands clutched tightly onto the wooden railing as she looked out at the river cutting through the valley below. Its waters shimmered under the sun's last golden rays, tempting here with fantasies of a simple life.

A gentle wind rose, whispering, urging her to listen and to understand its call. She closed her eyes, took a deep breath, and allowed herself to fully embrace the connection she felt to this place. Perhaps that was all she needed—not certainty or guarantees. But an open mind and an adventurous spirit to guide her towards a future filled with endless possibilities.

———

Tara stood at the edge of Redstone, her car packed and humming beside her. The sun's red-orange glow painted the town in warm hues, illuminating the streets filled with cherished memories. As Lucas and Sierra's paths aligned with the ley lines, she felt a sense of both joy and loneliness. Joy for their newfound platonic bond, intertwined with the greater purpose of protecting and understanding the mystical lines. And yet, a pang of isolation in her own journey for belonging and purpose. These mixed emotions propelled her decision to leave, to seek her destiny beyond Redstone's borders.

Taking in a deep breath of cool evening air, she tasted courage on her tongue as she stared into the rearview mirror, her reflection steady. "It's time to go," she whispered, affirming that this wasn't an end but a new beginning.

As she pointed herself towards Flagstaff, leaving the town behind, she felt a sense of freedom and liberation. No longer confined by the past, she embraced the open road ahead, each mile a step towards self-discovery and new adventures. Imagining all the places she could go and people she could meet, her spirit ignited with excitement.

Her journey took her through ever-changing landscapes—from familiar rolling hills to bustling cities and quaint villages tucked away from the rest of the world. In each new setting, she paused to soak up its unique energy and culture, often staying for a day or two before moving on.

One evening in the not too distant future, while admiring the sunset by the sea in a small coastal town with Ashley, she would experience a profound sense of peace. Sitting on a sandy beach, watching the waves crash against the shore, she would realize that her journey was not just about finding a new place to call home; it was also about understanding herself, her desires, and the meaning of family.

———

Chief Vega walked the bustling town square, taking in the mix of excitement and concern among the crowds that had come to see Sierra's nationally recognized exhibition, infused with the spirit of Redstone and the wonder of the powerful ley lines.

Vega took personally the growing responsibility upon his shoulders. These were challenging times, not just for maintaining safety and order, but also for navigating the transformative changes happening within the community.

Amongst the crowd, Vega made his way through, offering reassuring nods and words to calm those who approached him. His steady presence acted as an anchor amidst the buzz of conversations.

Finally reaching the steps of the historic town hall, Vega paused to look up at the old building. It had stood for over a century, bearing witness to the ups and downs of Redstone's fortunes. As he reflected on the legacy of past leaders before him, Vega felt a deep connection to his role in shaping the town's destiny.

Entering his office within the town hall, Vega climbed the stairs and took a moment to survey his surroundings. The room was filled with memorabilia from his career and tokens from Redstone's history. Pulling open his desk drawer, Vega retrieved a map of Redstone and its surrounding areas. Tracing the ley lines with his finger, he couldn't help but feel that they held both immense power and potential conflict. "How can I guide a town divided by fear and fascination?"

His pulled out a photograph from his early days in the police force, a reminder of his oath to protect and serve so that Redstone remained a peaceful and prosperous place. But now, with new complexities growth and heritage, Vega's role as a peacekeeper had evolved into that of a visionary leader.

As he pondered, the phone rang, interrupting his thoughts. It was the mayor, discussing preparations for an upcoming cultural festival meant to celebrate Redstone's heritage and its connection to the ley lines. Vega felt a renewed determination. He realized that he must go beyond his role as peacekeeper; he needed to be a unifying force that could bridge the divides and harmonize the town's diverse energies—both human and mystical—for a more unified future.

After hanging up, Vega made note of his reflections in his journal—a long-standing practice of his. "The ley lines don't just empower the land; they also reflect our fears and dreams," he wrote. "It is my duty to ensure they symbolize unity, not division."

———

Tense silence filled the community hall as Hiram Caldwell took the stage. The once vibrant "Redstone Reimagined" banner now mocked the town's struggles. Sierra Castillo and Ladawn Greer sat in the front row, their faces etched with a mix of skepticism and fragile hope.

Caldwell stepped up to the podium, his usual confidence

faltering. He took a moment to register the sea of faces, each one bearing the scars of his actions. In that moment, his past crashed down upon him. He gripped the edges of the podium, his knuckles turning white.

"I stand before you today not as a businessman, but as a man humbled by the strength and resilience of this community," Caldwell began, his voice raw with emotion. "I thought I could reshape Redstone in my image, but I was wrong. You showed me that the true value of a place lies not in its potential for profit, but in the hearts of its people."

A murmur arose in the crowd, surprise mingling with cautious optimism. Sierra leaned forward, her eyes narrowing as she searched Caldwell's face for any hint of deception.

"I cannot undo the pain I have caused." Caldwell turned to face Sierra. "But I can work to rebuild what I nearly destroyed. Starting today, I am dedicating my resources to supporting the very heritage I once sought to erase."

He paused, letting his words sink in. "I will begin by funding Sierra's cultural initiative, 'Echoes of the Ley Lines.' Her tireless efforts to preserve Redstone's history deserve more than just recognition—they deserve our support."

Sierra felt a lump form in her throat. She had fought so hard for this moment, yet now that it was here, she hardly dared to believe it.

Caldwell turned to Ladawn, his expression softening. "Ladawn, I know that no amount of money can erase the harm I have caused you and your family. But I want to ensure that your children have every opportunity to thrive. That's why I am establishing a scholarship fund in their names."

Tears streamed down Ladawn's face as she nodded, too overcome with emotion to speak. The pain of her loss still ached, but for the first time, a glimmer of hope began to take root.

As Caldwell continued outlining his plans for the town's future—

the parks, the school renovations, the investment in local businesses—a sense of unity began to build. The once divided community started to see a path forward, one that honored their past while embracing a brighter tomorrow.

Mayor Helen Jones stepped forward, her eyes shining with determination. "Let this be a turning point for Redstone," she declared. "But let us also remember that trust must be earned. We will hold Mr. Caldwell accountable for his promises."

Caldwell nodded solemnly, fully accepting that liability. As he stepped down from the stage, Sierra approached him. For a long moment they stood face-to-face—the guardian of Redstone's heritage and the man who had once threatened to destroy it.

"Thank you," Sierra said, extending her hand. "For listening. For understanding."

Caldwell took her hand, feeling the calluses born from years of fighting for her beliefs. "Thank you," he replied, "for showing me a different way. A better way."

The meeting ended and the townspeople began to disperse, a sense of renewed purpose filling the air. The road ahead would not be easy, but for the first time in a long while, Redstone could look to the future with hope. The battle for the town's soul had been won, not through force or intimidation, but through the power of unity, resilience, and an undying love for the land and its stories.

———

The wind whispered through the tall grasses as Hiram and Mika walked side by side. The ground beneath their feet was familiar, each step echoing with memories of their youth. The land stretched out before them, untouched and vibrant, the ancient stones still standing strong at the heart of the valley.

Hiram paused at the edge of the valley and inspected the scene. The heavy machinery was gone, replaced by the natural beauty that had drawn him and Mika here as boys. The old stones stood resolutely in the center, their presence a reminder of the delicate balance between progress and preservation.

Mika came to stand beside him, his eyes reflecting the warmth of the setting sun. "You did the right thing, Hiram," he said quietly, his voice filled with a mix of pride and relief.

Hiram nodded, a small smile tugging at the corners of his mouth. "It wasn't easy," he admitted, his voice thoughtful. "But standing here now… I know it was the only choice I could make."

The two men stood in silence for a moment, letting the peace of the valley settle over them. The land seemed settled now, its stillness carrying a quiet finality, its future secured by a decision that had been difficult but necessary.

"It's strange," Hiram continued, his tone reflective. "I spent so much of my life thinking that success was about building something new, something big. But now… I realize that sometimes the greatest success is in preserving what's already there."

Mika smiled, knowingly. "The land has always had a way of teaching us what we need to know, if we're willing to listen."

Hiram looked at Mika, seeing in him the same boy who had once led him through these canyons, full of wonder and wisdom beyond his years. "You never stopped listening," Hiram said, a note of admiration in his voice.

Mika shrugged, a modest gesture that belied the impact he had had on Hiram's life. "I just did what felt right. The land was here long before us, and it will be here long after we're gone. It's our job to take care of it while we're here."

Hiram nodded, the words settling into his bones. "I wish I had seen that sooner."

"You see it now," Mika replied, his tone gentle. "That's what matters."

They continued walking, the sun dipping lower in the sky, casting long shadows across the ground. The quiet between them wasn't empty—it carried the weight of shared battles and mutual respect.

They reached the center of the valley. Hiram stopped beside one of the ancient stones, resting his hand on its rough surface. The stone felt cool to the touch, solid, a testament to the resilience of the land and the people who had protected it for generations.

"We used to think these stones were markers for treasure," Hiram said, his voice tinged with nostalgia.

Mika chuckled. "In a way, we were right."

Hiram turned to Mika, a look of realization dawning on his face. "The treasure isn't something you can dig up or build over. It's this," he said, gesturing to the valley around them. "It's the land, the history, the connection we have to it."

Mika nodded, his eyes filled with a quiet pride. "And now, thanks to you, it's a treasure that will be preserved for future generations."

Hiram let out a long breath, feeling a sense of peace he hadn't known in years. "I guess we both found what we were looking for," he said, his voice soft.

"Yeah," Mika agreed, his tone matching Hiram's. "We did."

They stood there for a while longer, watching. The sun dipped below the horizon, bathing the valley in a warm, golden light. The sky above them faded from orange to pink, then to a deep, tranquil blue and the first stars began to appear.

Darkness settled in, but Hiram felt a profound sense of closure. He had come to Redstone with a vision of progress, of building something new. But now, standing in the place that had shaped him, he realized that the true progress was within himself.

"Ready to head back?" Mika asked, his voice gentle, as if sensing Hiram's thoughts.

Hiram nodded, turning away from the stones and the memories

they held. "Yeah," he said, a small smile on his lips. "I'm ready."

They walked back together, side by side, the path ahead of them clear and steady. The land around them, preserved and protected, stood as a testament to the choices they had made—not just for the project, but for themselves.

They reached the top of the ridge and Hiram turned for one last look at the valley below. The stones persisted, silent and strong, guardians of a land that would continue telling its stories long after they were gone.

"Goodbye, old friend," Hiram whispered, his voice carrying on the evening breeze.

Mika placed a hand on Hiram's shoulder, a gesture of friendship and solidarity. "This isn't the end, Hiram. It's a new beginning."

Hiram smiled, feeling the truth of those words deep within him. "Yeah," he agreed. "A new beginning."

Together, they turned and made their way back to the town, the future stretching out before them like the stars in the night sky.

Guest Editorial by Mayor Helen Jones

Published in the Redstone Weekly and on the Redstone City Webpage

Unity and Spirit: The Heartbeat of Redstone

Sitting in my office, overlooking the idyllic town of Redstone, I am reminded daily of the spirit and unity that pulsates through our community. It is a unifying force that not only binds us together but also propels us forward to face new challenges and adventures with courage and resilience.

Recently, we have witnessed remarkable transformations and accomplishments that have garnered both national recognition and local pride. From Sierra's groundbreaking cultural project, "Echoes of the Ley Lines," to the revitalization of Le Sanctuaire Deux into a lively community center under the capable leadership of Susan Andrews, Redstone continues to showcase its strength through our collective commitment and diverse contributions.

Our decision to protect the ley lines stands as a testament to what can be achieved when we come together with respect for our history and future. It was more than just preserving our environment or culture; it was a demonstration of our town's unified will to honor and integrate the old with the new.

But our unity does not just manifest in grand projects; it is also reflected in everyday interactions—the friendly greetings on the streets, support for local businesses, and lending hands of help and friendship. These are the moments that truly reveal the character of Redstone.

As we look towards the future, we stand at the brink of more exciting developments. As your mayor, I promise to nurture this spirit of unity and ensure that Redstone remains a shining example of community and innovation. The recent sighting of a mysterious figure observing our town reminds us that Redstone's allure extends far beyond our borders, sparking interest and intrigue wherever our actions may reach.

Let us move forward with the understanding that each one of us plays an integral role in weaving the vibrant tapestry that is Redstone. Whether you are a longtime resident or a newcomer, your voice and actions contribute to the ongoing story of our town.

To those who have stood by us through thick and thin—thank you for your support and love for our community every day. And to those who are just finding their place among us—welcome, may you find the same sense of hope and harmony that has guided us thus far.

Together, we will continue to face whatever the future holds with the same spirit of adventure and unity that defines us. Here's to embarking on this journey together, creating a legacy that future generations will look back on with pride.

With utmost gratitude and highest hopes,
Mayor Helen Jones

Guardians of the Sacred Land

Under a sky dense with stars, the desert holds its breath. Around ancient stones, the sands shimmer faintly, like traces of something alive and watching. The ley lines hum quietly beneath the surface, a pulse older than memory.

A jackrabbit, its fur dusted with the glow of these mystical paths, perches atop a prominent dune. It is more than a creature of the earth; it is a sentinel, its presence deliberates, almost reverential, as it sits bathed in the unearthly light. Its ears twitch, not just at the sounds of the natural world but in response to the faint melodies carried by the breeze—melodies that rise from the earth itself, ancient tunes of lost civilizations whose echoes dictate the rhythm of life here.

Above, a hawk circles languidly, its path synchronized with the ley lines below. It soars not just as a predator; it is a guardian, its keen eyes surveying the sacred land. Occasionally, its shadow crosses over figures that appear only at the edge of sight—spirits of the ancients, their forms blurred and ethereal, mirages that flicker in and out of existence.

The horizon begins to lighten, a profound transformation unfolds. Dawn spread across the desert in deep blues and purples, fleeting and surreal. For a moment, the land held its secrets close, cloaked in colors that felt almost imagined.

The plants and rocks respond to the dawn's magic. Thorny bushes and rugged boulders are outlined in a luminescent glow, standing as ancient sentinels in this sacred ceremony. The wind intensifies, now carrying a symphony of whispers, each gust laden with the voices of millennia, speaking in tongues lost to time but felt in the soul.

The creatures of the desert begin a delicate dance, a choreography that mirrors the swirling patterns of the ley lines. They move with a purpose instilled by generations, a ritual of reverence for the land that sustains and mystifies. Their movements trace the glowing ley lines, following a cosmic script written by the very stars.

The sun rises, its rays illuminate the desert, transforming the mystical night into day. The spectral colors fade into the morning blue, but the sense of something ancient and powerful remains. In this moment of daily resurrection, the desert reveals its deepest secrets and its true soul—not through grand declarations but through the subtle, mystical interplay of light and shadow, sound and silence, the visible and the unseen.

Here, in the stillness of dawn, the desert does not just exist; it speaks of eternities, of lives past and future, woven into the fabric of the present by the mystical, pulsing ley lines.

315

THE END

Special thanks to generous and talented editors who advised along the way: Bibiana Synder, Richard Roper, Nora Bellot, and Lesley Jones. I am sure that the outcome would have been much different without their expertise. Thanks to Veronica who endured many evening alone as this transpired. Finally, yet importantly, thanks to extended family who offered only encouragement.

www.ingramcontent.com/pod-product-compliance
Lightning Source LLC
Chambersburg PA
CBHW071237300726
48975CB00002B/456